WHISPERS IN THE DARK

A COLLECTION OF CTHULHU NOVELLAS

EDITOR: SCOTT HARRISON

SNOWBOOKS LTD.

Proudly published by Snowbooks
Edited by Scott Harrison

Snowbooks Ltd
email: info@snowbooks.com
www.snowbooks.com.

British Library Cataloguing in Publication Data.
A catalogue record for this book is available from the British Library.

Trade Paperback 978-1-909679-30-6
E-book 978-1-909679-12-2

First published 2015

WHISPERS IN THE DARK

A COLLECTION OF CTHULHU NOVELLAS

CONTENTS

Thana Niveau is a Halloween bride who lives in the Victorian seaside town of Clevedon, where she shares her life with fellow writer John Llewellyn Probert, in a gothic library filled with arcane books and curiosities.

She has twice been nominated for the British Fantasy award – for her collection *From Hell to Eternity* and her story "Death Walks En Pointe".

Her stories have been reprinted in *The Mammoth Book of Best New Horror* (volumes 22 - 25) and *Best British Horror*. Her latest stories can be found in *Interzone; Zombie Apocalypse: Endgame; Horror Uncut; Steampunk Cthulhu; Love, Lust & Zombies; Exotic Gothic 5; The Black Book of Horror* (volumes 7 - 10)*; Terror Tales of Wales; Terror Tales of the Cotswolds; The 13 Ghosts of Christmas*; and *Magic: an Anthology of the Esoteric and Arcane.*

NOT TO TOUCH THE EARTH

THANA NIVEAU

They were only a few hours out of Phoenix, well beyond the state line, when the rusty grey Pontiac started to protest.

The sun had been beating down on the desert all day without mercy, turning the car into a sauna. The air was stifling, heavy and difficult to breathe. It rushed through the open windows like heat from a furnace. Bettie fanned herself with the road map, but it only stirred the baked air around her and Will, and it required too much effort anyway.

Before them the highway rippled and shimmered like a boiling ocean, while on the radio Jim Morrison urged them to break on through to the other side. That was when the engine began rattling and knocking as though there were something trapped inside it. Bettie's father would have said it was gremlins.

Will exchanged a worried glance with Bettie and steered the car to a shuddering halt on the dusty shoulder. The plastic Krishna figure on the dashboard wobbled and fell off, hitting Bettie's leg on its short plummet to the floor of the car. She rubbed her knee.

Will smacked the wheel. "Damn," he said, arming sweat off his forehead. His long shaggy hair stuck to his face like spit curls. He sat back in his seat with a resigned expression. "Well, I guess that's that."

Bettie gave her boyfriend's hand a sympathetic squeeze. They'd had their doubts about Silver being up to the journey, but the rickety old jalopy had surprised them, covering most of the distance between New Orleans and San Francisco without any problem. But she seemed to have had enough now. Will turned the key in the ignition, but the engine refused to start. Steam hissed from beneath the hood, and Bettie couldn't help imagining a mechanic shaking his head solemnly like a doctor on TV. Silver had gasped her last.

Bettie sighed and retrieved Krishna from the floor. The little blue figure smiled back, playing his flute and dancing as though they had nothing to worry about, as though it didn't matter that they were stranded in the middle of the desert, only halfway to their destination.

She was determined not to let circumstances bring her down. She was hot and miserable and tired, but she forced herself to focus on the positive things. "We made it to California at least," she said. She beamed at Will as the realisation sank in. She could hardly believe it. "California!"

"Yeah," Will said, returning her smile. "It's amazing, isn't it?"

They stared out through the bug-spattered windshield at the unfamiliar landscape. It was forbidding, but eerily beautiful, like the surface of the moon. Joshua trees and cacti dotted the horizon, casting strange shadows across the sand and scrub. It was a world so far removed from Louisiana that it hardly seemed real. They'd seen a roadrunner just outside Tucson and Bettie had squealed with childish delight at the sight. They'd made a game of looking for coyotes and empty ACME boxes, but hadn't spotted either.

"Well," said Will, "looks like we'll have to hitch the rest of the way."

Immediately Bettie heard her mother's voice in her head, warning her of all the dangers lurking in the world, of all the people who meant her harm, and of all the bad things that could happen. She felt guilty about taking off with Will the way she had, but her mother was a classic example of everything that was wrong with the world.

She saw the bad in every situation and always expected the worst, as though she was constantly dogged by a dark cloud that was poised just over her head, ready to burst at any moment. Sometimes Bettie felt the shadow of that cloud too, but she was determined not to let it bring her down. She wanted to believe the world and the people in it were essentially good, and that good things would happen if you stayed positive.

But in spite of her optimism, the worst had come. So she and Will had split. If they went far enough, fast enough, maybe they could outrun the dark cloud.

Seeing her expression, Will touched her face. "It's a major highway. We won't be stranded out here all night. Someone will come."

"What about Silver?" she asked wistfully, stroking the torn upholstery.

He shrugged. "We'll just have to leave her here."

"Aww, poor old Silver." Abandoning the car felt like they were truly abandoning their old lives. It was scary but also exhilarating. In a way it was a bigger step than stealing away in the middle of the night had been.

"Come on." Will opened his door and hot air flooded the car. "It was time for a break anyway."

Bettie winced as her bare limbs came unstuck from the hot seat and they emerged from the car like explorers in a strange land. Bettie piled her long blond hair on top of her head and wound it into a sloppy bun to get it off her neck. She was used to the cloying, sweltering humidity of New Orleans, but the dry heat of the desert was a new experience. It was more intense, but it felt clean. It felt like her sweat was her own, and not just wet pollution settling on her skin from outside. She tucked Krishna into her embroidered bag and went to take a closer look at the Joshua trees.

They were strange and beautiful, stationed like sentinels across the pale expanse of desert and scrub as far as she could see. Their upraised arms looked furry in the late afternoon light, the spiny brushes at their ends like alien hands. The world was so still she might have been staring at a photograph. There was no wind, and not a cloud in the deep blue sky, only the powerful sun blazing overhead. Bettie could hear the rustling of hidden creatures scurrying through the brittle grass and she wondered what tiny dramas they were enacting. The world was so incomprehensibly huge; how could you ever know the millions of things you were missing all around you?

San Francisco had been Will's idea. That was where it was all happening. He'd been as far as El Paso once with his family, but Bettie had never even been out of New Orleans. California seemed a million miles away, a mythical haven where they would be safe. If they could get there.

Will interrupted her musing, slipping his arms around her waist. She closed her eyes and leaned back against him. His shirt was soaked with sweat but she didn't care. She loved the raw animal scent of him, the wildness deep within. She felt like a house cat next to a tiger.

"It's nothing like I imagined it," she said. "The desert, I mean."

"It's weird," Will agreed. "Kind of spooky."

"But beautiful."

They stood gazing out across the unfamiliar vista, transfixed. A lizard scuttled over rugged white rocks and cocked its head, fixing them with beady black eyes. They stared back.

After a while the purr of an approaching vehicle broke the silence. They watched as an eighteen-wheeler with North Carolina plates blasted past, rocking Silver in its wake.

"Better get our thumbs out if we want a ride before nightfall," Will said.

He unpacked their meagre possessions from the car while Bettie stood on the side of the road, ready to flag down a ride. Two cars went by without stopping in the first fifteen minutes and a third slowed down just enough to yell, "Get a job, you long-haired freaks!" But Bettie was determined not to give in to any negative energy. She and Will passed the time by looking at the road map and imagining all the things they could do once they got to San Francisco.

A squadron of bikers passed by trailing clouds of dust in their wake, as though they were being pursued by dust devils. The roar of engines dwindled as they vanished into the distance and after a while the road was silent and still. A bird cried somewhere overhead, an unfamiliar call Bettie had never heard before. In spite of herself she thought of buzzards circling and she shook her head to clear the thought.

But she needn't have fretted. Before long came the rumble of another engine, and soon a brightly painted van appeared through the heat waves. It was decorated with flowers and peace signs and a tattered American flag waved from the antenna. Even from a distance they could hear the Rolling Stones blaring from the speakers. Bettie jumped up and down, waving excitedly and the van drew to a juddering halt behind Silver.

A pretty girl wound down the passenger window and leaned out. Her long red hair was woven with beads and feathers, and her smile seemed as wide as the highway. The driver was a guy with long jet-black hair and the bluest eyes Bettie had ever seen. They looked like angels.

"Hi there," the redhead called. "You stuck?"

"Unfortunately, yes," Will said with a rueful grin. "Our car collapsed in the heat."

"No way!"

"'fraid so," Bettie said. "We were on our way to San Francisco."

"Hey, that's where we're going!" The redhead turned towards the driver. "It's fate, isn't it, Piper? Oh, you have to come with us – say you will! My name's Hialeah and this is Piper Dawn. Say hi, Piper!"

Piper raised a hand and murmured a shy "hello". It was clear Hialeah did most of the talking in their relationship. But her exuberance was catching, and Bettie liked both their rescuers instantly. She and Will introduced themselves and, with a last wave at Silver, they clambered into the van.

"Ready to roll?" Hialeah asked.

Will gave her the thumbs-up and Piper threw the van into gear, kicking up a spray of dust and gravel as they peeled away from the shoulder. Bettie watched until Silver was out of sight.

"Goodbye," she whispered.

"So where have you come from?" Hialeah asked, turning around in her seat. She had to shout to make herself heard over the music, but there was no question of turning it down. What was a road trip without music?

"New Orleans," Will said.

"Wow! That's a long way! I've never been there, but I always wanted to go. Is it true you actually eat crawfish?"

"It's true," Bettie said proudly. "And they're delicious."

"Far out," Hialeah breathed, sounding as amazed as if Bettie had said they ate dinosaur meat. "We've only come from Tucson. We're gonna start a band. I sing and Piper plays the guitar." She smiled even wider as a thought occurred to her. "Hey, you guys should join us! We can be like the Mamas and the Papas!"

"Or the Sons and the Daughters," Piper said.

Will shook his head with a laugh. "I'm not much of a singer," he said. "But I'll design the album art if you like."

"Hey, that's cool. I can't draw to save my life. But my voice isn't too bad. What about you, Bettie?"

"Well, I had a few dance lessons as a little girl. Ballet. Tap. Maybe I can be a go-go dancer?"

"Wouldn't my dad just love that!" Will said, grinning.

Hialeah cocked her head with a curious expression and Will explained.

"He's a preacher. Real blood and thunder stuff."

"Yeah," Bettie said, "and he thinks I'm some evil temptress who's led Will down the path of sin. He actually believes the peace sign is the devil's mark."

Piper and Hialeah exchanged a bewildered look.

"Wow, no wonder you guys split," Hialeah said. "We're on the run because of family problems too. My brother Dave left for Vietnam last week."

Will's hand tightened on Bettie's and, in spite of the heat, a chill went through her body. It felt like the dark cloud had found them after all, like it was looming just above them, swollen with bitter, poisonous rain.

Bettie swallowed. "Oh my God, I'm so sorry," she said.

"Nah, don't be. He joined up. The creep actually *wanted* to go kill people." Hialeah shook her head in disbelief. "You should have seen my old man. He was so proud. Like that's something to be proud of, you know? So then he starts hassling me and Piper, saying Piper should be a real man and join up too, blah blah blah, and I said what if *I* went over there to fight, would he be so proud then, and he said it would mean at least I wasn't a coward like some people. Can you believe that? Anyway, that's when we decided to cut out. Hey, what's wrong? What'd I say?"

Bettie glanced uneasily at Will. Without a word he fished in his pocket and held up the damning slip of paper for them to see.

Hialeah's eyes widened with horror. "No shit, man! Piper, look!"

"Jesus," Piper said, eyeing it warily, as though its

infection could spread. "I'm real sorry. That's some serious bad luck."

Will took the draft card back and tucked it away. "Yeah. Bad luck is right."

No one spoke for a while. On the radio Jimi Hendrix was wringing impossible sounds from his guitar and asking Joe where he was gonna run to now. The words made Bettie feel hunted. Haunted.

The song reached its end and Bettie didn't recognise the one that followed it. She breathed a little sigh of relief. Maybe it had broken the bad spell.

Hialeah's smile returned. "Well, you'll be safe in San Francisco," she said with utter confidence. "They'll never find you there! Say, why don't you burn that thing?"

"We were planning to burn it when we got to San Francisco," Will said. "Sort of an initiation into our new life."

"Why don't you do it now? Maybe it'll be good karma for the rest of the trip."

Bettie agreed. "I think it's a great idea. To be honest, I don't like you having that thing with you at all, Will." She stopped short of voicing her superstitious fear that it was the reason the car had broken down. Once she started letting ideas like that into her head she might as well spread her arms wide and wait for the ugly rain to fall.

"It's getting dark," Hialeah said. "Let's stop somewhere for the night. We can have a barbecue and drop some acid. We've got food and beer and everything. What do you say?"

Bettie looked at Will. A barbecue with their new friends sounded like the best thing in the world, but she was nervous at the mention of acid. "Oh, I'm not sure about that . . ."

"What's wrong?" Hialeah asked, clearly sensing her reticence.

"She's never tripped before," Will explained.

"Seriously? Wow! And I thought I was late to the party! Piper turned me on a few months ago and it completely changed my life. Trust me, Bettie, once you try it there's no going back. And you won't want to."

"She's right," Piper said. "Best thing that ever happened to me too. I think all the world leaders should try it. Then they'd understand. They'd see how connected everything is, how alike we all are. They'd realise how pointless war is. Who knows? Maybe it could even save the world."

It was the most Piper had spoken so far. Bettie had heard the same thing from others, Will included, but Piper's quiet passion seemed to give the words extra weight.

"I guess I've always just been a little scared of what

might happen," she admitted. "Or what I might do. What if I have a bad trip? Or I think I can fly and I jump off a building?"

Hialeah laughed. "Oh man, that's all just propaganda and scare tactics! And anyway, where are you gonna find a building to jump off out here, huh?"

"It's OK," Will said, putting his arm around her. "We'll look after you."

Bettie smiled and curled against Will's chest as Hialeah went on about how mind-blowing it would be, and how she couldn't believe their luck in finding each other. The girl changed subjects like a butterfly flitting from flower to flower in a garden. And she was so relentlessly cheerful it was hard not to believe that everything was as simple as she seemed to think it was. Then again, maybe it actually was. Maybe Bettie was just being uptight without good cause.

She did want to try it. So many friends back home had described their fantastic visions and transcendent experiences. But Bettie had seen strange things as a child without any chemical assistance, none of them good, so the thought of hallucinations frightened her deeply.

Only once had she made the mistake of confiding in someone. Her childhood best friend Janie had looked at her with such horror, and then betrayed her by telling her parents that Bettie was "looney tunes". What if she was right? Any little girl who saw monsters must be crazy, right? Anyone who saw things that weren't there, who heard voices, who couldn't tell the difference between dreams and reality, deserved to be locked up. Right? Bettie had saved herself – and her parents' shame – by forcing a smile and admitting that she'd just been trying to scare Janie. She'd always been an imaginative child, after all.

Well, she was hardly an adult at the tender age of seventeen, but maybe the scary visions had just been a childhood phase. It had been years since she'd seen or heard anything strange.

Outside the desert was flashing past her window and Bettie thought of all the things in life that could pass her by like that. She could easily stagnate and die in the bell jar of society. The whole world was changing; did she really want to sit on the sidelines and watch? Not be a part of it? Not be a force for good? For change?

She gazed out the window at the Joshua trees, the cacti, the stretch of road that would eventually lead them to a place of beauty, peace and love. The Mecca of their generation.

"OK," she said. "Let's do it."

Hialeah looked overjoyed. "Oh Bettie, it's gonna be amazing. I'm so glad we ran into you. It was destiny.

Hey, you know what? You guys should change your names like we did! You don't want to go through life with the boring names your parents gave you. Be your own person, reinvent yourself. That's what I always say."

Bettie closed her eyes as their hostess chattered away. She felt safe, as though the heavens had dropped a true best friend into her path.

From the radio the 5th Dimension invited her to fly up, up and away in their beautiful balloon. She wanted nothing more than to go with them, to sail the silver sky and be free. Everything about the moment seemed right. The van slowed to a stop on the side of the road and she gazed at the lengthening shadows and the vibrant orange light of the sun as it sank towards the horizon.

Hialeah hopped out of the van and fished around in her bag before finding a plastic baggie with several sugar cubes in it. She and Piper fed one to each other, then gave one each to Will and Bettie.

Bettie opened her mouth and let Will place the sugar cube on her tongue. "Feels like communion," she said nervously. Then she did the same for Will.

Through the dissolving sweetness she detected a slight bitter tang and had a moment's paranoia. She heard her parents' voices in her head, warning her of danger, poison, contamination, brain damage. She pushed it all aside. There was nothing to be afraid of.

Not anymore. The dark cloud was gone. Will and their new friends would take care of her.

Piper was unloading a cooler from the van and she imagined she could already smell burgers and hot dogs.

Bettie glanced nervously at her watch.

"Don't worry," Will said. "It takes a while."

"Will I know when it starts?"

Hialeah giggled. "Oh yeah. You'll know."

Piper set up a small hibachi stove, and soon they had a little fire going. Will took a deep breath and dipped the draft card into the flames. He held it up as it curled and blackened, and then a breeze lifted it away into the sky. Up, up and away. It disintegrated above their heads, the fragments winking out of existence like fireflies.

"Farewell, William Daniel Broussard," Will said softly.

Bettie felt a wave of relief and at the same time a dizzying sense that they had stepped off a precipice. There was no going back now. It was scary, but surely that was a good thing. Anything seemed possible.

"Who are you going to be now?" she asked. The idea of Will having a new name was exciting too, like having a lover who was also her boyfriend.

Will looked thoughtful for a moment. "Lucky," he said after a while. "It was my great-grandfather's name.

Well, his real name was Lucien LeBlanc but everyone called him Lucky. He lived to be 101."

"That sounds lucky to me," Bettie said, and she kissed him. "It's nice to meet you, Lucky." Just saying the name felt like an invocation.

The food was the best she'd ever eaten, the company the most pleasant. Even the warm beer tasted like champagne. Bettie felt like she'd known Hialeah all her life, like they were sisters.

She'd almost forgotten about the acid when she noticed a funny tingling sensation. Her skin felt strange, thin and vibrating, like a bubble that could burst in the slightest breeze. She touched her lips and noted with passing curiosity that her fingers were bleeding. There was no taste of blood, but ribbons of crimson streamed from her fingertips, vanishing into the sky. She described lazy figures in the air, red loops and curlicues, trying to write her name.

"What is it?" Will asked her, straining to see what she was seeing.

"Magic," she whispered, unable to elaborate. She saw the vibration of the words she had spoken, and more she hadn't. They drifted into the air with her blood, as though her thoughts were alive and floating into his mind.

"You're off," Hialeah said with a laugh. "Don't worry

about anything. Just go where it takes you. You're safe and surrounded by love."

Bettie barely registered the words. She blinked and then it was raining. Trembling liquid diamonds scurried over her face and she raised her head to see where the water were coming from. The stars winked above in oceans of pure sky, pouring their tears over her, purifying her. There was the sense of time slowing. Years passed as she stood beneath the downpour like a statue in a fountain. It seemed like centuries before she broke the spell. She touched her clothes and was surprised to find them dry. For a moment she was confused, but then something else caught her attention.

She lay back on the warm sand, hearing the footfalls of ants and other tiny creatures beneath the throbbing veneer of earth. It seemed that if she listened carefully enough she could understand what they were saying, speak their language. But the sand was in the way. She stared at it and realised that she could see the individual atoms that made up every single grain of sand. She could count them if she wanted to. They blinded her with impossible snowflake perfection.

Around her the Joshua trees seemed to be crowding closer, leaning down to her the way a person might to a small animal in a cage, whispering to her.

None of it was threatening. She was at the mercy of

the entire universe, and she knew with utter certainty that it was benign. More than that, it loved her, loved the tiny part she played in it, however insignificant it might seem to her.

From far away came the sound of music and reality intruded just long enough for her to realise that Piper was playing a guitar. It was a sensual experience beyond anything she had ever known. She could actually see the music. It was profound, transcendent. The notes became swirls and bursts of colour, an aurora borealis of sound. The words he sang spiraled outwards, inwards and into dimensions no one had ever seen before, paths she could follow forever. Overhead the stars wheeled, a vortex of incredible beauty. It was more than she had ever wanted to see, more than she thought she could take.

Bettie opened her mouth and nothing escaped but a sob. And another. Suddenly she couldn't stop the flow of tears.

"I can't go back," she whispered. "I've seen too much." She was suddenly terrified that someone would take all this beauty away from her, strip her of her newfound awareness.

Will was beside her, a smile like heaven and his own eyes as wide as hers with blissful, terrifying understanding. They shone like jewels, flickering in the light of the campfire. He took her hand and the warmth she felt was exquisite. He might have reached inside the basket of her rib cage and squeezed her heart. Their love was a splash of colour, drenching them both. She had to remind herself that he was no longer Will, at least not the Will she knew. He was Lucky. Reborn. What would she find when she looked deep inside for her true self?

Her bare feet sank into the sugary sand, the sensation blissful beyond imagining. They were ghosts, all of them, drifting through the world on the way to another dimension, a higher plane of existence. She could feel the change taking place in her mind, could feel millions of years of evolution passing in slow languorous seconds.

The music was alive, writhing on the floor of her mind. So raw, beautiful, intense. She felt like the beach beneath the onslaught of rolling waves, helpless to do anything but succumb to the sensory overload. Visions slid over her, pinning her down, receding, then returning to begin the process all over again. It was too much to see, too much to take in, but she had no choice. Her mind would expand to encompass it all. She didn't want it to stop.

A sudden intense sorrow gripped her and she felt herself crying again. Will's hand tightened on hers, but he didn't need to speak. His touch was a comfort beyond words. His eyes were closed and she wondered briefly how she looked to him inside his mind. She imagined he was both Will and Lucky, both her boyfriend and his ancient relative. He seemed to age before her eyes, his hair spilling over his bare chest like a silver waterfall, his face deepening with lines. She saw her own death in his.

"I'm dying," she whispered. She was in a barren wasteland, waiting for the rain that came only once in a lifetime. Tears. The blood of her soul. But the thought didn't frighten her. On the contrary, it was curiously reassuring.

Will smiled. Lucky smiled. "Yes. You're only dying."

Dolphins frolicked in the ocean of her tears and Bettie returned his smile. Her faced ached with the joy of it. She watched as her parents' daughter crumbled to dust. Old skins fell away, the casings of dried cocoons, prisons for butterflies that never spread their crumpled wings. Distilled to her essence, she felt the whole world pressing against her, wanting in.

She gazed up at the circling sky, at the labyrinth of diamonds she must find her way through. She had the sense that she was looking through time itself.

And that was when she saw them. The eyes.

They were not quite as bright as the stars, but they were piercing. They shone from behind the world, watching.

"Who are you?" she heard herself ask, her voice a pale echo of something once familiar.

"I'm Hialeah," came a female voice, and her new friend's face swam into her field of vision. "You're safe."

"No," Bettie said, struggling to grasp her scattered thoughts. She pointed. "Him."

Hialeah looked up into the sky and was quiet. Finally she said "It's just God."

But something in the girl's voice sounded uncertain, as though she wasn't actually seeing anything there but stars. Were these visions hers alone?

"Is it raining?" Bettie asked.

Hialeah stroked her hair. "If you want it to be."

She did. She wanted to drown in the tears of the universe, wanted to feel them sluicing over her body as she offered no resistance. Her part in the world was minuscule, insignificant. At first it had felt comforting but as she stared at the heavens a creeping sense of dread began to settle on her. Gradually her sense of oneness, of connection, began to disintegrate. The eyes watching her did not regard her as companion or lover. They saw her without seeing *her*. They were something distinctly *other*.

"I'm here," she whispered, desperate to feel the connection again. "Can you see me?"

"I'm here," Hialeah echoed.

Bettie felt a flash of frustration. *Not you*, she thought. Then she realised that she didn't have to speak aloud to communicate with her watcher. She didn't even need to keep her eyes open. She shut them and curled up in the sand next to Will, staring behind her eyes at the fantastic colours. Visions swam past like darting fish, too fast for her to register. Each one held a thousand secrets, a thousand answers. Each was a missed opportunity. But there was no way to catch them. If she reached for one, a thousand others flashed past.

The music had shifted into a darker register. It became discordant, almost grating, like sounds produced by instruments no one had ever heard before. The notes twined about her body, lifting her up. She floated in a timeless void, a speck of cosmic dust, utterly meaningless in the scope of it all. And yet something had singled her out. The others were still with her. She knew Hialeah and Piper were near. She could feel Will's hand. But none of them knew where she was. She was irrelevant in the world and yet somehow she knew she had a purpose. The presence – God, the universe, Nature – had plans for her. There was something she was meant to do.

The presence was beyond naming, beyond gender or any physical form she could visualise, but her mind felt as though it would unravel if she couldn't picture it, couldn't fix an image of it. She could feel herself coming undone at the knowledge.

Was this enlightenment? Was this cold emptiness all there was?

Beside her Will was murmuring, as though talking in his sleep. She heard the words "beast" and "apocalypse", then "Father". She pressed closer to him, but he seemed unaware of her. Were they each in a separate world, lost to the angels or demons of their own minds?

She opened her eyes and peered up into the maelstrom of stars. The watcher was still there, the only constant in the kaleidoscopic dreamscape. The eyes were focused on her, the pupils bottomless and black. Bettie felt herself pulled towards the malevolent gaze, felt herself floating, soaring into the abyss of their scrutiny. Her stomach swooped and she flailed her arms in terror. Looking down she could see the others far below, lying insensible in the circle of Joshua trees. Unknowing, vulnerable. Helpless.

"San Francisco," Bettie whispered frantically. The incantation worked and immediately she saw the Golden Gate Bridge in her mind, its brick-red towers and cables stretching across the water. It was a powerful symbol, an icon. It stood for hope. Permanence. Human triumph. It would rescue her from the encroaching despair.

But even as she imagined the sturdy bridge she saw

the waters beneath it churning with unrest. The surface rippled with the tremors of a disturbance far below and, as she watched, the bridge itself began to twist and writhe like a living thing. It was sinuous, snakelike. Soon the towers began to warp. The cables snapped, each one sounding like the crack of a whip as it came loose and flew, whistling, through the air. There was the terrible shriek of grinding metal, like violins raked by knives, and the screams of hundreds of people fleeing the disaster. But the worst was yet to come.

Something dark was lurking beneath. Something incomprehensibly huge. The black shape was spreading. It grew like an oil slick, staining the entire bay and seeping out into the Pacific Ocean. There was movement within the darkness. Multiple limbs thrashed as something rose towards the surface. And kept rising.

Burn, burn, burn . . .

When Bettie saw it clambering out of the water and onto the bridge she tried to scream, but her voice was gone. She drifted helplessly in the void, unable to do anything but watch in silent horror as the bridge folded in on itself, spilling the tiny antlike figures of people into the black water. The bridge groaned as it finally collapsed into the murky depths. And then Bettie was falling too.

Soon, soon, soon . . .

Falling, falling the endless miles from where she floated in space down to the cold expanse of water. She struck the roiling dark sea and screamed, icy water flooding her mouth, her throat, her lungs. She tasted salt and blood as she struggled against the waves, but the creature was pulling her down with its writhing legs, taking her with it.

Her only thought was a simple prayer for death to be swift. And painless.

* * *

She had no idea how long she had been screaming. Someone was shaking her and after a while she recognised Will's voice.

"Bettie, wake up! You're dreaming!"

Choking and sputtering, she struggled free of the watery nightmare and stared wildly around her. "What happened? Where am I?"

"You're safe. You're with me."

"But *where*?"

Will held her firmly and looked into her face. "We're in the desert. With Hialeah and Piper. Remember?"

She did remember. She remembered everything with terrible clarity. Pressing a hand to her chest, she breathed in slowly, carefully. There was no water. Nothing but hot, dry air. The van. They were in the painted van. Parked on the side of the road. Procol Harum was playing on the radio. Normality was returning.

"What happened?" she asked, sitting up.

Will laughed nervously. "You tell *me*. You seemed to have a pretty mind-blowing trip last night. We all watched the sun come up but you were beyond reach."

"What do you mean?"

Hialeah reached out to her from the front seat and squeezed her hand. "Totally catatonic. Just lost behind your own eyes. But you didn't seem upset, so we just left you to your visions. Lucky carried you to the van and we just assumed you were sleeping it off."

"Lucky?"

Will laughed. "Yeah, that's me. Don't you remember?"

She did. "Lucky," she said. The name was like an anchor, grounding her further in reality.

"We've been driving for a few hours," Hialeah said. "We're nearly there."

"Really?"

"We pulled over because Lucky couldn't wake you up," she added with a sympathetic wince. "It must have been some nightmare."

Bettie sat up and blinked at their surroundings. It was late afternoon, judging by the shadows. The landscape had changed dramatically. The Joshua trees and cacti were nowhere to be seen. Instead all around them was bland, featureless scrubland dotted with run-down gas stations and rickety outbuildings. How could she have slept so deeply?

"Am I still tripping?"

Hialeah shook her head. "I don't think so. Mine wore off hours ago."

Lucky and Piper both nodded to show that they were back to normal too.

"What on earth were you dreaming?" Lucky asked.

Bettie scrubbed at her eyes. "I don't know. I don't know where the trip ended and the nightmare began. It started off great. Colours and lights and infinity . . . I think I saw the face of God. I understood everything. At one point I was sure I was dying and being reborn. It was incredible."

Hialeah was nodding enthusiastically. "That's exactly how it's supposed to go."

"Yeah," Bettie said, "but then it turned ugly. There was something watching me. Something evil. I think . . . I think I might have been in hell." She shuddered and turned to Lucky, remembering something he'd said. "Did you see the end of the world?"

He frowned slightly. "Well, I did have one dark moment . . ."

"Was there a monster?"

"Not unless you count my father. I was in his church and the big crucifix on the wall was alive. There were bugs crawling on it, and my father was preaching fire and brimstone, hellfire and damnation, trying to convince me it was Judgment Day." He laughed uneasily. "I told him I didn't believe in any of it and then I just walked away. It felt so good to say it and the feeling stayed with me for the rest of the night. I felt so strong when it was all over. Like I'd literally banished him from my mind for good."

"Wow," Bettie said, feeling embarrassed. "Sounds like I'm the only one who freaked out. I'm really sorry."

"Aw, you just had too much to dream last night," Hialeah said with a wink. "Thing is, it wasn't even heavy stuff. Pretty low grade, actually. There's no way you should have been that far gone."

Bettie closed her eyes. She could still see the baleful eyes glowing at her from the stars, still feel the sharp grip of its legs, still see the horrible destruction it had wrought. At the time it had felt real and immediate, but now that she was awake and clear-headed it seemed less like an apocalyptic vision than a simple bad dream. The hallucinations must have bled into her dreams, that was all. Freaky, but certainly not impossible.

"Do you want to go back to sleep?" Lucky asked gently.

Her eyes flew open again. "No way! You said we were almost there. I don't want to miss my first sight of San Francisco!"

"Fab!" Hialeah cheered.

Piper grinned and threw the van into gear. They coasted back onto the highway and Hialeah started rummaging at her feet. "Here, these are for you." She turned around in her seat and held up a handful of cactus flowers. One by one she slipped them into Bettie's tangled hair. "You can't go to San Francisco without flowers in your hair!"

Bettie's eyes blurred with tears. "Thanks."

As they settled in for the last leg of the drive, Piper asked, "So have you thought of a name?"

Before she could answer Hialeah shouted "Star Child!" and Lucky suggested "Skyfire". A series of wild space-themed suggestions followed, but none of them felt right to her.

"Hmmm, I was thinking of something more – I don't know, literary."

"Well," said Piper, "you said you were in hell, but you came back. What about Persephone? She married Hades, but was allowed to come up for half the year, so spring and summer could happen."

Bettie remembered reading about Greek mythology in school and she had always found the stories unaccountably disturbing. The gods were so petty and vindictive, their punishments always far out of proportion to the so-called “crimes” against them. She remembered the story of Persephone very well, as it had frightened her as a little girl.

“Married to the King of the Underworld,” she mused. “That sounds a little creepy.”

On the radio the Supremes faded out and the next song began. They recognised the muted snare drum and psychedelic twanging guitar at once. It was practically an anthem for their generation.

“Maybe it wasn’t hell after all,” Lucky said with a smile. “Maybe you just fell down the rabbit hole.”

Bettie returned his smile. They sang along with Jefferson Airplane, about the caterpillar and the Red Queen and the dormouse, belting out the final lines of the song at the tops of their voices.

“My head got fed all right,” she laughed.

Lucky kissed her and said, “Hello, Alice. Welcome back.”

Hialeah crossed her eyes and made a crazy face, pulling her mouth into a wide grin with her fingers. “We’re all mad here,” she said, and everyone laughed with the easy camaraderie of people who were always meant to be friends.

“That’s perfect,” Bettie said. “It feels just right.”

The disc jockey was talking about California, about the beautiful day, the sunshine and the love that was in the air. And as the Beatles began to sing she met her own eyes in the dusty reflection of the window and a small shadow seemed to flicker across her heart.

The flowers in her hair made her think of Ophelia's "fantastic garlands" and for a moment she felt less like Alice than Hamlet's drowned lover.

* * *

They approached the city from the south. They'd wanted to arrive via the Golden Gate Bridge, but it would have meant a much longer drive and an impractical route. Instead they cut across to the coast road, where the view was breathtaking. None of them had ever seen the Pacific Ocean before. There was nothing to compare with the endless stretch of shining water and the foamy wild waves crashing on the beach.

From the moment they reached San Francisco they could feel the energy. It was a completely different world from either New Orleans or Tucson.

At first they drove aimlessly, marvelling at the sights. They exclaimed over brightly painted Victorian houses and the iconic cable cars making their way up and down the hills. All along the streets were people their age, with long hair and love beads and tie-dyed clothes. Some of them waved and made the peace sign with their fingers when they saw the van and recognised others of their kind.

All along the scenic route Alice had been quiet, admiring the view while at the same time trying to push away the intrusive memories of the end of her acid trip. She had tried to cling to her friends' words, to reassure herself that the horrors she had seen weren't real.

A girl named Bettie had been lost in Wonderland, but she had escaped to find it had been nothing but a curious dream. She was Alice now, conversant with madness, but not imprisoned by it.

They passed an official-looking building where a group of protesters were marching across the lawn. They were chanting and holding up signs saying MAKE LOVE, NOT WAR and EIGHTEEN TODAY, DEAD TOMORROW.

For a moment Alice felt a little flutter of unease at the reminder of why they had run away, but she closed her eyes and conjured the image of Lucky's draft card going up in flames. They were safe now, just like Hialeah had promised. No one would find them here.

"You're very quiet."

"Huh? What?" She looked around, shaking off the

fog of distraction. Lucky looked concerned. "Sorry. Just putting the ghosts to rest."

He put his arm around her, reassuring her with a squeeze. On the radio were songs of love and peace, and all around them was the most beautiful city in the world. There was no place in their new life for shadows and dark thoughts.

Outside a church they saw another protest. Some teenagers were sitting in a circle, completely naked, their hands upraised as if in prayer. A sign was planted in the ground nearby declaring LOVE IS NOT A SIN. Alice had never seen anyone but her boyfriend naked before, and the sight was shocking. She wondered if she could ever learn to be that free, if they would become like their parents' worst fears of the counterculture. Perhaps they could all join a commune, sharing each other's bodies as easily as they might share a loaf of bread. Surely that was the natural way to be, after all. The world seemed full of possibilities she had never considered before.

All around them the streets were alive with all the vibrant world-changing ideas she had only read about in the paper or seen on the news back home. She'd seen protests and demonstrations in New Orleans, but nothing on this scale. And when their little group finally reached Haight-Ashbury they were blown away. Haight Street was like a tiny city in itself, a city populated entirely by kindred spirits. Even the graffiti and vandalism seemed good-natured.

They passed a deli whose name had been changed with spray paint to "PSYCHE-Delicatessen", and a shop window featured an army recruitment poster with Uncle Sam redecorated as a long-haired hippie with tinted shades.

It was overwhelming. So much to see, so much to take in, so many new experiences on offer. San Francisco was like an acid trip itself.

They turned off the radio and rolled down the windows to listen to the street musicians. On one corner they heard a girl who sounded as though she'd had opera training. Her voice carried across the waves of street noise like a siren, drawing them in. Beyond her was a man in a woven robe, pounding furiously on bongos while people danced around him in a circle. Further on a guy stood on a plastic milk crate reciting poetry.

They listened to the words for a little while before a trio of laughing girls broke the moment, hammering on the side of the van. The girls were similarly dressed, in flowered tops and miniskirts, and they looked like sisters. One held a picnic basket and Alice imagined that they had stepped straight out of a fairy tale.

"Welcome, travellers!" the girls cried, their eyes

shining like marbles. "Are you here to change the world?"

"You bet!" Hialeah replied at once.

They gave a cheer. The one with the basket passed a brown paper bag through the window to Hialeah.

"What's this?"

"Brownies. We make them for everyone."

There was no need to ask what was special about the brownies. Alice and Lucky knew a guy back home who had been studying to be a chef. One night he'd sneaked back into the restaurant after closing to use his boss's pressure cooker. The resulting cannabis butter had made the most potent chocolate chip cookies they'd ever tasted. A single bite was all it took to make all the troubles of the world fade into insignificance.

"Hey, thanks," said Hialeah.

"You're welcome! Peace be with you all!" With that the girls skipped away, swinging their basket between them like three Little Red Riding Hoods.

Hialeah opened the bag and shared the brownies around. They were powerful if not very tasty, and suddenly Alice felt a pang of nostalgia for the brownies her mother used to make, for all the home-cooked meals she would never eat again. What were her parents doing now? Had they found her note? Was her mother crying? Her father cursing? Lucky's father would undoubtedly be praying, exhorting his congregation to pray too, for his wayward, cowardly son. She shook her head to banish the past. Maybe someday she would send a postcard home, just to let them know she was okay.

At the end of Haight Street they came to Golden Gate Park, where they got out to explore.

All around them people were dancing, singing, meditating, *being*. They seemed free of all rules and inhibitions, free just to be themselves, free to be happy, to live their young lives the way they should, with no fear of being sent to die in foreign lands.

"It's just like I always imagined it," Hialeah said. "I feel like I'm dreaming."

"Me too," Piper echoed.

Alice pressed close to Lucky, excited but a little frightened. "I kind of feel like I'm tripping again," she confessed. "Like my senses can't handle it all."

"Don't worry," Piper said. "We'll help you find your way back through the looking glass."

Lucky kissed her neck. "Alice," he whispered. "I love you."

Alice.

She imagined the name like a velvet cloak, as deep and as blue as the ocean, wrapping her in its soft embrace. It smoothed away all the lingering traces of the bland girl she had been before, and of the pain of missing the bland life she had left behind. She mustn't confuse familiarity with safety. An image from her trip returned and she sighed as she pictured "Bettie" written in the sand of a beach. Foamy waves obliterated the name, leaving behind a scattering of seashells that spelled out "Alice".

"I love you too," she murmured. The brownies had come on strong and their little group was feeling mellow, happy and intimately connected.

They wandered for hours, soaking up the vibes, enjoying the atmosphere and the friendly people. It was like coming home to a party where everyone knew them, had been expecting them, and welcomed them with open arms.

And yet, every so often, Alice had the eerie sense that a person was not who he or she seemed. Occasionally someone would eye her warily, as if sensing that *she* was the one who was somehow different, not one of them. That she didn't belong. The feeling always faded as quickly as it came, and she told herself it was just the brownies making her paranoid. It had been an eventful couple of days, after all. Traumatic even.

They walked through the crisp green grass of the Presidio and Alice gasped in amazement as they came upon an ancient Greek city at the edge of a lake. In the centre stood a huge and ornate rotunda, surrounded by urns and trees. A sculpted frieze of people in togas danced across the panels of the rotunda beneath a high, graceful dome. Curving around and behind it was an elaborate colonnade, also lavishly carved, and along the top was a repeating motif: an empty pedestal with four figures facing each other around it, leaning with their elbows on the flat surface. They looked as though they were communing, perhaps looking for a statue that had lost its way. Or summoning a new one to take its place.

The whole spectacular vision was inverted in the mirror of the lake, where the shimmering reflection was broken by the swans and ducks gliding across it.

"Have we gone back in time?" Alice breathed.

"Maybe," said Hialeah with a twinkle in her eye.

They followed the path to the rotunda, where they stood dwarfed beneath its grand dome. Statues of angels gazed down at them from between the curved arches and columns. The concave ceiling was a mandala of geometric shapes and Alice imagined that she could hear the whispers of all the people who had ever stood beneath it, their voices trapped there forever.

Piper sent a wild call up into the dome, startling a flock of pigeons, which flapped away noisily. The cry echoed around them for several seconds.

They wandered out again and, after a few minutes of awed silence, Lucky asked, "What is this place?"

"It's called the Palace of Fine Arts."

They all turned towards the male voice that had spoken. A man sat behind them on a bench, reading a battered paperback. He looked to be in his late forties, with short hair and a tie. There was something professorial about him and he reminded Alice of Mr Winters, her favourite English teacher back at school.

"It was built for an exhibition in the early part of the century," he continued. "It was only meant to last a few days but the people loved it so much they wouldn't let it be torn down." He stood up, offering them his hand, which they took it in turns to shake. "Name's Tom," he said. "Tom Lawrence."

"Pleased to meet you," Hialeah chirped. "I'm Hialeah and this is my boyfriend Piper Dawn. That's Alice and Lucky."

Tom smiled. "Ah, I do envy you young people. Sometimes I wish I could just change my whole identity too. I'm guessing you're new in town?"

Lucky nodded. "We just arrived today. We've only been here a couple of hours but already it feels like home."

"San Francisco does that to people," Tom said knowingly. "I've been here all my life. You couldn't drag me away, not for anything."

Alice noticed the book he was reading. *The Stars My*

Destination by Alfred Bester. "Oh, I love that book!" she exclaimed.

Tom gazed down at the cover like it was an old friend. "My wife Helen gave me this book for my birthday several years ago."

"I read it in school," Alice said. "It totally blew my mind! Where's your wife now?"

Tom closed his eyes. "Gone to the stars herself," he said, his voice tinged with sadness. Alice noticed he was still wearing a wedding ring.

"Oh, I'm so sorry."

"Helen was very ill and this was the last gift she ever gave me. I cherish it. I've reread it every year since she died and I'll keep reading it until it falls apart in my hands. Then I'll buy a new copy and read it again. I can keep her with me forever that way." He was smiling wistfully as he said it, but when he raised his head to look at Alice something darkened in his expression. He looked uneasy, even a little frightened.

A chill went through her bones, like someone had walked over her grave. And from somewhere she was sure she heard the strange discordant grating.

It's you, a voice hissed.

Alice took a stumbling step away from Tom. "What?"

You're the one.

The air around her felt icy all of a sudden and she

felt something shudder in the ground beneath her feet. Slowly a shadow engulfed the park, blocking out the sun. There was a roar in her ears, like the sound of a violent storm. Stinging needles of rain pelted the earth. Only the rain wasn't rain at all but spatters of blood and flesh, as though the storm had ripped the world apart and torn the people in it to shreds. She realised with a sick feeling that she wasn't actually *seeing* it so much as *hearing* it, like a hellish orchestra tuning up for a grisly performance.

"Hey." It was Lucky. He was shaking her by the shoulder. "Are you all right?"

She blinked and shook the moment off like cobwebs. The sun was shining. There was no shadow, no whispering voice, no disharmony. When she looked back at Tom he seemed like nothing was wrong. He was telling Piper and Hialeah about other sights – Alcatraz and Coit Tower. And Lombard Street, the crookedest street in the world. As though nothing odd had happened at all.

"Yeah, I'm fine," she mumbled.

"You went all pale for a moment. I thought you were going to faint."

She forced a smile. "Really? Must just be the heat. I'm okay." She sealed the lie with a kiss and told herself she would make it true. No one else seemed to have noticed anything.

She looked back up at the Palace, determined not to let any weird thoughts or visions bring her down.

It was the most beautiful place she had ever seen. Truly magical, like something from a fairy tale. The rich buttery columns might be made of icing, like the tiers of a wedding cake. The trees might be sleeping dragons, the swans princesses hiding from wicked queens.

Above them the sky was endlessly blue, the reflection below sparkling like sapphires. She felt at one with it, with the romance of the place and the sense of communion with those who had built it and those who had preserved it. She imagined that, whatever bad things might happen to her in her life, she could always seek shelter here in her mind. All she need do was close her eyes and she would be here. Were there boys in the jungles of Vietnam right now wishing themselves here?

The idea made her eyes fill with tears and she had the sense she'd had in the desert of being unable to take in the sensory bombardment. Her heart swelled with emotion and she remembered the feeling of helpless insignificance beneath the stars. She could almost see them shining beyond the blue of the sky, the unfathomable depths in which this place was only the tiniest speck of microscopic dust. And although she tried hard to repel the memory, she saw the eyes, those black, black eyes that had watched her so coldly, so indifferently, those eyes that had *seen* her. Again there was the awful feeling of being watched, of something noting her presence. Her ears prickled with sounds that wanted in.

Glancing out towards the lake she was startled to see crowds of people. She hadn't noticed anyone here when they'd arrived, although they must have been there. A place like this would never be deserted. There were tourists pointing and exclaiming, hippies sitting on the grass, a couple in wedding attire being photographed outside the rotunda.

She watched a little boy feeding ducks at the edge of the lake and the sudden horrible thought came to her that he might fall in. But that wasn't all; the image spiralled into something much worse. She saw his lifeless body floating face-down in the water, the ducks swarming over him, quacking noisily as they pecked and tore at his skin with their bright orange beaks, staining the water crimson.

She shook her head to banish the sight and looked around frantically for the boy's parents. They stood a few feet behind him. They were staring at her, their eyes cold and accusing.

Her stomach twisted at the thought that she had somehow projected the terrible image into their minds.

Turning away she saw a man in a red tracksuit watching her. He stood on the path circling the lake as though he too had been interrupted by the awful pictures from her mind. And as soon as she saw him, she saw him dead as well, lying broken and bloody beneath the feet of a stampeding mob.

Run, run, run . . .

She couldn't block out either the voice or the visions. With a sense of awful dread she turned back towards Tom. He was dead. What was left of him was scattered over the park bench in bloody chunks, as though a bomb had gone off in a butcher shop. His cherished book lay in a scarlet puddle on the ground, only the title had changed. *Death's My Destination*, it said.

She choked back a scream as madness picked at her mind like sharp, bright fingers. That wasn't the title, she told herself, just a line in the book. It wasn't a prophecy because she was no prophet. None of this was real.

But averting her eyes from him offered no peace.

All along the colonnade people were flailing blindly, attacking one another and falling to the ground. They writhed and struggled, clawing at their eyes, howling and crying like animals. Everywhere she looked there was chaos. Screaming people, panic, terror, death. And above it all, beyond it all, something was watching.

Soon, soon, soon . . .

Alice squeezed her eyes shut tight.

It's the brownies, she told herself. *Flashback. Nightmare.*

But she knew better. Whatever she had encountered during her trip had found her here, had tracked her like a predator. Then the worst thought of all struck her. What if it had been with her all her life? What if expanding her consciousness had merely made her aware of it at last? Why didn't the others sense it? Tom had seen it in her; why didn't they?

She opened one eye cautiously and peeked out through the nearest arch. All she saw were people. Normal people doing normal things. No blood, no death. And no one was staring at her.

With a sigh of relief she realised that none of the others had noticed anything was amiss. It was as though she had stepped out of the world for a moment, into a kind of private hell. But the vision – or whatever it was – was gone now, and she told herself it was just her mind playing tricks, even if she didn't really believe it. The alternatives were too awful to consider. If there wasn't some malevolent presence out there dreaming of the apocalypse then her friend Janie had been right all along. She really *was* looney tunes.

So she imagined a box where she could lock the terrible sights away, just like turning off the TV. She tucked them inside, closed the lid and locked the box. Gone.

"How far are we from the Golden Gate Bridge?"

Lucky's voice pulled her from her rumination and she felt a rush of protective love for him. Sweet, gentle Lucky, who President Johnson had sentenced to death. San Francisco would save him. It would save them all. Maybe that was all the visions meant.

Tom pointed. "It's just over there. About two miles."

"Well, I'm game," Hialeah said.

Lucky nodded. "Me too. Bett – I mean, Alice?"

She smiled at the use of her new name. She'd already come to think of Will as Lucky. And he was. They all were. Lucky to have escaped the war, lucky to have met Hialeah and Piper, and lucky to be here. Lucky to be alive.

"Absolutely!" she said.

The others were already heading off, but something held her back. She looked back at Tom, who was watching her, his forehead creased with concern. After a moment he fished in his pocket for something and held it out to her. It was a scrap of paper with a name and address scribbled on it. LUANA, it read. FORTUNES TOLD.

She looked quizzically at Tom. She'd never have pegged him as the type to believe in such things.

"I saw her after Helen died," Tom said, as though confessing a great secret. "I was sceptical when I first went but now, well, like the song says, I'm a believer. I think you should see her. She helped me."

Alice didn't know what to say. She stared at the handwritten slip of paper, her eyes following the loops and curls of the words. If this woman really could tell fortunes, maybe she could help make sense of things.

"Thank you," she said, tucking the paper into her bag. "I will."

She walked away, looking back only once. Tom was still watching her. He raised one hand as if to say farewell and Alice didn't like the finality of it. He looked haunted. She waved back and then hurried to catch up with the others.

After walking for a while they could see the bay. White sails dotted the blue expanse of water and off to the right was a rocky island crowned by an ominous squat grey building. Alcatraz.

They stared at it in silence for several minutes. It was no longer a working prison, but Alice wondered if anyone still lived there on the island. It looked so cold and forbidding, so isolated. Were the waters of the bay really teeming with sharks? Was that why no one had ever escaped? She could almost imagine that the jagged sails were the teeth of giant sharks lurking beneath the cold waves, and she turned away before the image could gain strength.

At last they saw the Golden Gate Bridge, its long red span wreathed in fog. This far away it looked impossibly delicate, like a model made of matchsticks and fine thread that could fall apart in a breath of wind. It was strange to see something so familiar, so iconic, in reality at last. She'd seen the bridge in countless photographs, paintings and in films. But to finally be within walking distance of it was truly inspiring.

They reached it within the hour and it felt like the end of a pilgrimage. Tom had said it was exactly a mile across and they'd walked miles already. Alice's feet were sore, but she didn't care. The excitement of being here soothed away the nagging pain.

The heat wasn't as oppressive here as in the desert, but it had still made them thirsty and sweaty. They found an ice cream stand in the park at Fort Point and treated themselves, gobbling their cones hurriedly before the ice cream could melt. Then they set out across the bridge, to see the magnificent view that countless people before them had seen.

Although the sun was still high overhead, there was a fearsome breeze sweeping in from the Pacific, and it was a long, chilly walk to the centre of the span. The fog below made it seem as though the bridge were thousands of feet in the air and they were crossing clouds and not water. The wind tore through the mist like scissors through rags, shredding them, and through the holes they could see the choppy water of the bay. Alice couldn't even imagine the desperation of escaping prisoners from Alcatraz braving it. Or worse, the people who probably jumped from this bridge into the icy depths. She pushed the thought aside and pressed on, sticking close to Lucky.

But it wasn't long before the cold wind got the best of them. Hialeah cried off first, shivering in her skimpy dress. Piper had given her his jacket to wear but it was no match for the elements. Even Alice finally had to admit defeat. Her feet and legs were really beginning to hurt from the day's trek and they couldn't afford to get to the other side and then collapse from exhaustion.

"Besides," she gasped, "I'm starving."

"Me too," said Hialeah. "All we've had to eat all day were those brownies."

Piper gazed towards the city. "I wonder how far it is back to the van? We've still got some hot dogs."

"However far it is," Alice said, wrapping her arms around herself, "I'm freezing. Sorry, Lucky."

Lucky seemed the least tired of them all. "It's okay," he said reluctantly. "We can try again another day. This is our home now, after all, and we can come back any time we want to."

Alice kissed him, liking the sound of that. "Home," she murmured. She was shivering but happy. She had forgotten all about Tom and the disturbing visions at the Palace of Fine Arts.

As they made their back towards Haight-Ashbury, footsore and hungry, Alice felt content. Tonight they could eat dinner in the park with their makeshift family, then fall asleep under the stars. Just like creatures that were wild, and most importantly, free.

* * *

They settled into their new life easily. It was the Summer of Love and all around them was friendship and acceptance, music and drugs, love and sex. It was paradise.

There was no threat of war here, no oppressive authority figures to tell them what to do or how to wear their hair. No teachers to tell them what to think.

Their school was the world and their world was Haight-Ashbury.

Fog blanketed the city every morning until the golden sun rose to banish it. The nights were chilly, but it was a small price to pay for calling Golden Gate Park their home.

A commune had sprung up in a little grove of trees deep inside the park and Piper had got them a four-person tent for shelter. Every night was like a camping trip. They ate food cooked over a fire and listened to the music and the voices all around them. If any member of the commune needed something, there was always someone happy to provide it. It was such a simple way of life, so easy and free.

Piper and Hialeah had staked out the corner of Haight and Belvedere Street, and they performed there during the day, graciously accepting the coins tossed into Piper's guitar case. They called themselves The Dreamseeds.

When they ran out of money Alice found a job in a bakery just opposite the park. There was nothing like the smell of fresh bread every morning. The pay wasn't much but the owner, Mr Castillo, was generous and kind. Every evening he gave Alice a loaf of bread to take home with her, along with any cakes or cookies he couldn't sell. A widower who had lost his only son in Vietnam, he was very sympathetic to the flower children. He allowed them to decorate the front window, and one morning he woke to find that the bakery had effectively been renamed "All You Knead is Love".

Lucky had a harder time finding work. With no ID he could only do cash-in-hand jobs in the area. Again the commune saved him. He wasn't the only refugee from the draft, and before long someone put him in touch with an operation in Chinatown that specialised in fake IDs. Afterwards he had a driver's licence in the name of Lucien LeBlanc.

Days passed in a blissful haze, becoming weeks and then months. New Orleans soon felt like a distant memory, like a past life. The leaves began to change colour and the air grew crisper. Occasionally Alice wondered how her parents were. She had come to think of Mr Castillo as a father figure and over time she confided everything to him. He wholly understood her reasons for running away.

"Sometimes it takes just as much courage to walk away than it does to stay," he said wisely. "Try not to judge them too harshly. They only want what's best for you."

"But they don't know me at all. I don't think they ever did."

"I'm sure they'd be comforted to know that you're happy."

"I'd like to think so," she said wistfully. "Sometimes the temptation to call home is almost overwhelming, just to say hi, and let them know I'm okay. But with Lucky – well, you know. I just can't risk it."

"I understand, *chica*," he said, putting an arm around her. "Lord knows my son and I didn't always see eye to eye, and I'd give anything to go back and undo all the foolish things said in anger."

Alice nestled into his chest, enjoying the comforting feel of his embrace and the fresh-baked bread smell of his clothes. "Yeah. But kids can be stubborn. The more you tell us not to do something, the more we want to do it."

Mr Castillo sighed. "True. So true. I just wish Carlos had listened to me that one time."

"Hey," she said, "even if he hadn't chosen to go, he might have been called up like Lucky. You can't blame yourself."

They were silent for a while, happy just to share a quiet moment. Alice gazed across to the smiling face of the little blue Krishna figurine, who had come with her all the way from New Orleans. Now he danced on top of the cash register beside a little statue of the Virgin Mary. She liked to think that both brought them luck.

It wasn't long before the bell clanged above the bakery door and a group of school kids burst in. They headed straight for the glass case, pointing and exclaiming at the array of doughnuts and bragging about how many they could eat.

Mr Castillo smiled. "No rest for the wicked," he said with a laugh. He kissed Alice on the top of her head and went out to confront the manageable chaos of the shop.

She smiled as she watched him sort out their order and count their change. *Life is good,* she told herself.

* * *

As time went on she hardly ever thought about that strange trip she'd taken in the desert, the eyes that had peered at her from the icy depths of the sky, the awful visions she'd had afterwards, the terrible sounds that had pierced her ears. Sometimes she would catch a person staring at her, watching as if in fear of something she might do. In the end they always looked away and Alice told herself she had just imagined it. There was none of the paranoia and death imagery of that day at the Palace of Fine Arts.

But one day something happened that brought it all back.

She hadn't dropped acid again and no one had

pressured her to give it another try. She was content with the lighter treats on offer, the ones that made her feel mellow but weren't profoundly mind-altering. Everyone else around her tripped, though, and for the most part they had pleasant psychedelic experiences. They grooved to the music and the colours and the wild visuals, and sometimes they wept at the awesome beauty of the world and everything in it. Sometimes she envied them, but fear kept any temptation well in check.

She didn't know the boy who freaked out. He was someone she'd seen around the streets, someone who seemed easygoing and laid back. Certainly not the kind of person who would do what he did.

When she heard the screaming she thought at first that there had been a car accident. A crowd was clustered around a shop front, and raised voices were telling someone to take it easy, to put something down. She thought she heard the word "screwdriver".

As she got closer she saw several people running away, and a girl was hunched over in the gutter, being violently sick. She raised her head as Alice passed, her face pallid and stricken. "Oh God," she moaned, "his eyes!"

Two volunteers from the free clinic were pushing their way through the crowd and Alice heard the clatter of an object on the sidewalk. A large screwdriver rolled to a stop against a fire hydrant, its metal tip dripping with blood. A pulpy mass lay nearby in a pool of what looked like black ink. Her stomach lurched as she pieced the scene together, and she looked up in time to see the boy being dragged away. His eye sockets streamed with crimson and his shirt was drenched in gore. He was screaming something about eyes. Cold eyes that watched, that *saw*. The words made no immediate sense to Alice but they still felt chillingly familiar.

"They see everything! They're coming!"

There was a roaring in her ears then, like the crash of huge waves on a beach. It was followed by a high-pitched whine, a new note in the symphony of horror she'd first heard in the desert.

Behind her eyes she saw flickers of movement against the darkness, like thousands of arms gesturing frantically. No, not arms. Legs. And not human ones. For a moment she had the sickening thought that tiny creatures were living inside her eyes, scurrying along the nerves into her brain. She blinked away the image, disturbed by the idea that the vision wasn't even hers, that the boy had somehow projected into her mind what he was seeing. Was he seeing them even now, without eyes?

As the volunteers guided him towards the clinic, he suddenly went quiet. He turned his head slowly, deliberately, his empty sockets fixed on Alice, as though he could see her in spite of his mutilation. His lips were moving and it took her several moments to work out what he was saying.

"Run, run, run."

* * *

Alice dug through her bag until she finally found what she was looking for.

LUANA. FORTUNES TOLD.

The card gave an address on Hyde Street, near Ghirardelli Square. Mr Castillo showed her where to find it on the map, but if he was curious about why she was looking for a fortune teller, he didn't ask.

A cable car took her most of the way to Fisherman's Wharf, and it should have been a delightful, picturesque journey. Instead Alice found herself staring uneasily at the tracks, unnerved by the thought that she was riding an impossibly long and ancient snake, one whose bones made up the heart of the city. The sky overhead had darkened, with clouds the colour of lead. In the distance thunder rumbled like a beast. Everything felt ominous, portentous, and suddenly she wanted to turn around and go home.

But the boy had taken her back to that day at

the Palace of Fine Arts, when she'd had that awful apocalyptic vision.

Death's my destination.

She remembered vividly the sight of blood and chaos, of people torn apart and scattered across the park like so many scraps of meat. Mostly she remembered Tom. Kind Tom who seemed to have heard the same voice and who had given her Luana's address. She remembered how haunted he had looked as he'd waved goodbye, as though she were heading into some kind of danger from which he knew she would never return. Something was coming. Something terrible.

Run, run, run . . .

Soon, soon, soon . . .

Her stomach began to flutter as the cable car came to the street she wanted, but she stayed on until it reached the turnaround. There it followed the curving tracks in a slow U-turn and began the reverse journey back up the hill.

This time Alice stepped off at the right street and stood staring around her at row upon row of painted ladies. They didn't seem real. They looked like gingerbread houses, and she imagined that all their bright colours would have corresponding flavours: cherry, blueberry, apple, banana. But the idea of a gingerbread house suddenly reminded her of the purpose it had in the fairy tale: something tempting and tantalising meant to lure unwary innocents into the clutches of evil.

She felt frightened and completely out of her depth, recalling the voice that had whispered inside her mind the day they had arrived.

It's you.

"Stop it," she growled, disgusted with herself. *What* was her? *What* was coming? She refused to believe that everything around her was some elaborate trap, that evil beings even existed, let alone that they had sought her out for some diabolical purpose. What was so special about her anyway? Surely evil found evil people, ones who were only too happy to commit murder or start wars and slaughter millions of innocent people.

At last she found the address. It was a narrow Victorian townhouse, sandwiched into a row of others in the same style. It was painted in vibrant shades of purple with fancy gold trim all around. Stairs led up to a bright red door with a bay window beside it. Two more bay windows looked out from the floor above and the house was topped by a gabled roof. It looked like the kind of house a child would draw – a tall box with a triangle on top.

Instead of curtains the bay windows were hung with strips of fabric printed with Hawaiian flowers and zodiac symbols. A small sign in the corner of one window advertised Luana's services.

Although there was no question that this was the right place, Alice hesitated. A thousand fretful thoughts ran through her mind like mice in an attic. She didn't even know if she believed in things like fortune telling and astrology, but surely it could do no harm. Lucky's father would have disagreed, of course. He'd call it the work of the devil. The memory of his small-minded ideas spurred her on.

She climbed the short flight of stairs to the door and rang the bell. From within she heard a musical tinkling that echoed the wind chimes on the porch. Footsteps soon followed, then a smiling woman opened the door. She looked to be in her fifties and was what her mother would have called "pleasingly plump". She had dark skin and long black hair and she wore a flowing chiffon dress patterned with tropical flowers. She fixed her wide brown eyes on Alice and stared for several seconds.

Alice shank a little under her scrutiny before she was able to stammer out a greeting. "Um, hello. Are you Luana?"

The woman nodded. Although she was still smiling, her eyes suddenly seemed a little darker and her forehead was slightly creased. Was Luana reading her mind?

“My name’s Alice. A friend gave me your address and said you had helped him. I . . . I’m not sure if I . . . Well, I mean . . .”

Luana opened the door a little wider. “You are looking for answers,” she said. “Come in and we’ll see what we can see.”

From within came a medley of scents. Cinnamon and incense mingled with the slightly musty smell of old books and candle wax. There was also the lush fragrance of exotic flowers. Alice closed her eyes and breathed deeply, savouring the aromas.

Luana led her into a sitting room with three mismatched couches and a small table covered with yellowing lace. It looked like an old wedding veil. Books surrounded them, crammed onto sagging shelves. Huge showy blossoms flaunted themselves in pots scattered around the room, further illuminated by the flicker of candle flames. The room was warm and humid, and Alice felt as though she’d stepped into a greenhouse.

“Tea?” Luana asked.

“Yes, please.”

Luana poured a deep red liquid from a teapot into a tiny nested glass bowl. The design was such that the tea seemed to float inside an even smaller bowl within, giving it the appearance of something magical. Luana passed it to Alice, who held her nose over the wisps of fragrant steam.

"It's hibiscus," Luana said, "with rosehip and pomegranate."

Alice sipped it carefully and sighed at the strange but comforting blend of fruit and flowers. "It's delicious."

Luana smiled. "It's my great-grandmother's recipe. From Honolulu. It's said to calm the nerves." At that she gave Alice a meaningful look. "And something tells me your nerves need calming."

Alice winced. "Is it that obvious?"

"Perhaps not to everyone," Luana said with a shrug. "But I know someone with a burden when I see her."

"A burden. Yes. I guess you could call it that."

Luana gestured towards one of the couches and Alice sank gratefully onto a pile of embroidered cushions. Outside a breeze stirred the wind chimes and their tinkling melody enhanced the feeling of serenity in the room. She didn't know what to say or how much to tell. She'd been rehearsing it in her head all day but it didn't sound like anything but pure madness.

At last she simply blurted it out. "I see things. *Saw* things. When I was little I would wake up from nightmares without realising I was awake. I couldn't tell what was real and what wasn't. But then it stopped happening and I assumed it was over. Until a few weeks ago." She took another sip of tea and then she finally spoke the words that had been haunting her. "I think I saw the end of the world."

There was no reaction. Luana merely watched her, listening with a serious expression. Alice couldn't tell what the look meant.

After a few seconds she felt self-conscious and she gave a nervous little laugh. "But like I said, that was weeks ago and obviously it hasn't come true. So I have no idea if it was just a bad trip or what. I'd hate to waste your time if––"

Luana held up her hand. "I believe that some people do see visions of the future," she said, "whether good or bad. But there's no way of telling when something will occur. If it ever will. And even if it was just a bad trip, you can't live your life in fear, dreading every day and waiting for something terrible to happen."

Alice felt a wave of relief at the other woman's understanding. "That's it exactly! At first it was just like that. I was worried all the time, like someone was always standing behind me in the shadows, you know? Just waiting to pounce. It got better over time, and usually I can forget about it, but every once in a while I'll catch someone's eye and it's like they can see into my mind, see what I see. Or what I saw."

"Have you told anyone about these visions?"

She shook her head vehemently. “No one. Not even my boyfriend.”

“It’s a heavy burden to carry alone,” Luana said sadly. “Especially for one so young.”

“It’s awful. And then yesterday this guy . . .” She shuddered at the memory. “Well, I think he saw the same thing I did. He blinded himself, but he still saw *me*. He looked right at me.”

“Some people have sight beyond their physical eyes. Will you give me your hands?”

Alice did as she asked, placing her trembling hands in Luana’s. Luana closed her eyes. After a while she spoke, her voice low and husky.

“I see emptiness, water. A deep, vast coldness. It’s black. So black. Infinite, eternal.” Her eyes flew open then and she released Alice’s hands, drawing back with a little gasp as though breaking free of a trance.

“What? What is it?”

Luana pressed her fingers to her temples. “Forgive me. There is such power in you. For a moment it was too much.”

Alice didn’t know what to make of it. Could it just be an act? A part of her wanted to believe so because the alternative was simply too frightening. But Luana’s words had been eerily specific and her intuition told her the woman was not a con artist.

Luana offered her a weak little smile. "Shall we see what the cards have to say?"

Alice swallowed the last of her tea and set the little bowl down on a rickety side table. If the tea had made her calmer, Luana's spooky vision had only wound her nerves tightly again. "Okay."

Luana went to one of the bookshelves and took down a battered wooden box. She spread a thin black cloth over the table. In the centre, drawn in what appeared to be chalk, was a large five-pointed star inside a circle.

"This is a pentacle," Luana explained, touching the middle of the star. "It represents the earth. Our world and all that we can know."

From the box she took a deck of what looked like large playing cards. They were frayed at the edges and clearly very old. Alice had never seen tarot cards before, but she had always been curious about them. Luana shuffled them with practised ease and set the deck down on the table. With one fluid movement she swept them around into a circle, their obscured faces a story waiting to be told.

"Choose six cards," Luana said. "Just close your eyes and let your instinct guide you."

Alice did as Luana instructed. She pictured the fanned cards in her mind and slid her fingers over them. Immediately one seemed to glow and she pressed down on its corner, teasing it out a little from the others. Gradually she traced her way around the circle, waiting for each one to feel right before choosing. When she had drawn six cards she opened her eyes and Luana tucked the other cards back inside their box.

"Very good. Now we'll lay them out. This card ––" she held up the first one Alice had chosen "––represents you." She placed it face-down in the centre of the pentacle. "Now, if we start from the point at the bottom, and follow the line up, we will see the situation that is causing conflict. Here." She tapped the upper left point of the star. "Keep going and we can see the past, the heart of the matter and the future." She traced the star with her finger as she placed the corresponding cards at each point she indicated. "And then we have the final outcome." She put the last card at the bottom point of the pentacle. "Are you ready?"

Alice stared at the cards, a little frightened and a little awed. All she could do was nod.

Luana turned over the first card. It was upside-down and it showed a heart pierced by three swords. Alice watched the other woman's face carefully. Luana was unable to hide the little flicker of a frown.

"What is it?" Alice asked. "Is it bad?"

"Not necessarily. It's a difficult card, a card of sorrow and conflict, but then you are in some distress, are you not? Something painful has come to the surface, something that is causing you a lot of suffering."

"That's certainly true," Alice said.

"Let's see what the nature of the problem is." She turned over the next card. It showed a golden wheel surrounded by mythical beasts. Some were clinging on, others sliding off. This card was also upside-down. "The Wheel of Fortune," Luana said. "Now, this is interesting. It suggests something deep and mysterious at work inside. Fate if you like. A sudden change in fortune."

"Why is it upside-down?"

"Well, luck can be either good or bad. Perhaps this is what's causing the inner turmoil."

Immediately Alice thought of Lucky. "You mean coming to San Francisco was a bad idea? My boyfriend and I ran away from home to get here."

Luana considered the two cards. "I'm not sure it's as simple as that," she said slowly. "We'll have to look at the spread as a whole before we can interpret it fully."

Alice didn't like the way her tone had changed. She had started off sounding so confident. Now she seemed guarded, as though she wasn't telling Alice everything. Was she getting other impressions from the cards?

"This represents the past," Luana said, and turned over another inverted card.

Alice tilted her head sideways to see it. "That doesn't look too bad," she said hopefully.

Eight gold cups were stacked in the foreground as a figure moved away from them into the distance.

But Luana's expression told her there was nothing positive about the card. "It's a herald of abandonment, of giving something up, leaving it behind. It means sacrifices must be made."

The words chilled her. Sacrifices? Like what? Her life? Lucky? "But you said that's the past, right?" she ventured.

"Yes. So you've lost something already."

Luana sounded so grave Alice had to force a laugh to lighten the mood. "Yeah. My sanity. Hey, I'm sure all this means is that I just had a bad trip. People have them sometimes."

"Again, it's not that simple. Something has been taken from you. Something . . ." Luana shook her head. "I don't know."

This time Alice was sure there was something Luana wasn't telling her. She sat back in her seat. "Look, you're really starting to freak me out. I'm not sure I want to know what the rest of it means."

But Luana ignored her. She stared down at the cards, her expression dark and apprehensive, almost trancelike. “The heart of the matter,” she said softly, turning over the next card.

It showed a moon hanging over the water, and it too was inverted. Alice could tell from the way Luana’s hand trembled that it wasn’t good.

“I’m so sorry,” Luana said. “I had hoped to give you some reassurance but . . .”

“What does the Moon stand for?”

Luana took a deep breath and ran a hand through her hair. She was clearly reluctant to tell her. “The abyss,” she said. “The blackest depths of the soul. It’s a confrontation with madness.”

Alice suddenly remembered Hialeah’s demented Cheshire cat-like face when they’d decided on Alice’s name. They’d laughed so hard, but there was nothing funny about it now.

Madness. Just like her visions. Just like the horrors she’d seen in the park, the eyes that had watched her from the cold and empty cosmos. Before she could stop her Luana had flipped over the next card, the one that represented the future. As with all the others, it was upside-down.

“The World,” Luana whispered. Her hand fluttered to her throat and she stared at the card in silence. “This is all wrong,” she said at last.

The words made the room seem suddenly very chilly.

"Wrong how?"

"I'm not entirely sure what I'm seeing. There's a pattern here but it's very strange. It doesn't make any sense."

Alice hated to ask but she had to know. "What is it?"

Luana pointed to each of the cards one by one, tracing the lines of the pentacle. "From the beginning of conflict we have a dire twist of fate, a downward spiral with something awakening in the subconscious at the heart of it. All the cards are reversed, suggesting the darker aspect of each one. But I don't sense a personal connection to you as such. It's almost as though the cards aren't really about you at all but something else. Something much bigger."

The words made her flesh crawl and it was several moments before she could ask, "Like what?"

Luana looked up at Alice and her eyes were clouded, her face haunted. "The World should symbolise completion of a cycle," she said. "Integration."

"But it doesn't?"

"That's just it. I think it does. I think it's the final stage of a journey – one that doesn't end well." Luana looked just as unsettled as Alice felt. "And whatever this journey is, it isn't yours. Something is using you."

Alice stared at the array of inverted cards, each of them hinting at disaster, madness, tragedy, chaos. Only one card was yet to be revealed. The one Luana had said meant "final outcome". It sat before them like a veiled threat.

"I don't want to see it," Alice said, her voice barely a whisper.

Luana's expression changed to one of determination. "You have to. Even if it's not *about* you, it was *meant* for you."

Her hand hovered above the final card and then she grasped the nearest corner, took a deep breath and turned it over. It was blank.

Luana's eyes widened as she stared in horror at the empty black face of the card. Then she turned slowly to face Alice. "Who are you?" she hissed. There was both fear and anger in her voice.

"What are you talking about?" Alice gasped. "I'm nobody! Nobody at all!" But even as she babbled her insignificance she could see that Luana was genuinely terrified.

"Get out," Luana said, her voice quavering. She pointed towards the front door. "Get out and don't come back."

Alice rose from the couch as if in a daze. She couldn't understand what had happened or why Luana was so frightened.

"Look, I need your help," she pleaded. "I have to know what's going on. You're the only one who can help me."

Luana's face had gone white. "I can't help you," she said. "No one can. It's too late."

* * *

MARCH FOR PEACE! WE MUST CHANGE THE WORLD!

The flyer had appeared overnight. It was plastered throughout the Haight – on buildings, telephone poles and car windshields – an invitation to an antiwar demonstration the following week. The plan was to block the evening rush hour traffic across the Golden Gate Bridge in both directions. Such a stunt would undoubtedly get plenty of media coverage and, more importantly, the government's attention.

"Hell, yeah!" was Hialeah's response. "Count us in!"

Alice's stomach gave a little flutter as she and Lucky looked at the sheet of paper. She felt like a small animal that sensed danger everywhere, saw threat behind every pair of eyes.

She hadn't told anyone about her visit to Luana, even though Lucky had woken her from nightmares in the days following the reading. And when Mr Castillo asked how it went, she merely laughed and said it was all a bunch of star sign mumbo-jumbo. She even half believed it had just been a scam, although what Luana could possibly have hoped to gain from it was a mystery. Maybe the woman was just crazy. Alice couldn't afford to think otherwise if she hoped to stay sane herself.

But the flyer gave her a genuine jolt.

They'd been in San Francisco for several weeks now but none of them had participated in anything on this scale. Most rallies were peaceful and took place without incident, but protesters were always in danger of getting arrested. If that happened, the police might find out who Lucky was.

They'd already had one narrow escape from a performance that got out of control at Pier 39. The cops had turned up in full riot gear, frightening and angering the crowd. The four friends had split up and run, none of them knowing whether the others had been busted or not, until they met up again in the park that night. The event had sufficiently scared Alice and Lucky that they hadn't left the sanctuary of the Haight since, but it had turned Piper and Hialeah into rebel activists.

"You can't live your life in fear," said Hialeah, echoing what Luana had said. "Lucky's ID will pass muster. Even if he did get busted the pigs couldn't do anything. He's completely legit now."

"Yeah," Lucky chimed in. "I was talking to Mandrake

about it the other day. He's got a fake ID too, and he said he got arrested at a protest last year. Disturbing the peace. He spent the night in jail and they let him out the next morning. No question about the ID at all."

Alice chewed her lower lip as she stared at the flyer. She did want to go. Very much. It was going to be huge. History-making. The whole world would be watching and she didn't want to be left out. More than that, she knew Lucky wouldn't want to miss it. He'd told her more than once that he felt guilty to have escaped when so many other guys his age were in the jungle now, risking their lives against their will and being sent home in pieces.

"Let's do it," he said. "It's going to be the biggest peace march ever staged. Hundreds – maybe even thousands of people. How are the cops gonna find me in that crowd?"

He did have a point. Just hearing the projected numbers made Alice's heart race with the excitement it promised. Thousands of people staking out one of the world's best known and beloved landmarks. Thousands of voices demanding an end to war. How could the president – the *world* – not listen? Here was their chance to make a mark. If they never accomplished anything else in their lives, this single event could stand as a testament to a time when they stood up to be counted, when they put themselves in the firing line to make their voices heard, when they risked everything for the greater good. It would be something to tell their children.

Alice held her head up high as she came to a decision. She would not live her life in fear. "Okay," she said. "We'll go."

To her delight, Mr Castillo not only approved; he wanted to go too. He had already pasted the flyer in the window of the bakery and he was making a giant batch of cookies iced with peace signs to take to the demonstration the next day.

"I wish my parents had been as cool as you," Alice told him, not for the first time.

"I'm sure they would be proud of you," he said.

Alice wasn't so sure of that. They'd called Lucky a coward for not wanting to join the army. Not to his face, of course. But it was obvious in their frosty demeanour whenever he came over to see their daughter. Their tight-lipped smiles betrayed their disapproval more than any of the cruel words uttered by Lucky's own father.

Mr Castillo saw the doubt in her expression and placed a comforting hand on her shoulder. "In principle if nothing else," he clarified. "You're standing up for what you believe in, both of you. And that's something to be proud of. *I'm* certainly proud of you."

Alice's eyes watered at that, and she hugged him back. "Thanks," she said. "I think I love you, you know."

That made him chuckle. "I love you too, *chica*. I couldn't be prouder if you were my own daughter. Now let's get to work. These cookies aren't going to ice themselves."

* * *

It was time. Time to make a stand, time to make their voices heard, to make their presence count.

Hialeah had spent the morning with some girls she'd met at a music gig and when she returned Alice's jaw dropped. She was completely naked. Naked and painted. Every inch of skin was covered with a fantastical mosaic of flowers and butterflies. Vines twined down and around her arms and legs, with painted fig leaves placed strategically over her breasts. Her red hair hung long and loose down her back.

"Well?" she asked, eyes twinkling. "What do you think?"

She turned in a slow pirouette and swept her hair out of the way to show off the magnificent winged stallion prancing across her back, its long golden tail swishing across her left shoulder blade.

"I can't believe it," Alice said at last, marvelling at

her friend's audacity. "Are you really going to go – like that?"

"Of course! So are Marietta and Jack. Erin's painting them now."

Alice had no idea who Marietta and Jack were, but Hialeah had so many friends it was impossible to keep track. The commune was like an enormous extended family.

"Well, you look amazing and I truly admire your bravery."

Hialeah laughed. "I'll probably freeze to death before I get a chance to feel nervous."

"Has Piper seen it?"

She nodded. "He loved it. But I couldn't talk him into doing it himself."

"Well, don't even think about trying to talk *me* into it," Alice said. "Lucky and I are going with Mr Castillo. He's making some coloured aprons for us with songs painted on them in food colouring. I can't wait to see!"

"He's a real treasure," Hialeah said fondly. "Hey, if I get cold can he make me a 'Foxy Lady' one?"

"What? And ruin all Erin's hard work?"

Hialeah looked down at herself and traced the stem of a rose that circled her navel. "Yeah, you've got a point. It is beautiful. Such a shame it won't last forever."

"Nothing will." The words came without a thought, casting a shadow in Alice's mind as she said them.

Was it her imagination or had the vines and roses moved? She stared at Hialeah's painted skin and for a moment she was sure she saw them writhe like snakes coiling around their prey.

Soon, soon, soon . . .

"Hey, you okay?" Hialeah asked.

Her voice snapped Alice out of the moment. There were no snakes. Just flowers and other decorations. She shook off the ghostly feeling and arranged her features into a smile again. "Yeah."

"Good. Because there's nothing to worry about. Lucky will be fine."

She was relieved that Hialeah had misunderstood her sudden dark spell. But perhaps that was all that lay at the heart of it anyway. And Hialeah was right. In all the chaos and clamour of what was sure to be a history-making protest, how could Lucky possibly be singled out?

"You're right," Alice said. "I'm just a worrier."

"Well, it's time to stop fretting and enjoy yourself! We'll see you later. Piper went on ahead with his guitar to stake out a spot for us to play. Look for us by the south tower, the side facing the bay."

"Okay."

Hialeah gave her a tight hug and the girls went their separate ways.

At the bakery Mr Castillo was dressed and ready and eager to go. He wore a bright yellow apron, the title and lyrics to "Mellow Yellow" written across it in elegant script. He threw out his arms in a "ta-da!" gesture.

Alice gave a delighted laugh. "It's fantastic!"

"I'm glad you approve. Lucky's was a little more work but I think you'll like it."

Hearing his cue, Lucky appeared from the back room. He was the living embodiment of "Purple Haze" in a violet apron with Jimi Hendrix's words scrawled crazily around the title of the song. Lucky smiled as he showed it off, clearly proud of the artist's handiwork.

"I still can't believe you made these," Lucky said. "It must have taken you all night."

Mr Castillo waved away the compliment. "The old never sleep," he said. "And anyway, you kids make me feel young again. My own parents never allowed me to be creative. Okay, *chica*, ready for yours?"

"I can't wait!"

The apron he held up for her was pure white, and the lyrics and song title weren't even necessary. Painted across the front was a famous rabbit, wearing a herald's tabard decorated with hearts and an Elizabethan ruff around his neck. In one hand he held a scroll of parchment, and in the other, a trumpet. Jefferson Airplane's words danced around him as though coming through the bell of the horn.

Alice's eyes went wide as she took in all the detail. It was her very favourite illustration from *Alice in Wonderland,* and for a moment she wondered how Mr Castillo could possibly have known that. But the grin on Lucky's face gave the game away.

"It's incredible," she said at last, moved by the thought and effort that had gone into it. "Absolutely perfect. Thank you so much."

"There's nothing to thank me for," he said bashfully, although he was clearly overjoyed by her reaction. "Now let's go and stop this silly war!"

* * *

The turnout was astonishing. Alice had never seen so many people in one place in her life, and every single one of them was gathered there for the same purpose. It was a glorious day. The sun was high in the sky and the fog had long since burned off. Alice felt full of hope. Nothing bad could possibly happen on a day like this.

Many of the protesters wore flamboyant costumes or body paint like Hialeah. Many more carried signs or flags or flowers. One girl was dressed in an elaborate

Victorian mourning dress with a black veil and a beauty pageant sash spattered with fake blood. It said "Mrs America".

The widow made Alice think of Tom, and she wondered if he might be somewhere in the enormous crowd. She glanced down at her White Rabbit apron and tried to imagine what song he would be.

The sheer number of people was intimidating, and Alice stuck close to Lucky and Mr Castillo, afraid of getting separated and lost in the crowd. They began making their way along the bridge but they only got as far as the first tower, where the density of bodies meant they could go no further. Just beyond it she saw Hialeah and Piper. They had made it a little further out along the bridge and they waved, urging their friends to push through the crowd to join them. But Alice was happy to stay where they were and fortunately Lucky and Mr Castillo were too. They stayed by the tower and offered the peace sign cookies around. They were gone in minutes, either eaten or brandished in place of placards.

Mr Castillo looked a little out of his depth and Alice was just as overwhelmed. The protesters blocked the traffic like a human dam, and voices carried across the crowd in waves, competing with the angry honking of car horns. More than one car door opened to liberate someone who excitedly joined the protest. One teenage boy climbed out through the back window of a fancy car and onto the roof, shouting "Hell, no, I won't go!" His parents screamed at him to get back in the car, but he dived into the crowd and was swept out of sight by a sea of hands. Alice's heart raced with excitement. It felt like they were at the centre of the world.

From somewhere in the middle of the bridge a group was chanting "Hey, hey, LBJ, how many kids did you kill today?" The voices grew as others picked up the chant, but it was soon overtaken by the more popular "One, two, three, four – we don't want your fucking war!"

And still the people came, and kept coming. Like an irreversible tide they poured onto the bridge. It wasn't just kids and hippies either. One group of older women wore matching placards around their necks that said STOP KILLING OUR SONS. Some of them waved photographs of guys Lucky's age. Alice's heart swelled. She hoped they were safe, that they might still come home. Maybe today would see to that.

"This is incredible!" Lucky shouted. She could barely hear him over the noise.

"I know – I can't believe it!"

It wasn't long before they heard the whop-whop-whop of helicopters circling above and police shouted down at the crowd through megaphones. They needn't have bothered; their shouts were nothing but a blur of tinny voices, lost in the roar of the protest. Sirens added to the din but the police cars had no hope of pushing through the mob. There were fire engines as well, parked like circled wagons down at Fort Point. She wondered if they intended to turn the fire hoses on the crowd.

Alice felt tuned in to the whole scene, a tiny part of a much greater whole.

The moment was an absolute triumph. The protest was too massive not to make national headlines. The world could not ignore their thousands of voices. She was only one little cog in the mechanism of change, but so was every other person there. Each single one had stood up to be counted. That had to make a difference.

But even as her heart soared with happiness she felt a creeping sense of déjà vu. She had felt small before, but it hadn't been comforting; it had only made her feel meaningless and insignificant. Dwarfed by the incomprehensible magnitude of the universe. That feeling was back now. It poisoned her sense of wonder, turning it to unease and then to dread.

The World.

Something is using you.

I think it's the final stage of a journey – one that doesn't end well.

The skin on the back of her neck began to prickle and her hands felt cold, clammy. All at once she felt disconnected from the energy, as though a tether had been cut, isolating her from the others. All around her people were chanting, singing, shouting, but the voices were nothing but a rush of air in her ears, like the hollow sound of noises heard underwater.

She moved to the edge of the bridge and peered down into the bay. And froze.

The water was absolutely still. Not a single wave marred the smooth surface, not even so much as a ripple. And far beneath the silky blue she saw something glinting. Something icy and alien. Something she had seen once before.

The eyes met hers through the fathoms and held her. She stood rooted to the spot, staring, unable to look away as the pinpricks of white grew slowly and steadily. Something impossibly large was rising to the surface.

Lucky was somewhere behind her. She tried to speak, to call his name, but she couldn't move at all. Helpless, she could do nothing but watch as the eyes came nearer and nearer. The bay seemed as deep as the deepest ocean, as though something had made a hole in the world, letting the endless void of space creep in. She knew with a kind of cold certainty that she was seeing *through* the water of the bay, through the ocean and the centre of the earth, to the endless black universe beyond. And something was coming through that hole, tunneling through it like a monstrous parasite.

As it made its slow, inexorable ascent, Alice had time to realise many things. She knew exactly what was going to happen and just how bad it would be. The things she'd seen in the desert hadn't been hallucinations. The whole thing had been a premonition. Tom had seen it in her. So had Luana and the boy who'd blinded himself. Alice herself had seen glimpses of it in her nightmares as a child. But the thought that disturbed her most was the idea that she had been the catalyst. When she had locked eyes with that terrible presence in the desert, it had connected with her in some way. Perhaps it needed her in order to come through.

You're the one.

She shuddered. The bond was an appalling violation.

She still sensed nothing from the rising creature, nothing at all. No malice, no hatred, no sadistic glee. And that was somehow worst of all. There was nothing but cold indifference. Emptiness.

Her mind ached to detach from it, to break free from the unbearable dispassion. Neither she nor the thousands of innocent people gathered on the bridge meant anything to it. She wasn't even sure it registered them in any meaningful way. Like a germ invading a cell, it had simply located a way into the world and, once there, it would destroy anything and everything in its way. Her awareness suddenly seemed a very tenuous thing, as though her mind could snap like a thread if she thought too hard about it. The lure of madness was there and a part of her longed for it, for the escape it might offer.

She flashed back to the tarot reading. The Moon. What had Luana called it? The abyss. The blackest depths of the soul. Her stomach twisted.

On the other side of the water the creature was still rising, its eyes still fixed on her. Time slowed as it came closer and closer, growing larger with each interminable second. In the desert she had felt her mind stretched nearly to its breaking point, unable to comprehend what she was seeing. Now she longed for it to break, to spare her the revelation.

There was a day at school once when her class had drawn the sun and the planets in chalk in the parking lot. The relative sizes had been incredible. Miss Bertram had said that if the sun was the size of a basketball, earth was barely the size of a peppercorn. But it was the distances that had really blown her mind, both then and now. She could barely imagine a hundred miles, let alone a hundred *million*. And that was just their own solar system. How much further had this creature travelled? And for how long?

Worse still: what other horrors were out there in the infinite blackness?

She didn't have time to wonder much longer before the surface of the water began to shiver and clusters of enormous bubbles drifted to the surface, ascending faster than the eyes.

When the first bubble reached the surface the water began to churn, just as it had in her vision all those weeks ago. It seemed like another lifetime. More bubbles roiled up from below, bursting like depth charges and sending up immense plumes of foamy seawater. The bridge trembled beneath the onslaught.

It was only then that she registered the screaming.

All around her was chaos. People were running in all directions, panicking. She heard "Earthquake!" cried over and over. But what was coming was far worse than that, worse than any of them could know.

There was the crunch of metal and breaking glass as cars slid into one another on the shuddering bridge, the howls of pain and terror as people were crushed beneath wreckage or trampled in the stampede.

Where was Lucky? Mr Castillo? Hialeah and Piper?

She still couldn't move, couldn't tear her eyes away from the ones rising to meet her. They gleamed with unnatural light but the eyes themselves were like black punctures in a pale writhing body. As it came nearer it drained all the blue from the water, turning it a sickly waxen shade as it finally broke the surface.

And she was face to face with it at last.

Its head swarmed with fleshy bristles and uncountable rows of teeth filled the ragged pink hole of its gaping mouth. It rose up out of the water like a colossal centipede, waving thousands of short spiky legs. Each segment of its glistening white body was the size of a skyscraper, each leg the length of a tree.

For a moment the masses of people behind her were eerily silent, transfixed as they stared at it in horrified disbelief. The silence lasted only a second. And then the creature began to clamber up on to the centre of the bridge.

Alice tried to scream with them but no sound would come. She felt a coiling sickness in her guts, as if she'd swallowed an enormous worm that was thrashing around inside. Somehow she knew she was connected to the monster, that it was using her in some way, leeching energy from her. Her eyes filled with tears, mercifully blurring the hideous sight. It became a vast pale smudge, like the fog that engulfed the bridge every morning.

Cables snapped and girders broke like matchsticks beneath the thing's immense weight. Cars and people crashed down into the water as the bridge began to come apart, as though it were made of nothing more solid than frayed rope. The people running along it didn't have a chance. They would never reach safety before the whole structure collapsed.

And even if they did, what then?

The creature scuttling across the bridge would make its way into the city, crawling easily over houses and buildings, leaving a trail of devastation in its wake.

From somewhere far away she heard Lucky's voice. He was screaming. The sound tore through the thousands of other screams, unravelling her. She had heard that scream so often in her nightmares, in her obsessive imaginings of the many terrible ways he might die in Vietnam. It had all been for nothing. They'd run away to escape one horror only to run straight into another. Now there was nothing she could do but listen.

His screaming ended as suddenly as it had begun and Alice knew with a sickening agony that he was dead. Crushed by falling debris, trampled underfoot or possibly even drowned in the icy bay. The ground seemed to fall away from her and all she could do was pray he hadn't suffered much. It was the last sane thought she would have. As she watched the monster clamber across the disintegrating bridge and all the helpless people stranded on it, her mind began to splinter.

The madness freed her from her paralysis, and

suddenly she found she could move again. She watched with strange fascination as the bridge fell apart around her. The main suspension cables snapped and whistled through the sky like giant whips. Without their support the centre span split like a drawbridge in reverse, forming two huge ramps that poured their contents into the bay. The creature sat at the heart of the chaos, its fanged mouth opening and closing on the bodies that slid into it.

Under the strain of the weight the towers started to break and bend, then topple inwards.

The far tower went first. It came apart and fell with a grinding shriek of metal that seemed to go on for hours. The screaming bled into a single voice, and the people who remained clung to whatever pieces of the structure they could grab onto. They looked like ants dangling from blades of grass, so easy to dislodge with the slightest movement. For a moment she thought she recognised a bright yellow apron down in the bay, but then a wave caught it and pulled it under.

The south tower began to shudder violently then. Alice clutched the railing as the foundation rattled below. She could only watch as the tower above her crumbled and fell piece by piece into the bloodstained water, crushing everything beneath it. Everything but the creature, which was moving across the sea of bodies towards her.

She stood alone on the remnants of the tower's anchorage as though stranded on a jagged island. Behind her the road stretched out across Fort Point and into the city. People were running, screaming, panicking, trying to get away from the bridge. Some were still shouting about an earthquake, others about Armageddon. It was a chorus of the damned.

Far below, the water was filled with bodies, very few of them still moving. They were like tiny specks of coloured sand in a swirling sea of red. Alice felt curiously detached from the sight, as though she were dreaming. The colours were so vivid and fantastic, just like in her other dream, the one she'd had in the desert.

You're only dying.

The empty eyes of the monster swallowed her gaze as it moved past her, making its way up what remained of the south span. It crawled up the sloping debris to the abutment, crushing the elaborate latticework of red iron girders as it went. It paused then and turned to look back, and Alice imagined that it saw her, just for a moment. Then it continued on past her, its multitudes of legs wriggling, its mouth working ceaselessly.

She watched it pass with something like sorrow. Luana was right. It had never been *her* journey. She had played no real part in the creature's emergence and she was no part of its plan; she was simply a witness. And now that the gateway was open others could follow. Even now she could hear the water of the bay churning and she imagined the thousands of pallid squirming forms that would soon crawl through the hole in the world.

Her ears streamed with blood as the last pieces of the bridge tumbled into the darkening water and the noise rose to a deafening pitch.

After a while it began to sound like music.

Johnny Mains is a British Fantasy Award winning editor, author and horror historian. Mains was project editor to Pan Macmillan's critically acclaimed 2010 re-issue of *The Pan Book of Horror Stories*. Mains is the author of two short story collections and the editor of six horror anthologies, the latest being *Best British Horror 2014* and *Dead Funny: Horror Stories By Comedians*, both out now, from Salt Publishing.

THE GAMEKEEPER

JOHNNY MAINS

For my father, Jock

'You may kill or you may miss
But at all times think this:
"All the pheasants ever bred,
Won't repay for one man dead."'

— Mark Beaufoy (1854-1922)

PROLOGUE
(1970)

He pulled up the handbrake of the Land Rover, but left the engine ticking over. Though he came here at least three times a week, the undeniable beauty of the valley never failed to grab him. His mind wandered, as it normally did when he came to Top Field, about the days when he used to fish the river that cut through the Stour Valley. Those days were long gone. The last time that he had fished for pleasure, he couldn't remember.

Roger Casement glanced at his watch and calculated that he had about an hour and a half to check all of the snares before it got dark. Then he lit up a cigarette and breathed the smoke in deeply. The snares could wait.

CHAPTER 1
FIRST SHOT
(1946)

Father and son walked through the heather and scrub, rarely talking, for the climb would rob them of any conversation until they reached their destination. Breakfast felt heavy in the youngster's belly, not heeding his father's sage words that they should march on an empty stomach. Have a light bite at lunch so as not to feel drowsy in the afternoon, and then be rewarded when dinner came, with a hearty, sleep-inducing meal.

Father was three steps ahead, his new Lloyd rifle slung over one shoulder, the strap made out of strong hemp. Roger Casement wanted his father to stop, to rest – to realise that the small boy didn't have his legs, couldn't make his way through the rain-drenched beech fern as fast as he could. His wax cotton trousers were holding out, as his father said they would, but still Roger had his doubts.

A pheasant broke free from the underbrush ahead of them, clamouring loudly as it flapped its wings to find height and safety. Father and son followed the bird as it flew up and up, into the mist that was forever prevalent in this part of Scotland.

Father stopped, letting Roger catch up. The young boy breathed in and out heavily.

"Who introduced the pheasant into Britain, son?"

"The Romans did, Father."

"Very good. And where do pheasants originate?"

"Russia, Father."

"Very good." Father started to walk again.

* * *

Father unfolded the thick greaseproof paper slowly and handed, with grubby fingers, a ham sandwich to an eager Roger. The early heaviness had faded away, and it was with surprise, as he received the food, that a pang of hunger twisted his insides. Roger took a big bite, savouring the baked ham and thickly spread butter. He chewed slowly and thoughtfully. It was good bread; it didn't turn into a chewy paste like the bread that Mother sometimes bought from MacFarlane's.

Father placed his sandwich on his knee, reached for his battered thermos, and poured a cup of tea, the steam disappearing into the damp of the day.

"We don't have far to go. Down to the edge of the loch and then ten minutes from there we'll be at the point."

Father took a swig from the thermos' cup then passed it to Roger. The tea was scalding hot and almost too sweet with sugar. His insides were fire for a few seconds, but then it passed and he was left with soothing warmth.

Once lunch was finished, they began walking again, a little slower. Half an hour later they reached the edge of the loch, the ancient woodland curving around its left hand side. They then went straight up the hill, through the thick scrub of bracken and heather, before the undergrowth became sparser with great slabs of granite breaking through the earth. The hill becoming rockier; careful footsteps were needed. The going was wet and slick underneath and, if one was to slip, it could easy be a broken ankle or wrist.

* * *

At the top of the steep gradient there was a small ramshackle hut, moss covered and decaying. Stark and alone. Roger wondered how they would ever manage to get anything from there; deer would never be foolish enough to come close to the place. Arriving, Father pushed the door open. It smelt of damp, but there was a strange sweet undercurrent, almost to the point of being sickly. Inside, the walls were wet. The floor was smooth granite, dry, save for a few patches where rain had dribbled in and down through the planked walls.

There was a small table and a chair, both covered in green mould. The window was small and draped with black netting. Two cushions, that bore host to a grand gathering of earwigs underneath, were under the window, for kneeling on. They looked damp, but not too bad.

Father pulled a cloth out from his pocket and started wiping the rifle down reverentially. He paid special attention to the metal sights, then the trigger, and finally the stained wooden stock of the rifle.

Only once the rifle was prepared to his satisfaction did he load the ammunition.

"And now, we wait," Father said softly, looking out at the whispering strangeness of the bleak landscape that spread out for what seemed like forever before them.

It's a known fact that children have little patience, but at times like this, Roger had somehow built and prepared a place in his mind where he could go into. Retreat and be safe. Looking at him, you would think that he had fallen asleep, and there were times that his father, glancing across at his son, smiling softly, had thought the exact same thing. But no, he was awake, and alert – just somewhere else. It would only be simple things that Roger focused on; he was, after all, only eight years old, years away from being able to explore more challenging ideas and issues in his 'blank box', as he liked to call it. Roger would set himself sums – mainly long multiplication, or if he was tired, repeat the eight times table over and over, as he had always found that one to be the hardest.

On other occasions he would make up stories – the location was always the mountainous highlands of Scotland and there would always be some thrilling chase. Splashing through rivers, slipping on treacherous heather as he scrambled up steep inclines, using the surrounding forests as camouflage as he heard the deep, swarthy voices of the enemy come closer and closer, brandishing...

"I have one, son," Father whispered loud enough to bring Roger out of his reverie.

Roger crouched catlike, and silently made his way over to the window. His father was staring down the barrel of the gun, his breathing slow and mellow.

"Where?" Roger asked, staring off into the distance, and not able to see anything.

"Three o'clock, standing next to the outcrop of rocks. Stag, maybe four or five years old." Father adjusted his kneeling position ever so slightly. Roger looked down at his father's knees. The wet had soaked a good patch of material and Roger thought that Father might have trouble walking for a few days after this – the wet and the cold would do its damage.

More amazed at his father's diligence to the kill than actually looking where the kill was, Roger murmured that he saw the deer, but didn't really. It was a lie that passed over Father's head, a little something that meant absolutely...

crack

Roger hadn't prepared for the shot, although he knew it would come. When Father had something in his sights, he would always fire, even if he thought it was a shot to nothing. Roger's heart seemed to jump out of his mouth, and then in the next instant adrenalin flooded through his body, made the hairs on the back of his neck stand up, made the small of his back wet with sweat.

"Yes!" Father hissed, still staring down the sights. Once he was pleased that it was a definite kill, he brought the barrel of the rifle back in through the window and laid it down on the floor. While the gun would get wet, it would be taken apart later on in the day and given a meticulous cleaning – so a little bit of water in the meantime wouldn't harm it any.

"Come on, let's get it," Father said, patting his son on the shoulder. He was smiling that little half-smile that crept up onto his face when he was genuinely pleased with something. Normally Father "was a very hard to impress man". His stoic features and flinty grey eyes betrayed nothing, especially in business.

They left the hut and hurried towards the kill. With

every footstep Roger felt nervous excitement building.

It was a clean shot. There was no knife work needed. The stag was dead. The shot was to the neck. The exit wound, when Father lifted the head up to look, was the size of a fist.

"Instant kill, it wouldn't have felt a thing," Father said softly. Roger nodded, but didn't need any comforting.

"We'll gut it here, make it easier to take back to the shed, and we'll hang it there for a week or two and get the meat nice for eating."

Father pulled out his knife with the horn handle and knelt down again. He started cutting round the anus of the deer first, being careful with the blade as to not penetrate the colon or the bladder. The knife only went in an inch or two deep, and once he had cut round, he pulled on it gently to make sure it was free.

Father rolled the stag onto its back, and then slowly cut through the skin of the animal and downwards, making sure not to slice into the stomach. His knife work was calm and assured, his free hand pushing the stomach and intestines down and working his way to the testicles and around them until he came to the anus. The intestines slowly started to spill out. Father moved the stomach and the intestines to one side and then started to cut his way through the diaphragm very carefully, freeing it up. He put his hand into the chest cavity and grabbed onto the heart, and then, with his knife hand, started to slice through the oesophagus. Father pulled everything out and dumped it onto the ground next to the carcass. It squelched and slopped as it landed. The stomach and all the intestines followed it.

"That'll soon be gone," Father said, pulling hair from the knife, wiping it, then his bloody hands, on the ground.

Once the animal was empty, he hefted it up, 'moaning' with a twinkle in his eye about having to let the blood from it, and they walked slowly and carefully back to the hut. Roger opened up the door and walked inside, looking up to the ceiling where the hanging pole ran across the middle.

"I don't think you'll be able to hang the deer from here, Father," he said, pointing to the problem as Father struggled in with the animal.

Father studied it carefully and sighed. "You're right. The slightest bit of weight and it's apt to pull the whole roof down on top of us and we certainly don't want that to happen."

"What will we do? Shall we leave it?"

* * *

Roger walked ahead, carrying the rifle, finding the right way down and Father followed, ever so carefully, the deer slung around his neck and shoulders. He held onto the legs to balance it and him out. His face was beetroot red and he was panting heavily with the exertion.

"This had better...be...the best venison we've eaten this year, I'll...tell you...that for...nothing," Father gasped, pausing every so often to get his breath back. He didn't let the deer drop to the ground, as he knew that if he did, he wouldn't have the strength to pick it back up again and would have to leave it where it landed.

Roger then made a mistake, a small one that he didn't realise he had made, but a mistake none the less. He went over a slightly uneven patch of ground with a small but sharp-looking rock sticking out from it. Easy for a young boy to negotiate, but his father, not seeing the rock, stood on it. His ankle twisted underneath him and he fell to the ground heavily, crying with pain as the weight of the deer made him fall that much harder. The deer fell to one side, and Father started rolling down the hill. A single bramble branch, as thick as an index finger, caught his trigger hand and ripped a deep furrow across his palm.

"Father!" Roger blurted, looking around as soon as he heard the shout, and ran towards him.

The head of the Casement family lay sprawled on the wet earth. His face was turning a dark purple. He gasped for breath, struggled to sit up. His eyes flitted this way and that, panicked. His left leg lay at an unnatural angle.

Bone had rent through the tough fabric of his trousers.

"Roger...I can't...brea..." he started to shake. His legs, including the broken one, started to thrash violently. His right hand clasped his chest. His breathing was now a weak rasp, sounding like the last, perfunctory swipe of sandpaper on a piece of smooth wood.

"I...love...you..." his father said, then his head fell down and he stopped breathing.

Roger stared at his father, stunned. The boy waited for his father's chest to rise again. It would be all right, he had just forgotten to breathe. He would be okay again in a moment...

It was almost as if the last breath from his lungs caused the mist to suddenly descend – it seemed to swirl in from nowhere.

The young boy knelt down and placed his ear against his father's mouth and listened for the faintest sign of life. There was nothing. As Roger fell back on his haunches, the tears came and with it, a total, devastating loss swallowed him up.

* * *

Roger knew if he could drag his father down to the loch, it would be easier for someone to bring his body back home from there. He placed the rifle on his father's chest, breathed in deeply, grabbed hold of the sleeves of the waxed jacket, and pulled. The corpse moved, but only slightly. Roger surveyed the hill below him and knew if he could get the body to the beginning of the wet slabs of granite that sloped down the hill, the wax on the jacket and the trousers would help aid him – but... Roger stopped with horror as he looked at the white bone poking through the torn material. It seemed to glow in the damp mist.

"I will not leave you, I will *not* leave you," Roger shrilled and pulled again. The sheer terror that coursed through him gave him a strength that no boy of eight should have. Then, no boy of eight should have to pull the corpse of his parent down a lonely Scottish mountain.

* * *

Darkness came quicker than the boy had expected, and he had to leave his father behind, take the rifle, and make his way first to the loch and then back to the Bristol 400, the family car which was parked there. He knew that Mother would call for help eventually, and she knew roughly where they would be. All Roger needed to do was sit tight and wait.

Roger tried the handle of the door and was thankful that it wasn't locked.

The tears felt like they would never end; tears of

confusion and emptiness, of being utterly alone, and the knowledge that his father was out there in the darkness.

Roger thought he might die crying. That whoever found him would find him drowned.

A sob hitched in his chest. The car began to lift, gradually, but steadily – a clear foot and a half in the air. Roger screamed and scrabbled to the window. He peered out into the black as the car dropped; all four, thin, tyres hitting the ground at the same time.

Roger was thrown back, smacking his head against the far side door. The car lifted again, and was slammed down a few seconds after.

The ringing in his ears could shatter glass. Roger felt like his eyes had been plucked out, and the ringing became distant, otherworldly.

When Roger came to, it was daylight. He rubbed the back of his head, and his bottom lip quivered when he saw a crimson smear on his hand. He sat up and wondered why it was so bright.

Snow.

Roger's heart sunk and he burst into tears, more out of frustration than anything else. He reached across and tried to open the car door, but there had been at least nine inches of snowfall and the door wouldn't give as he tried to push it against compacted snow.

He didn't know if anyone was looking for him now, and, more importantly, how long would it take to find his father? The small boy knew that the snow could last until February or March if there was a season for it, which meant that his father wouldn't be found until it thawed, and the snow turned to water and left the hills, and the rivers would burst their banks and the loch would swell.

An icy blast had filled the car, so Roger pulled the door shut which had been open a scant inch, and thought about his options. He was hungry; his stomach beginning the slow frenzy. He was wearing adequate clothing, he was warm and waterproof (to an extent) and his boots would be leak free for maybe a few good hours.

Roger tried to think of the path the car had come after Father had driven off the road, but the snow was too great. Until there was at least a hint of a frost, he wouldn't be going anywhere.

The car being lifted? Purely his imagination. It couldn't be anything else.

He thought of Mother, going out of her mind with worry, never realising that her husband was dead. Roger started to cry again, and this time the tears didn't stop for a while.

* * *

The noise filled the car, waking Roger. He cupped

his hands over his ears and screamed to try and drown the noise out. He looked out of the window as blocks of snow all around were being sucked up into the air, twenty, thirty feet before vanishing. He pushed the door open. The snow that had been impeding before was simply not there.

The noise drilled through him. It was the sound of a thousand foghorns, all blasting at once. He grabbed the rifle and his canvas bag (forgotten when he first went up the hill with his father) and ran, his feet slipping on the slight residue of snow that was left, a dusting.

Slabs of snow continued disappearing – it had to be from everywhere, and for one, horrendous moment Roger thought that his father may be lifted with the snow and taken also. But he was heavier than the snow, he was heavier...

Roger started running, blinded by terror, and didn't see the hole that opened up in the ground in front of him. He fell straight through, not touching the sides and landed hard.

When he came to, his hands were burning, and realised that he was still gripping onto the rifle. He breathed in deeply and winced as he tried to move. A shrill pain ran up his back.

The foghorn noise, whatever it had been, had stopped. Roger looked up from where he had fallen. There was no way he would be able to climb back up. The sides were as smooth as silk, no purchase.

Roger let go of the gun and got up. He looked around him. The light from the hole not really illuminating anything. He felt around on the floor. Again it was smooth, until he felt the rough fabric of his satchel. He pulled it towards himself and undid the metal buckles, the clacking noise soothing him a little as he undid them.

His hand clasped the flashlight immediately, but the back of his hand also brushed against greaseproof paper, the crinkling making his heart leap with joy. Roger had always made himself a 'provisions' bag – a penknife, flashlight, spare batteries, matches and marbles – and his mother must have sneaked something into the bag for him whilst he hadn't been looking.

Letting go of the light, he pulled out the still-mysterious foodstuff and unwrapped it – the tang of oats and fruit made him instantly salivate. He bit into the flapjack and chewed, his mouth exploding, and then he paused. He didn't know when he was next going to eat, and maybe he should wrap it up and save it for later...but no...his hunger took over and he devoured the slab in another three mouthfuls.

Once the paper had been scrunched up and put back in his bag, he pulled out the Eveready flashlight and pressed hard on the rubber button. It sprang to life, lighting up a good-sized area in front of him.

He placed the light on the floor and redid the bag,

slinging it over his neck, then picked up the rifle and did the same, but over his shoulder this time. He thought he wouldn't be able to get at the rifle if he had to get the hemp strap from around his neck.

He looked up at the hole above him, thinking that the tunnel might lead to somewhere at the bottom of the valley, making it easier for him to be rescued.

Roger started walking, slowly at first, making sure that the torch was pointing down at the ground, so that he wouldn't be caught unawares by any sudden change in gradient. His little heart thumped rapidly in his chest – he was caught up with the unknown excitement of what he was doing; it was almost as if his father had died many, many years ago and was now nothing but a half-remembered memory.

It was a tunnel he was walking down, about three times as high as Roger was, but it wasn't wide. Someone with some heft would have got through, but it would have been a struggle for them.

His torch light was strong, unwavering; but even if it was to fade, he had five batteries in his bag which would last him for many more hours to come.

Roger felt a change in the tunnel. He was now walking downhill, not at too steep a gradient, but his thigh muscles were starting to strain slightly.

* * *

As soon as Roger stepped into the cavern the foghorn noise started again, but this time it was more vicious, like a million screams erupting at once. He ducked back into the tunnel to try and muffle the worst of the noise, but it held neither comfort nor compensation. He put both fingers into his ears and shouted as loud as he could, to try and get above the level of noise.

After a while the foghorn's screaming stopped and was replaced by a confused babbling, and then silence. Roger banged his little fists feebly against the wall, incomprehension stretching his poor mind to near breaking point.

Once he realised that he wasn't going to be able to go back to where he came from, he turned off the torch, forced it through the hole-flap in the bag. It wasn't needed. The cavern was so light, it could almost have been an open air cave.

It was large, bigger than anything Roger had seen in his life. It stretched out for at least a mile, but Roger couldn't see the other side from where he was standing. There were many obstacles that needed to be overcome, massive rocks to try to negotiate his way over, massive stalagmites that looked like souls trapped in ice everywhere.

Roger made his way slowly into the cavern, his wonder again overcoming any fear that he felt. He was aware, though, that the air around him seemed thicker, like he was walking through molasses. He cinched his jacket to him more closely. It was colder here than it had been outside or in the tunnel, and it was *snowing*. He walked to the first pillar and noticed that there were strange carvings on it, definitely not in English. They certainly didn't look like the Egyptian hieroglyphs that Roger saw in his schoolbooks. He touched it. It was smooth and cold...and made him feel sick. He staggered back and fell onto the ground, the bolt of the rifle digging into his back, making him cry out. The pillar started to glow in front of him. It turned a dark blue and began to crumble.

And then, standing before him in the midst of the broken and crumbled mineral, was something that was human in shape, very small, hunched and twisted like the old fisher women who worked on the harbour of Mallaig. It was naked. Its skin a cyanotic purple. It shuffled out from the debris, hands sensing the space before it. It had no eyes. Its mouth looked like nothing more than a scuffmark on leather.

It started to bleat. Roger thought that the noise came through a small breathing hole between the thing's eyes.

Roger scrabbled away from it, turning over onto his knees, the unwieldy rifle strap sliding off his shoulder. He picked the gun up and turned to face the recluse from the rock.

All of the stalagmites in the cavern started to glow an almost daylight blue – the light cast from them was so intense that Roger thought that if he shut his eyes he'd still be able to see the scene before him.

The speleothems started to crumble and topple, yet without making any noise. Massive chunks of debris bounced along the surface of the cavern floor. And from each – hundreds, no, thousands of twisted creatures, granny-sized, awoke from their sleep of millennia, with those same smooth faces; no eyes, and scuffmarks for mouths.

Roger ran to his right, away from the nearest shambler, whose face had now turned a blood red, viscous fluid seeping from the skin where the head met the torso. It had no neck. As it swiped its hand past the place where Roger had been only a second before, worm-like appendages appeared in the palm of its hand; three small tentacles covered in hundreds of very sharp slivers. They seemed to sniff the air.

Roger lifted the rifle. It was heavy, but he was not without practise. The teachings of his father automatically took over, and his brain seemed to relax with this familiar motion. But with it came a poem that his father had taught him, a poem that was familiar to all gun users. The first line haunted him as his hand pulled back the bolt of the rifle and fed the bullet into the chamber. *Never, never let your gun pointed be at any one.* But the poem wasn't enough to stop him wanting to save his own life, and once the bolt was back in its rightful place, he held the butt of the rifle by his hip, and as he squeezed on the trigger he jerked the front of the gun up.

The blast was deafening, almost as loud as the foghorn screaming that had assaulted his young ears back when he was in the car. The kickback ripped the gun from his hands. Noise seemed to suck the air out of the cavern and this was followed by the hellish scream of the shambler as the bullet ripped through its body at where a human's stomach would have been, had it one.

It fell to the ground.

Roger was surprised that there was no blood. There was *always* blood from the animals he and his father had shot. The others stopped shuffling. They began to gibber and started to retreat and crawled over each other, an algorithm of limbs, and scrabbled towards the centre of the cavern.

The ground beneath his feet started to tremble. Roger started to run. He didn't know where he was going – he just wanted to be as far away from those *things* as possible.

The snow started to fall more heavily, and from the cavern's epicentre a snow whirlwind began whipping past the stalagmites that hadn't crumbled.

Roger stopped running and simply stared at it

dumbly as it came towards him. He felt his jacket freeze as the wind lashed him. It picked him up and spun him round, throwing the young boy to the other end of the cavern. Roger was dazed, but with it enough to see the wall open like an eager mouth to accept him, beyond was utter darkness.

In the dead space the whirlwind became more feeble, bereft of power and was no more. However, Roger didn't fall. He hung there, suspended in the infinite blackness. In this place there was no gravity.

The young boy came to, hazily. He kicked his legs to find purchase. He brought his hand to his face and couldn't see it. He yelled for help, but from his mouth came no sound.

From the darkness, hundreds of thousands of times the size of the boy, an eye slowly opened. It was every colour and no colour; depthless, ancient and terrible. Roger's mind collapsed in on itself. A not-unwelcomed unconsciousness took him.

Roger travelled through the darkness, his hair had fallen out, his clothes dissolved – and on his back burned a deep arcane mark. The young boy passed through stone and soil as if they were simply water and once in the afternoon air of a calmer Highland day, gently came to rest on the ground, by the loch.

CHAPTER 2
KILL SHOT
(1970)

He found a fox in the third snare. It was barely alive. The snare had caught the fox open mouthed and had tightened round the back of its head, tearing into the commissure of the animal's mouth, at least half an inch deep between upper and bottom jaw.

Roger looked at it and knew that the struggle had been a ferocious one, the earth underneath it torn up. Roger nailed all of his snares to good tree branches or trunks as, with one or two little tugs, the fox could get away but die a much slower death. But probably quicker than this one.

He broke the shotgun and put a cartridge in, raised it and stared briefly at the animal which was panting in long ragged gasps, its snout covered in dirt and bubbles of bloody saliva. The noise of the gun caused some pigeons in the trees up above to take flight. He laid the shotgun on the ground and pulled a pair of wire cutters from the pocket of his Barbour Border Blue wax jacket.

He knelt down, hunched next to the dead animal and snipped the snare and wrenched it from its head. He picked the fox up by its back legs, grabbed the shotgun and walked back to the Mk 1 Land Rover, opening the back door and slinging the dog fox in.

Roger decided that he would leave the rest of the snares until daybreak. He thought that the chances of there being a fox in another snare unlikely, but not impossible. Only two or three times in all the years he had been gamekeeping had he caught more than two foxes at a time.

He got in the Land Rover, lit a Piccadilly, started the machine up and drove steadily across the field. If he was lucky he'd get back to the car before dusk.

The Rover P6's boot was lined with torn open potato bags. The fox went in; that would be put in the freezer until he and the family came back from their weekend away, then thawed and worked on. Roger was a keen taxidermist, amateur, but learning with every job that he undertook. He wouldn't be able to use the body of the fox, as that took the brunt of the blast, but he'd certainly be able to use the head – with a little fixing, that tearing to its mouth would be unnoticeable.

* * *

"Dad!" Shaun, his son, ran out to the car. Even though it was complete and utter darkness, the boy ran fast to meet him: sure footed as a mountain goat. The child waited by the boot of the car as Roger turned off the engine, got out, and went to the back of the car, rubbing the boy's head affectionately.

"He's a bit small, Dad," Shaun said after looking at the fox in silence for a minute. His torch was clasped firmly in his left hand, and not for one second did the beam waver.

"How do you know this isn't a vixen?" Roger enquired.

"Even though he's a bit small, he's heavier *and* longer. If he wasn't as long, I'd have said it was a vixen, due to pup, but I'm much cleverer than that, Dad," Shaun said with a knowing smile.

Inwardly Roger beamed. He picked the fox up by its hind legs and walked with his son to the back of the house, to the coal shed and the work hut where the garden tools and the chest freezer was kept.

* * *

"So did you have a good day then?" Roger asked his wife, Amanda, who was sitting on the sofa reading *The Godfather*. He sat down on his chair, put on his slippers and lit up a cigarette, looking at his wife as she put down the book and smiled at him.

"The usual, trying to contain Shaun's enthusiasm..." Amanda winked at him.

Shaun came into the living room a minute or so later with several sheets of paper and a pencil. He sat at the table and started to draw a quite effective picture of somebody fishing, with trees lining the side of the river.

"Are we all packed for tomorrow?" Roger asked, inhaling deeply on his Piccadilly. "I've got to go onto the estate first thing to check on the snares that I didn't get round to this evening, but as soon as I'm done we can head off. Going to go at daybreak so we can be off just after breakfast, if you want?"

"That's fine, so you want to take Sir with you tomorrow?" she said, cocking her head at Shaun.

"Would he get up that early, though?" Roger asked, already knowing the answer.

* * *

He woke, bright as a button. He lay there in the dark, confused for a moment, trying to frantically remember if he had been dreaming or not. If there had been a dream, it had long gone; he felt like he had drunk ten cups of Camp or Bev coffee in a row. Beside him Amanda slept gently, her head close to his shoulder; he could feel her breath on it. Roger lifted back the thick woollen blankets and slid out of bed, fumbled for a second for his watch, a Bulova Trident, which had belonged to his father. He walked out of the bedroom, crept quietly down the stairs, and turned on the living room light. He stared at the scene before him.

The carpet was moving. It rippled metallic silver.

He rubbed his right eye with the heel of his palm, swore under his breath, and went back up the stairs to put on his slippers. There was no way he was going to walk through the room in his bare feet.

Back in the bedroom he stepped on the creaky floorboard and woke up Amanda.

“Roger?”

“Shhh, need to get my slippers. Go back to sleep.”

“What’s up, is there anything wrong?” she asked groggily.

“Silverfish, the whole of downstairs has silverfish.”

“I’ll let you deal with them,” Amanda thrashed about for a second then pulled the blankets over her head. Roger grinned and went back down the stairs.

Most of the silverfish had scuttled away to whatever place they came from as soon as the light had been turned on, but there was still a good few thousand there. Amanda’s book, which she had left on the floor instead of putting on the little table next to the sofa, was damaged. No doubt they would have feasted well on its binding.

He crossed the room, the hard soles of his slippers

crushing silverfish here and there. He went through to the tiled hallway and brought out the Hoover – that had always been a bone of contention, when buying it, Roger had wanted to go for the tasteful green model, it would fit in with the rest of the house, had been his argument. Instead he had found himself loading a pink Hoover into the boot of the car. "It's hardly as if you are ever going to use it," Amanda had said playfully.

Roger plugged it in and pressed in the round button on the upright with his foot and started cleaning up the mess, the noise of the machine jarring him. Silverfish tried to scuttle away, but they were soon sucked up into the Hoover.

It was a bit of a wrestling match, but he managed to get the room looking better, and once the upright had been put back in the cleaning cupboard, he used the fireplace brush and pan to sweep up the bits of crushed carcass and threw them into the still-warm fireplace.

* * *

Shaun was awake when Roger went to get him. The young boy was sitting upright, reading *The Beano*. He leapt out of bed when Roger told him he could come and do the snares with him.

"Why were you vacuuming so early in the morning?"

"We were invaded, son. Invaded by a host of creatures

from another planet. It was me against them, but I think I managed to get the better of them, for now..."

"Don't be so silly, Dad, I'm not eight..."

It was going to be a good day. The morning sky was clear, no clouds to sully it. The Rover purred through the country roads at a steady pace. Roger looked at the fuel gauge and made a mental note to fill up the tank before they set off down to Carlisle and to the cottage they had booked.

The car entered the estate up by the 'top field' and drove down a little used dirt track that made the car bounce about, lifting both Casements off their respective seats.

Once they arrived at the stables, they collected extra snares, traps, feed bags, and other tools of the trade, then jumped in the Land Rover and drove deep into the estate, past several rookeries and open fields.

The vehicle stopped at a gate at the entrance to a large scrub of woodland, and Shaun jumped out, climbed up, opened the latch, climbed down, then with one foot placed on the lowest rung on the gate, pushed off with the other and rode it until it hit the wooden breaker on the other side of the earth drive. He held the gate, watched as his dad drove the Land Rover through, and then swung the gate closed behind the machine, coughing a little at the thick smoke that belched out of the exhaust pipe.

Once he jumped back into the Land Rover the vehicle crept carefully down the road of brown and brittle pine needles, and they soon left the bright morning behind them as they made their way into the wood.

They came to a clearing, and Roger performed the familiar manoeuvre of driving in as tight a circle as he could so they now faced the way they had just come. Pulling up the handbrake he turned off the engine and father and son sat there, listening to the engine cool down and tick over.

As Roger hadn't brought either a shotgun or rifle with him, he took the spade out from the back, just in case they came across a fox or badger that was caught in a snare and still alive. A couple of swift blows to the head normally saw an end result.

They walked a diagonal right through the woods, came out the other side and immediately came across the 'run', little paths through undergrowth that foxes had been using for generations.

It was these runs that held the best chances of catching foxes – there was the lamping at night – where Roger would go out with one of the farmers with rifle and a powerful beam, to try and draw the foxes in with the sounds of a distressed animal, which they mimicked by rubbing a saliva-wet piece of polystyrene across the driver's side window. The little trick never failed to work. The noise sounded like an injured rabbit. Sometimes the rewards could be three or four foxes in one night, but it was a long old night, many miles covered, and if Roger had anything on the following day, then he'd just have to stay awake and suck it up. Sometimes the fox shooting could go on till the sun rose.

While Roger didn't have a problem with Shaun coming out to see the snares (his son had seen many dead animals before, many caught in the snare – once a rabbit, whose midriff had been bitten by the snare and in its struggle to try and get free had nearly cut itself in half) he did have a problem with taking him out at night. He thought that the shooting of foxes, and the inky blackness of their blood in the back of the Land Rover where they'd end up, might spook the boy too much and give him nightmares.

There had been one late jaunt on the boy's seventh birthday when they had gone rabbit shooting, and Shaun had shot his first rabbit, a baby one. The noise it had made really seemed to scare the child, a high pitched screeching, and as the bullet had torn through its nervous system, it was thrashing and bouncing all over the place before it crashed to a sudden stop and died.

It hadn't put the child off shooting again, but it did slow him down for a while. Roger did, however, decide that until Shaun was a little bit older he'd only do the daylight sojourns; probably not realising that the blood and injuries seen in the cold light of day were often hidden in the darkness.

* * *

There was a fox in the last snare and it was dead. The wire of the snare was hidden in its fur, but there was a line of matted blood betraying where the wire had bit. It was lying on its side, one orange eye glazed and vacant. Roger handed Shaun the wire cutters. The boy approached the animal and put his fingers into the animal's fur until they found the golden coloured snare. He snipped through it. Roger pulled out a fresh snare from his other pocket and anchored the end part around the tree, over and over, twisting the wire so that it could never be pulled free, then held the hoop up with the same piece of split twig that had been used to hold up its predecessor.

He gave the spade to his son and picked up the fox. It was another dog, this time a heavy one: old. They dragged it back to the forest where they came across a blown down tree, the roots ripped up. Roger threw the fox into the hole, dug some earth up, and covered it. On a hot day the stink might carry, but it wouldn't offend anybody.

"Can you remember shooting your first ever fox, Dad?" Shaun asked as they walked back to the Land Rover.

"No, I can't say that I do," Roger said quietly. And that was the truth, he couldn't. The memories of his childhood were extremely hazy. He'd been told some of the stories by his mother, of course, but they were—

"Are we going to do any shooting or fishing while we are away?" Shaun interrupted his train of thought, which was a good thing. Roger didn't like to dwell on his formative days. The ones that he could remember were very dark indeed.

"We won't be taking the guns with us, but I'm sure we'll certainly be able to squeeze in a spot of fishing when we arrive this afternoon."

"I'm really looking forward to it. I hope we catch lots of fish!"

Roger loved his son's exuberance.

* * *

They arrived at the cottage a little bit later than planned. Amanda started getting the rooms ready. Roger and Shaun walked by Blitterlee Golf Park and into Silloth to pick up bread, milk and that evening's dinner.

There were rabbits on the golf course, jumping about, but not as many as there might have once been. Numbers had been decimated by myxomatosis. There were still large pockets of survivors – where the Casement's lived being one of them, but they did untold damage to farmer's crops and had to be culled.

Silloth was a pleasant place. They went into the newsagent and Roger told his son to pick any book that he fancied from the revolving book stand while he picked up a newspaper for his wife. Shaun studied the paperbacks intently and came to rest on a book with a wedding cake on the cover. It wasn't just any wedding cake – it had a model of a bride and groom as skeletons: a deliciously macabre decoration. There was also a kitchen knife plunged into the cake and blood dribbling from the incision.

"I'll have that one please, Dad." Shaun said.

Roger shook his head when he saw what his boy was pointing at. "Are you sure there's nothing there more suited to your age?"

"Dad!" Shaun mock-wailed, exasperation evident on his face.

"Fair enough then, just don't show your mum."

Loaded up with some white chocolate mice and Black Jacks, Shaun was as happy as happy could be.

* * *

The cottage belonged to the owner of the gun shop where Roger got his cartridges and bullets. It was a solid little place, hidden in a little dip in the otherwise flat landscape, and was an excellent sun trap. By the time they got back Amanda was out in the garden, lying in faded bra and knickers, catching a decent heat.

Later, dinner was chicken casserole. The family laughed and ate well, and after dinner they drove the car down to the beach and watched the waves crash in.

Shaun played on the sand, kicking his football about. Roger and Amanda had a blanket wrapped around them, hugging. Amanda's brown hair was pulled back in a ponytail and tucked down the back of her jumper so it wouldn't be a portable swing for the little midges that appeared almost the second they'd arrived.

* * *

Father and son fished on the Sunday morning. There was a good river about six miles inland and they caught a few tiddlers here and there. Certainly nothing to eat, and nothing to shout about.

They drove back early Monday, Shaun had been carried from bed to car and was asleep for most of the journey. He'd been reading his horror book with a torch under the eiderdown and had scared himself so much reading one story that he hadn't been able to sleep, only collapsing with exhaustion at around five in the morning. Amanda walked in, saw the torch light still on and the horror book, and had given Roger a playfully stern telling off.

A great, short, family break.

And never did they think that by the end of Monday evening Roger would be arrested for shooting and killing someone.

CHAPTER 3
LOST AND FOUND
(1947)

Roger came to. He opened his eyes but couldn't see. He whimpered in his darkness as his body woke and pain enveloped him. His back burned like bad suntan.

Little by little his vision came back; blurred, like Vaseline on a film lens. He stared at his hand. It seemed to be covered in a very light purple fluid. He brought his hand to his face and cried with exertion.

Two hours later he was fully alert and sitting up. As he looked about him he saw that it was a beautiful summer's day. Jagged, broken, memories of being far up in the hills with his father. And it certainly wasn't summer when they had gone up to find a deer to -

He scrambled to his feet, unmindful of his nakedness and of his pain, and screamed, "Father!"

He looked around and saw the hill that he and his father had climbed up on the other side of the loch. He started running, but collapsed after a few hundred metres.

Roger began to crawl.

* * *

The ghillie, Andrew Smart, was enjoying a rare day off, fishing the loch, sitting in his boat, marvelling at how still the day was. He was fishing for brown trout. Two good sized fish were in his bag and would be cooked well that night.

He took a sip from his hip flask of whisky and decided that he'd best take the fish home. It was going to be a scorcher of a day and he didn't want the trout to spoil. He brought the boat back to the jetty, but didn't see the dirty, naked boy until the boat was alongside it.

"Jesus Christ," Andrew yelled, getting up in a hurry and nearly rocking the boat over with his jerky movements. He clambered up onto the jetty and, resting on hands and knees next to the child, felt for a pulse under his jaw.

It was there; feeble, skipping. Then Andrew recoiled with horror when he saw the mark on the boy's back. He withdrew his hand, crossed himself, and seemed loathed to do what he *was* going to do next, pick the boy up and get him to help.

The boy came to and groaned. Compassion kicked in and overrode any feelings of fear and revulsion that Andrew had. He picked the wisp of a child up and ran to the car, placing him in the back and putting his tweed jacket over him.

He knew who the child was. Everyone knew who the missing child was.

Roger Casement.

The boy had been gone for eight months.

But where had he *been*?

* * *

Doctor Hogarth was in his back garden, tending to his flowers; watering the ones that seemed to be out of sorts. Then in the distance a car horn blared and didn't let up. Hogarth thought there might have been a crash. He downed his watering can and walked round the side of the house, into the front garden, and out of the gate. He spotted the car, recognised it instantly. It was driving straight for the house. Hogarth nipped back into the house- even at sixty nine he was still light on his feet - and fetched his heavy black bag. He was out and ready by the time the car had screeched to a halt in front of the house.

"It's the bloody Casement boy," Andrew babbled, jumping out of the car, opening up the 'suicide door' and pulling the boy out. "I've found the Casement boy!"

"Bring him in," Hogarth said, thinking fast. It wouldn't do to have the boy laid out on the grass for all the neighbours to see. "First room on the right, lay him out on the table."

Andrew looked scared as he took the limp boy into the house. He walked into the parlour cum dining room: sepia pictures of dead relatives adorned the wall. Silk flowers in expensive glass vases sat on the large table. Hogarth removed them and placed them on the floor, whipped off the table covering, and Andrew placed the boy gently on the wooden surface.

"Where did you find him?" Hogarth asked, looking first at the boy's bald head, as Andrew looked at him, unsure, scared.

"By the jetty."

"Was he responsive?"

"I don't understand."

"Did he say or do anything when you brought him here?"

"He moaned a couple of times. Cried out for his father when we were driving here. Apart from that he's been as quiet as a church mouse."

"Did you mention his father to him?"

"No."

"Fetch the boy's mother. Stop in at the Reverend's on the way there. Tell him to come here straight away. She'll need some assistance."

Once Andrew had left, Hogarth looked at the boy with some curiosity. First impressions dictated that the boy looked to be in extremely good health, didn't look malnourished; and although he was covered in something, it had dried. Hogarth peeled a six inch section from his thigh. He walked to the window and twisted it too and fro in the light. It looked like petrol on water.

The boy coughed. Hogarth placed the 'skin' on the window sill and rolled the boy onto his side. He saw the mark on his back and tried to remain professional.

The poor boy.

The burn, if that's what you could call it, was at least half an inch deep. But it wasn't a burn in the traditional sense of the word. There was no blistering, no discolouration around the mark, or indeed any swelling of the skin. It was almost as if Roger had been born with it and had carried it with him for all his life, which wasn't the case. Hogarth had been present at the boy's birth, had seen him through a particularly bad case of jaundice, and as many colds and bugs that you'd care to name. His doctor's stethoscope had been placed on bare chest and back, and that mark had never been there.

Doctor Hogarth wondered who would do such a thing. He realised that the story was going to become a lot bigger once word was out, that there was going to be a lot of outlandish talk. He'd have to get Smart to tell him exactly what happened when he'd calmed down somewhat and stopped being the local hero for finding the boy. Even though Roger had really found *him*.

He left the boy and went to get his camera, his new purchase of only the week before. He made sure that the Bosley was in sound order and then took several photos of the mark. Hogarth had the feeling that the mark would be quickly swept under the carpet, that an excuse for it would be plucked from thin air and accepted by all and sundry.

He'd take the camera and drive to England. Take a holiday to visit his son who was lead researcher at the Esoteric Sciences department at one of the Universities there. And the boy, Hogarth would talk to him in the future; work on his memory a little. He didn't think that he'd remember much- anything at all – but there were ways in which to trick the mind to bring up its secrets.

Hogarth brought a blanket through and covered the boy. He then picked up the phone and told the operator to send for an ambulance, and to get hold of Sergeant Howie.

Elspeth, the operator was very curious as to what was going on.

So was Hogarth.

* * *

The search for Roger Casement had been huge. Two hundred people scouring the area. His mother had phoned in the police and from there the search had begun. But the weather deteriorated very quickly, making it impossible to do anything more than a rudimentary search of the lower slopes. The car was found, door open, but it was the absence of any snow that had really puzzled the searchers. The storm had been magnificent, but it appeared that everywhere but here in the region had been affected.

The hole that Roger had fallen down had either not been discovered, or had closed up. And so they searched. Roger's father was found, and it was then that all life seemed to leave the quiet, but hopeful, Anne-Marie Casement when the news was broken to her.

That the gun wasn't found with the body was a concern. But if the boy did have it in his possession, then at the very most, if he was lost, he'd have the ways and means of being able to catch his own food, and the noise in the valley would be heard.

Days passed. Weeks passed. The search tapered off, as all searches do when nothing is found. Frantic urgency slowly turning to a deep despondency.

Marie buried her husband and was left to mourn. The community rallied round, as communities always did when tragedy struck.

One or two people continued to search – a thankless, fruitless, task – and as the days began to get lighter and the weather warmer, one or two people thought that a small pile of bones might be found.

Others held the belief the boy would never be found, there too were many places to hide a body if you needed to. That there were many people living hidden, secret lives in the valley – the strange community, for instance, who lived a very 'free' existence up by the old ruins of Fort Duibh. The police, led by Sergeant Amos Howie (whose young son Neil had played with Roger on many an occasion), raided, with some force, the collection of drifters – mainly made up of soldiers unable to face the prospect of integrating back into normal society after the war, and women that they had picked up along the way. While there had been several firearms found, mainly relics from the First World War, there was no sign of the missing boy.

* * *

Andrew and his erratic driving nearly resulted in his death on Spoon Bridge, but he managed to wrestle control of the car at the last second and drive out of the sharp left-hand turn that immediately followed the bridge, otherwise they would have been picking bits of him from the sheer rock face.

In the days and weeks that followed, he would become - in a very small, but intense community way - a hero. He would appear in both newspapers for the area, would be given a free dram (or five) whenever he popped into the local hostelry, The Crooked Lamb, and the fact that he had beaten his own wife black and blue to the point of her losing their unborn child three years before – well, some places can have amnesia for a while.

Again, the car tore up the scrabbly roads, kicking up great clouds of dust. The drive to the Casement home was a relatively straightforward one – apart from the very end, where the car would have to be parked and Andrew would have to climb up the steep hill to the cottage, where the house was, on the outskirts of a small copse of trees.

Anne-Marie was in bed, asleep. She spent most of her days in bed now. When she did get up and face the day, she would sit at the window, looking out at the mountains in the distance, often crying. She rarely had good days, and when she did it would never take her long to find something to upset herself. She felt that she had no right to be happy as long as her son was out there.

The banging on the door didn't wake her up, but the stone that broke the window did.

"Mrs Casement! I found your boy, I found your boy!"

CHAPTER 4
THE VAN
(1970)

As Amanda was unpacking and washing clothes, and Shaun was playing with his toy cars up in his bedroom, too tired to come and check the traps, Roger put his rifle and shotgun in the back of the car and headed off: to check the snares, see if there were any repairs needed to any gates, and maybe even get a couple of pigeons for a nice pie later on in the week.

He stopped off at Featherstone's and filled the tank, then chatted to Archibald Reiver who had been released only the week previously after a heart attack felled him as he was putting wood through the circular saw. If the heart attack hadn't killed him, the loss of blood from slicing his three fingers off nearly had. Because of the heart attack, they didn't sew the fingers back on, the operation would have killed him. In fact, the doctors were quite wondrous of the fact that he had pulled through as quickly as he did.

"That's my shooting days over too," Archie sighed

wistfully, holding up his heavily bandaged hand up to prove his point.

"You've still got your trigger finger though," Roger said.

"Yes, but what am I going to balance the trigger guard on in future; it's going to be near impossible for me to take a decent shot."

"You'll adapt. Once you're back to punching fitness, come out with me, we'll get you back into it. Just because you have a handicap doesn't mean that you're handicapped."

"Are you sure?" Archie asked, doubt tightening his face up.

"We'll start you off using the 16 bore that Shaun uses. It's all about building up what you have left and getting it to such a level that when you go back to the 12 bore it's not going to be a shock to your hand or yourself. And it'll become second nature again, believe me."

Those were the words that Archie needed to hear. The doubt slowly seeping away, to be replaced by calming relief.

"That's really kind of you Roger, I owe you one."

"No, don't be silly, it's just one friend helping out another."

After Roger left Featherstone's he made his way to the estate, but decided to do the snares up at Blunderstone Rookery first: he wouldn't need to go and get the Land

Rover from the Estate's stables. Then he'd go and see Gavin Leader – the owner of the Estate and who he had been gamekeeper for – and tell him what had been caught, and the amount of foxes that had been shot. His boss was a well-known eccentric and lived life with his head in the clouds. But when it came to matters of pest control and the hunt, which he allowed to ride on his land, he was most attentive.

He pulled off the main road, about three miles away from where the Estate's main house was, and drove down a scrabbly road stopping at a wet, moss covered gate.

He pulled the shotgun out from the back of the car, jumped the gate, and walked a good mile and a half until he came to the snares. Roger often wondered if another gamekeeper would be so attentive to a lonely stretch of woodland as he was, but he recognised that it was one of the main ways that the foxes came into the estate from the hills; that was if they made the journey across the main road without being struck and killed by a vehicle.

He walked the mile up to the Rookery, his walking boots only very occasionally slipping on the almost non-existent, goat eaten grass.

Amazingly, and in a new record for the Estate, he found foxes in three of the nine snares he had laid up there, all dead. He dumped them in a pile by the gate that led to an arable field while he broke a branch from an oak tree and a fashioned spike on either end of it with his knife. Once that was done he took the head off from the best looking fox and impaled it hard onto the spike. In a while there would be a very nice skull to bleach. Shaun would be allowed to have one; in fact he had a good collection of skulls, from remains that they had found during their outings; rabbits, stoats and even a badger.

Once that was done he dragged the bodies back to the moss covered gate by the car. The next time he drove by in the Land Rover he'd pick them up and dispose of them. They'd stink the vehicle out for a while, even if they were put in a fertilizer sack to try and deaden the smell, but the truth was that it was only noticeable to those who had never come into contact with the smell before. Shaun was immune to it, although he had thrown up on the first occasion he had come into contact with his first dead animal: a rabbit, whose spoiled corpse was festering with hundreds upon hundreds of writhing maggots.

Even Amanda had stopped making a point of bringing up the smell that he brought back in his clothes. It was one of the reasons he smoked more on the job than on other occasions. Roger hoped that the smoke would negate the persistent linger of death.

Once he had finished at the Rookery he drove to the other end of the Estate, driving very slowly up the steep incline of Stobbie hill. He parked sideways on the hill. He would be the only vehicle here today, and this road wasn't even used by the people who owned the land.

He took his binoculars and rifle out this time, thinking that if he bedded in for an hour or two until dusk he might spot a fox out for a bit of back-shift mischievousness. He reached the top of the track which ended in a derelict wooden fence. He opened it rather than trying to jump over it - the rotten wood would crack, and he'd break something himself.

He walked over three fields, then entered Chosen Wood. The smell of pine trees soothed him as he walked through, some branches scratched his face gently as he walked between them. On the other side of the wood was a much smaller field and instead of being bordered by a dyke, was marked by ancient hawthorn. At the other end of the field was a steep drop, jagged rocks, felled trees, treacherous underground.

But the view was perfect, he could see another past of the Estate spread out before him – plenty of open fields. To the left of the boundary, far away in the distance was the road. Cars droned by.

Roger placed his rifle on the ground gently, lit a cigarette, sat on a tree stump, and was hidden by a large clump of Moor grass, that was about six foot in height – but he continued to have good visibility.

The light slowly started to bleed from the day and

entered the magic hour. Everything around him seemed to be softened by the low sun. And it was then he noticed the Bedford van crawl into one of the fields far below him.

Roger stubbed out his cigarette and used the binoculars that hung from his neck. He focused on the van, which was at one point a British post van, but had been repainted green, reminiscent of the colour of telephone service vans. The license plate read DYR 512C. With the sun being so low he couldn't see who the driver was; the windscreen was marred with reflection or the window itself had been replaced with tinted Plexiglas or had been sprayed with tint from a can.

It came to a halt at the furthest edge of the field, unseen to everyone bar Roger. It was almost as if, he thought, that whoever it was had come here before. It was a part of the Estate he never had need to go to – it was never a main route through for foxes. And this was private property. He'd report it to his boss and would let him phone the police if he felt it prudent. He got up from behind the grass and squat-shuffled away from the stump, slowly and carefully, right until he was at the edge of the drop.

The back door opened slightly and a girl fell out onto the ground. Roger took the binoculars away from his eyes and shook his head, almost as if he was trying to clear something away before he put them back up to his eyes again. There was a man standing in front of her. The driver? Roger refocused the binoculars. The girl, dressed in a simple flower print dress was trying to crawl away from the man. She appeared to be crying. He grabbed her by the hair and lifted her up by it, she was beating at his arms. Then he punched her to the ground and undid his trousers.

Roger reeled back with shock. He looked back to the rifle and reached for it. He'd let off a round, try to disturb him. He thought about how long it would take him to get to her if the driver left her behind, he would never be able to get to her by going down the incline, and he would break a leg for sure. He'd have to run to the car and then get the Land Rover and then have to drive to her. It would take about twenty to thirty minutes. That's if the driver left her there.

Roger grabbed the rifle, took the cloth coverings off from the telescopic scope, tucked the rifle in and looked down it. He was raping her and he had a knife to her throat. It was then that Roger knew without any doubt that he – the driver – was going to kill her. He breathed in and out deeply, the air about him seemed to change, almost starting to shimmer. On his next breath, though, his lungs felt heavy as if they had forgotten how they worked.

* * *

Roger sat in the room, his hands before him, cuffed. A cigarette between his fingers, he sat across from Sergeant Hamish Dolan who lived in the same street as him.

"Archie Reiver's son? Angus? No, I can't believe that." Roger felt another wave of sickness grab him. He hadn't recognised him. Not through all that *mess*.

"Look, Roger," Hamish said softly, pointing at the cuffs, "they'll come off you and you'll go home. From what you've told me,you weren't to know that what you were seeing was fake; that it was all a set up. But why the fuck did you take the shot in the first place? You're a gamekeeper, not a soldier, your talent is between you and you – but you could have killed the girl, you could have killed her." Hamish paused and took a cigarette from the packet on the table and lit it, taking a deep breath and exhaling just as quickly.

"I didn't think. It was instinct." Roger sighed, placing his cigarette into the heavy crystal glass ashtray. Smoke stuttered up in the space between them.

"What happened?"

"I was seeing it as clear as I am seeing you. The light was fading, and it was fading fast, but with the scope on the gun, I could see the freckles on her face. She was screaming. You could see that she was screaming and thrashing her head about, but the noise wasn't drifting up to me before you ask, the wind was blowing in the wrong direction for that. The driver, well he had ripped the top part of her dress off, he was on his knees, the knife was at her throat, but he was letting her thrash about, he was, as far as I could make out, grinning. He then raised the knife, and that's when I took the shot. I honestly thought that he was going to kill her.

"This was the weird thing. Normally, when I go to shoot a fox, take in for the wind, and look down the scope for a long time and then make the right adjustments for the shot, because if you shoot blind, the bullet will end up either going into the ground 500 metres in front of it, or it'll continue for a mile or so, way above it until it hits a tree or something. The distance that he was at didn't bother me, I've hit further, I think I lifted the barrel of the gun and squeezed the trigger. A part of me was thinking that I would never hit him, that I was way off target, that it would frighten him off, and he'd leave the girl. The thought of my hitting her never even entered my thoughts. I was trying to protect her, not kill her."

"Well, you're a good shot, right centre of his forehead."

"The bullet would have hit him a split second before the noise followed, so he would have been pushed off her before she had realised what happened. The noise, well it's the same with every other gun shot – it's a loud crack, and you think that it's loud enough to wake the dead. It's worse at night when you squeeze off a shot, because it's two, three in the morning, and you think you're going to wake up every one for miles around, and you probably do. But it's the country, and people round here are familiar with the noise they expect it, they - "

"So, you shot him."

"Yes, sorry. So he went flying back. I didn't realise it was a head shot then, the gun kicked and it took me a second to readjust my line of vision after I ejected the casing and loaded another bullet into the breech. Then I remembered that I had the binoculars, so I put the gun down and looked through them, and it was then that the back door of the van opened and someone came out holding a cine camera and he was shouting and yelling. And then the girl, well she looked like she was still screaming, and she had the guy that I shot in her arms, and it was then I could see that I had taken the top off his head off. He had blonde hair, but it was mostly red.

"I didn't know what the fuck was happening, I promise you. What kind of people go onto someone else's property to film a pretend snuff film? You've got the film now, haven't you?" Roger asked, his hand trembling as he picked up his cigarette and took a puff from it.

"Yes, we're looking it over," was all that the policeman would say.

"I only shot at him because I thought he was going to kill the girl. You have to believe that. Well, the guy holding the camera jumped out of the back of the van, and it was then that I noticed the black panel on one of the doors, I hadn't noticed it before, and it must have been a darkened window for him to shoot from – make the whole film look more real and dangerous to those viewing it. He started remonstrating at the woman, and then looked in my direction, but he would never have been able to see me. And then he dropped the camera at her feet, ran to the van jumped in it and did one of the tightest circles I've ever seen anyone do – if he'd had to reverse he would have run her over - and he left the field much faster than he entered it. I got up, picked up the gun, and walked slowly down to the car and made my way to my boss, Gavin Leader, and told him to phone the police. Then we both made our way in the Land Rover to the field. He was driving, I just wasn't able by then. I was in shock and my head was churning up something funny, and I felt like I was about to explode."

* * *

Roger opened the passenger door to the Land Rover slowly. There were only minutes of daylight left. Gavin turned on the headlights. The woman in the blood covered frock didn't notice. She seemed comatose.

As he slid out of the vehicle, and his feet hit the grass, he expected the ground to open up underneath him. Instead it felt spongy, like he was standing on a field-sized bowl of jelly.

His back was burning. Roger lifted up his arm and, with the flat of his hand, tried to soothe the spot. It seemed to aggravate it.

The sickly light from the Land Rover made the scene before him seem more alien than it was – but then it wasn't every day you killed someone, was it?

ohmygodwhathaveyoudone?

The top of the man's head was missing from above the eyes. Tufts of eyebrow had been taken along with it. Beyond, in the darkened shadows lay the skull, the brain matter, the hair, the rest of the eyebrows. Some of it might have ended up on the van that tore out.

Roger took another step. And it was then that the vacuum dispersed. Jagged memory and the familiar stain of time catching up, swallowed him.

CHAPTER 5
THE SKINNING
(1949)

The stranger took a room at The Crooked Lamb, paid a week in advance, and was led by the hostelry owner, Nora Lofts, to a clean but sparse room. The makings of a fire were already built up in the fireplace, a washbowl and full jug on the washstand in the corner of the room.

There was nothing *suspicious* about the stranger, he was very polite, wore a finely tailored suit, and when he was asked what he was in the area for, he gave a very plausible explanation that he was from London and had decided to spend a few weeks away after the death of his wife. Eliciting just enough sympathy as not to draw more than a curious look. He could hear them now: "You can't come to a finer place to forget about the death of your wife."

The stranger, Peter Swan, who gave his name as Archibald Swithern, was tall, just a shade under 6 foot, clean shaven, and conventionally handsome. He would certainly never have had a problem in finding a wife, had he ever decided to. In reality, his only use for women was sexual, an exploitation to be used during ceremonies.

He had first heard about the vanishing and re-appearance of the boy six months before. He had been invited to the opening of a new club in Regent Street, next to the publisher's Home & Holbert. Eldon Holbert was a scholar and publisher recently returned from America, when Archibald met him. The man described meeting an author, Frank Jeffert, who had pitched to him on the basis of letters from his sister. The woman had been residing in Britain when the boy's tale caught her imagination. She had detailed the disappearance of the Casement father and son, somewhere in the wild Scottish mountains and the strange sudden re-appearance of the boy.

Speaking in the comfort of their leather wing-back chairs, next to a fire in the smoking room, nursing generous measures of whisky, Peter and Eldon wondered why news of this hadn't made the newspapers or *Pathé*. It certainly had the makings of one of the biggest stories of all time – the boy didn't know what had happened to him, had no memory – the husband found dead, a suspected heart-attack, but who could be sure?

"In the end, I had to say no to the book. Frank wanted money for an all expenses visit to Scotland to research, then write the book which might take anywhere up to a year, and I'm sorry, it could have been the biggest best seller of them all, but I simply don't have the money to fund folly's journey," Holbert sighed, taking a last swill from his whisky and lifting the glass into the air so as to get a refill.

Peter would have gone to Scotland sooner, but there were other, more pressing matters to attend to. And in all honesty, to put some more time between the boy and what happened to him could only be a good thing. It would give the community a little more time to settle. And he had research to do.

Alone, in the warm room above the Crooked Lamb, Peter Swan undid his suitcase and removed all of the clothes and small bag containing carbolic soap, toothbrush and Solidox toothpaste. Once the case was free from such clutter, he took a small knife from his pocket, undid it, and poked it into the top left corner. Something clicked and the bottom freed. He dropped the knife onto the bed and took the false bottom from the case.

He smiled as he removed the book, his tongue burst free from his mouth and he licked his lips slowly, sensually, as the feel of the volume enveloped him. Arcane spells and blasphemous passages, bound with the skin of sacrifice, seemed to come alive in his hands.

He opened the book and turned the pages until he came to the passage he was after, and read it, near murmuring. It was written in an ancient script. No layman, and especially not the simple folk of the village, would be able to understand such noble and sacred text. Once slaked, he laid the book gently on the bed and removed a roll of velvet and undid it next to the book, revealing a black handled knife, his athame.

* * *

Research. It was easier than he had expected. Being a Doctor himself gave him the required air of fellow respectability, allowing him to send off for papers relevant to the case. And when he found the name of the doctor who had first seen the boy, he wrote to him, only half-expecting an answer.

Dr Hogarth,

I hope that this letter finds you well. My name is Dr Swan and my particular field is malnutrition in youngsters. While we live in a time in which certain elements of the community dwell in real poverty, my attention was brought to the case of the missing Casement boy. It was reported, very briefly, that you were the first person to treat him when found.

A fortnight later and Doctor Hogarth had written a four page letter back to him, uniformly boring – aside from the description of the mark on the boy's body, and the dynamite, the one piece of evidence that was needed to propel Peter Swan to this neglected part of Scotland, a photo.

* * *

Peter Swan spent a few days driving the local area, going deep into the valley where the search for the boy had taken the police and the villagers, to the surrounding towns and outlying communities, trying to build a picture in his head of what had happened, how it happened and why, out of nowhere the boy had suddenly appeared.

He went back to The Crooked Lamb every evening, played nice with Nora Lofts, accepted her meals, and even shared a pint of ale or two with the locals who regarded him quietly. He was quiet in return, playing the widowed husband to perfection, saying that he was even going to try and start writing a novel, so might stay a little while longer if the mood took him.

He had stalked the Casement house, of course. Had seen the mother, hanging out clothes on the washing line, walking down to the store to get that week's provisions. She always looked drawn and tired, her face as white as the sheets she hung out to dry on the lines strung from tree to tree.

The boy he had seen only the once, sitting on top of

the coal shed, swinging his legs. From his vantage point, hidden up in the scrub that surrounded the hills that shielded the cottage from sight of the main road, Peter trained his binoculars on the boy. He seemed to have a good weight to him, but his face had a far off, almost blank quality to it, like a polished stone.

Peter also stalked the home of Doctor Hogarth and wondered if he should pay him a visit. Not to talk about the case any further, purely to kill him and get rid of the letters that he sent him. The more he thought on it, the more he realised it didn't matter, that once the rite was performed and the gateway was open, a few letters enquiring about the Casement boy would be the least of anyone's worries.

* * *

He decided to strike early in the morning. When they were both asleep, or had just awoken and their responses would be sluggish. Peter Swan's last night in the Crooked Lamb was one spent in utter silence, meditating, reciting an ancient rite over and over in his mind, preparing himself for the task that lay ahead.

He had fasted for the whole day, no food or water had entered his system. He had used a light laxative to help rid himself of any toxins that might be stored within. When the time came to finally meet the darkness, he wanted to be completely free of the trappings of man.

The black candles that he lit had completely burned out by the time that early morning came. He dressed slowly, not putting on underpants, vest or socks. When the time came for the ceremony, he had to be fast and to execute everything quickly. He packed his knife, his tome of arcane magic, two fresh candles, and a stick of chalk, into his small leather carry-bag. Leaving the suitcase wasn't going to be a problem, much as not killing the doctor wasn't going to be a problem.

The night before he had parked away from the pub, so as not to wake anyone up and alert him to his early morning travelling. There was always the risk that the morning breeze might carry the noise of him starting the car back to the Crooked Lamb, but Nora would no doubt see the suitcase where it always was, neat, and on the dresser, and think no more of it, that he would be back later on in the day and perhaps wanted to take a trip into Inverness.

His excitement rose and he drove closer and closer to the Casement home. He pulled into a forest lane about a mile away, got out, and stripped off. He went into his satchel and brought out a tin of black shoe polish, and started to cover his face, ears and neck with the stuff. He then rubbed his hands over his nipples and cock, which was, by now, solid, full of blood. He then drew as best as he could an upside down pentangle on his chest, and in it, the sign that he had seen on the photo of the boy's back: the old runic sign for *serpent*. The one true indicator that the Casement boy was delivered to the darkness and brought back to the Earth to show Swan the way, to help him unlock the lower doors to hell.

Swan, in his savagery and excitement, had now become quite, quite insane.

* * *

He is thankful that there are no animals on the property, no dogs to be startled and growl at him. He likes dogs more than humans and it would grieve him so to kill one; although that would never be a problem - beckon the dog, knife in the windpipe, stroke its fur on the way down, down, down.

The door is unlocked like he knew it would be, all doors are unlocked in this part of the world; in the cities less so. Although you will find a fair amount of folk who still think there are nobody but nice people out there.

He opens the door slowly, it doesn't squeak, it opens onto flagstones that are smooth and don't hurt his feet as much as the scree leading up to the door. He wipes his feet on the largest of the flagstones, from them fall pine needles, dirt, a few bits of grit.

He pads silently through the kitchen and it leads into a spartan living area: two chairs, an open fire, whose ambers crinkle and glow red. The stairway is an open one, directly in front of the front door of the house, and he climbs up it, sure footing, one at a time. His leather bag in one hand, his other hand out in front of him, his guide into the unknown. His heart is racing, unhealthily so. His shoe polish-blackened cock points the way forward, his face disappears into the gloom that pervades the stairs.

He reaches the top of the stairs and freezes, listening for the rise and fall of sleep. He gently places the satchel on the floor, his hands work silently, undoing the heavy metal clasp, folding it back onto itself, making sure that the leather strap takes the weight of it and that it doesn't clatter. He opens the bag up bit by bit, and when there is enough space, he reaches in, pulls out his knife. He unsheathes it, lifts the blade to his mouth, kisses it, places the flat metal against his tongue, the metal is bitter, makes him salivate.

He takes a deep breath in and screams as loud as he can.

The mother screams in her sleep, then wakes up, falling out of the bed. He hears the thump, kicks open the door and runs into the room. She looks up at him, her eyes glassy, then she screams again. He grabs her by the hair and smashes her head against the bedpost.

"Mum?"

He hears the scared yell from the boy. He snarls in delight, then goes into the next room. The boy is sitting up in bed, his blankets wrapped around him, for defence, for comfort. The man screams again, into the petrified boy's face. Then punches him in the side of the head, knocking him clean out.

He drags the boy into the mother's bedroom as it is the larger of the two. He takes the boy's nightclothes off: striped, linen pyjamas. Scratchy to wear, no doubt.

Once the boy is naked he kicks him onto his front. The mark is there, it is angry looking and doesn't look as if it has really healed. He moans with pleasure when he sees it and wants to reach down to touch and caress the scar, but dares not to. It is not his to touch.

He goes to his bag and brings out the candles, the book and with the knife, takes them into the room. He curses when he realises that he did not bring matches with him, and has to go downstairs to the kitchen to find some.

He lights the candles, then goes back to his bag and brings out a piece of chalk and draws a circle around the boy. In it he draws three, upside-down pentangles, each with different marks, one of them identical to one on the child's back, the mark of the serpent.

He takes his book and opens it, flicking through the pages slowly till he comes to the one he needs.

He closes his eyes. He breathes deeply, gets his heart down to a manageable beat. When he opens them, Peter Swan starts to speak, starts to invoke his master, the one true lord of the darkness:

Lord Satan, by your grace, grant me, I pray thee the power to conceive in my mind and to execute that which I desire to do, the end which I would attain by thy help, O Mighty Satan, the one True God who livest and reignest forever and ever. I entreat thee to inspire thyself to manifest before me that you may give me true and faithful answer, so that I may accomplish my desired end, provided that it is proper to your office. This I respectfully and humbly ask in Your Name, Lord Satan, may you deem me worthy, Father.

* * *

In its waking slumber, deep in the nothingness, the eye searches and finds the cause of its itch. It recognises the speck that is before it and still wishes to let it live to see ascension.

* * *

Peter Swan drops the book, lifts the knife up, and goes to kill the child. The child comes to, and rolls over onto his side, shielding the desired kill spot. The child screams, blood pouring from his nose, his mouth.

"May you deem me worthy Father!" Peter yells, and

thrusts the knife down. It reaches to about a centimetre away from the child then stops, as if it has hit a wall.

Pain. Pain like he has never felt before consumes Peter Swan. It burns from the top of his head down to his toes. Consumes him, fills his lungs. He feels like his eyes are popping out of his skull, and then they do. He is blind. He begins to scream and scream and scream, and then it stops suddenly as his tongue falls wetly onto the floor. He is lifted up into the air, only about a foot. The air in the room starts to thicken and something wrenches the occultist sharply to the left. Then, in an instant, the skin is peeled from him, every inch of his body suffering indescribable agonies. Roger stares at the limp puppet and manages to smile weakly. Then in an instant, the body and skin vanish into thin air, leaving a gush of blood that falls from the spot where Peter Swan went to.

Roger blacks out.

CHAPTER 6
THE START OF THE SLOW SPIRAL
(1970)

Amanda came to pick him up at the police station. They hugged and then Amanda burst into tears. Roger asked where Shaun was and was told that the next door neighbour had him.

In the car, as Amanda drove back, all Roger could think about was Archie. His friend Archie. Both now having to live with the fact that Roger had destroyed everything that was once good between them.

Amanda had been putting Shaun to bed when the news came through, she had listened with dawning horror as the scant details of what had happened were relayed to her.

Her first question was why nobody had come straight to the house to tell her. The reply, a rather haughty and snippy one, was that her husband had used up the police station's resources and that other officers were being drafted in from other towns to deal with everything. She was lucky that she was getting a phone call, the voice said before hanging up on her.

Panic took Amanda, but she was a stronger woman than that. She went to the kettle, which had just boiled, made herself a cup of tea, and went to the battle scarred kitchen table and sat down, her hands wrapped around the mug. The heat was burning her palms, but she didn't really notice.

From what she was told it had been an intentional killing, but one taken because Roger had thought it the right course of action. She knew that her husband was a peaceful man, hadn't even so much as raised his voice to her in all the years that they had been together, was nothing but amazing with Shaun, so she knew that for him to do something like this, he would really have had to have believed that someone's life was at risk for him to take another's.

She didn't finish her tea, but got half way, then shouted to Shaun, who was playing in his bedroom, that she was going to go next door for a while and if the telephone went he was to come and get her straight away.

The neighbours were the Lambs: Hugh and Maria. They had only got together in the last three years. Hugh was an ex-director of the local water company. He'd resigned when he was fifty and spent most of his days since then reading books on birds, while his wife (regarded by the community as very exotic, because she came from Venezuela) was a nurse in the hospital in Haven, ten miles away. They had met during one of the dances that infected the local area every once in a while. There had been many attempted wooings of Maria by the local gentry; most of them rich farmers with lots of land and who suffered long lonely nights due to divorce or social ineptitude.

But she had met Hugh and they had hit it off immediately, and not long after that she had moved in with him, causing the little community a few raised eyebrows. But as Hugh had said on many occasions, 'a bird could fart and the whole valley would know about it', and it was true. There was an unwritten, sometimes horrible rule, that your business was *everybody's* business.

Hugh had always lived in the house 'next door' – even though it was a quarter of a mile away – and had been living there when Roger and Amanda had first moved into their house, three years before Shaun was born. They had been friendly, but Hugh was a private person, and had been ever since the death of his first wife, Aisling – or Dreamy, as was Hugh's pet name for her.

But once Hugh had met Maria, he had come out of his shell somewhat and was a highly intelligent, erudite and funny chap to have around, and Roger and Hugh used to disappear to the pub on the odd occasion (it was good to see Roger out somewhere other than his gamekeeping all the while) while the two women put the world to rights over a bottle of wine; Maria's English getting better and better every time she came across.

She was crying by the time she reached the cottage, Maria had just pulled up in the Triumph.

"What's wrong?" Maria hurried out of the car as Amanda collapsed at her feet.

* * *

Amanda had taken the phone off the hook. She went to the bathroom and drew a bath for her husband.

He undressed, turning around; the scar on his back seemed angry, almost as if it was going to bleed. She kissed him gently on his cheek and shepherded him in.

He looked at her with big doe eyes. He was a lost little child, and the enormity of what happened had robbed him of any masculinity.

"Can you burn the clothes, please?" he asked, his voice tired with emotion.

"Yes, of course, I'll do it in the morning."

"Now please Amanda. Do it now."

Amanda left the bathroom silently, scooping up the clothes on the way out and padded down the stairs and out the back. She dumped the clothes by the door and went to one of the coal sheds. There were three in total.

Two were used for coal, the other for any odd bits of junk. She dragged out a rusty, well used oil drum and with some considerable effort got it to a safe distance away from the sheds. She then got the drum on top of some orange bricks, went and got the clothes, threw them in, popped in some kindling and some newspaper, then threw in a match.

It wasn't long before flames were shooting out the top of the bin. She felt a presence, and turning around, saw the dark outline of her husband standing at the window, staring at the fire.

* * *

Amanda had asked if he wanted anything to eat. Roger was going to say no, that he wasn't hungry, but an incredible twist of hunger took him and he went down and sat at the kitchen table as his wife went about fixing him up a sandwich.

Roger lifted the sandwich from the plate before she had even placed it down on the table, and it was gone in a matter of seconds. Once the sandwich was gone, he stared at her, and she didn't look away, didn't flinch.

He burst into tears and she comforted him, held him, both thinking of the body that lay in the morgue with the top of its head blown off.

* * *

It was a long night, and neither of them slept. At three in the morning they were visited by two policemen who had slowly come to the realisation that the gun that had been taken from him at the scene might not be the only gun that he had on the property.

They looked sheepish as they were brought into the house and taken to the gun cabinet where they removed the twelve bores and Shaun's sixteen bore and another high powered rifle.

Amanda offered them tea and they accepted – which was the last thing that Roger wanted – but they all sat around the table, the law and the law breaker, the hero who would never be charged.

Once they had left, their drinks hurriedly slurped, Amanda went up to bed, her shattered frame crawled under the blankets and she lay there, staring into space, the dread of her husband's act had settled on her as heavily as a lead-lined tomb.

The killing would be around the community in the morning, if it wasn't whispering its way through the pubs and homes and steadings already. Word whipped through like wildfire when it was given the oxygen to breathe, hence she had taken the phone off the hook when she went to collect Roger from the police station. There would be the busybodies who would phone to see how she was doing, but all the while their little antennae would be quivering and reacting for the slight little thing that they could take and twist and pervert for their own good. There were no real friends in a community, even if you had known and grown up with them half of your life. Everyone was ready to spill the beans and gossip given half the chance, the main reason was out of boredom, there was simply nothing else in the area to do other than spread idle tittle-tattle. God knows that Amanda had played her part in it, and now, for all of those times, she had felt deeply ashamed that she might have spread a little brand of misery by her speculations and denunciations on what should have really been private matters.

And Shaun. What to do with the boy?

When Roger had opened his mouth to speak, Shaun was mentioned. And both agreed that they should tell him as soon as he was back in the house and that, if he wanted, they wouldn't send him to school once the holiday's had ended.

Indeed the whole family might have to get away for a while whilst things had settled down a little, but what Roger didn't say, but what Amanda had certainly thought, was that their time in this little corner of the world might have come to an end, that the black cloud that had appeared over their household might never go away.

Roger stayed at the table after Amanda had retired and thought about the past. The first time he had arrived in the area. The first time he had met Amanda. Their first kiss. Shaun being born. Remembering the first time he had been truly accepted as a part of the community, part of the landscape, if you will.

And what about the future?

Gavin had said that there would always be a job for him, but in the time being he was going to call on the services of a mutual friend to take over the running of the Estate until such times Roger felt that he was able to come back.

* * *

"I'm not in any trouble, am I, Dad?" were the first words out of Shaun's mouth when he walked into the living room where Roger was sitting.

Hugh and Maria had come along. Maria had brought a casserole with her and the three of them went through to the kitchen while father and son sat opposite each other.

"What is it? You're scaring me." Shaun started to sob, and Roger's heart *truly* broke. He held out his arms and his boy ran into them, and they cuddled and the boy sobbed hot tears into Roger's neck, and he knew that he would have to get what he had to say next so, so right.

If there was a false step, it could damage the boy more than could ever be repaired.

"Yesterday, I went out to do the snares. You know where the line runs and ends up before the valley drop?"

Shaun nodded.

"Well, I was up there, and you know how you can see everything for miles from there. In one of the lower fields, one that's never used and we don't have any snares down there."

"Ye...s." Shaun looked confused. The talk wasn't going in the direction that he thought it would. He thought that a relative had died or that he had done something wrong. And from what was being said, it was none of those things, so...

"There was a van that drove into the field and it parked up. The back door of the van opened up and a woman was thrown out of the back. She appeared to be in great distress. And there was a man who wanted to do things to her. Bad things. He had a knife." Roger paused as Shaun's eyes widened as he took in this information.

"I didn't want to see the girl die...I didn't want the girl to die, so I thought I'd fire a shot off, try to scare him away."

"But instead you shot him?"

"Yes. He had a knife against her throat. I thought that he was going to cut her throat. So I shot him."

"Well, that's good, then. The girl you saved: is she

fine?" Shaun smiled and reached and patted his father's hand reassuringly.

Roger took a deep breath in, and closed his eyes for a second, searching for the best way to put the next bit to him so that he would understand, but also that he didn't utterly destroy his son's faith in human kind.

"I killed him, Shaun. And he was acting. He was... the girl he was with and...and...another person, who was filming from the van, and who I couldn't see, were making a film. They were making a film, but I thought it was real life, so I took the shot...I –"

Roger broke down, heavy sobs, Shaun wailed and grabbed his dad and started to scream, "Are you going to go to jail? Are you going to jail? It was a mistake, it was a mistake wasn't it?"

Amanda rushed out from the kitchen and knelt down on the floor next to them. Hugh and Maria looked on, tears in their eyes as the Casement family tried to hold onto what was left, to stop the cracks from becoming chasms.

* * *

Roger went to bed at midday. They had spent the morning consoling Shaun. Roger *had* been arrested, but he was yet to be *charged* with anything. The Police, along with the Department of Public Prosecutions would have to do their investigating. There would have to be a statement taken from Shona, the girl Roger had 'saved', and from what he had heard from the police officers who had come to collect his guns, she seemed to be in a catatonic state and was unable or unwilling to talk to anyone.

Sergeant Hamish Dolan had said that he didn't think that this would go to trial, as Roger was leaving the station he however did tell him that he had to be on his guard if he wasn't charged.

"There will be a lot of people in your corner, and they are the ones that would have done the same in your situation. But there will be the Reiver's and they are a big family and one or two of them will be out for blood. And unless there is a hatchet to be buried, as far as they are concerned, your name will be mud and blacklisted forever more."

Roger lay on the bed, fully clothed. His back was burning in the place where his scar was. His mother (a joke of a woman if there had ever been one) had said that he had fallen off a shed as a kid and cut himself on some rusted tin sheeting on the way down. His wife had accepted this story, as he had supposed he also had. But on days like this, he knew deep down there was something more.

Roger didn't remember much, if any, of his childhood. He remembered nothing about his father dying, knew nothing about him having a heart attack while out stalking deer, and that from the age of eleven he was in all sorts of trouble, he had been packed off by his mother to go and stay with that staple of dysfunctional families, an elderly aunt, whose first line in discipline was a beating with a hickory branch (which Aunt Alice had said, with some relish, came from a tree in China when she went there with her father, and it had been used on her to no ill effect) – and being locked in a bedless room for days on end with only soup and water to survive on.

He ran away more times than he cared to imagine, and after an abortive attempt at living with his mother again, where she flew off the handle for no reason, attacked him, and blamed him for killing his father – he left for the last time and...

sleep

sleep

sleep

Roger drifted down; fell down the hole of his childhood. It was pitch black. He felt around, his hand found a wall, it was as cold and as smooth as chrome. He staggered forward, blind, his feet not coping with the frictionless surface on which he walked.

And then he was in freefall, and he was surrounded by fractured, gibbous memories that had been unlocked, freed by delicious trauma – a smell of crushed fern and heather, a heap of stinking guts pulled from a Stag, eyes glassy, bleating at Roger to stop gutting it, that he was killing his own father.

Roger twisted in his sleep, his clothes sodden as his body broke out in a complete, all over sweat.

His father looking at him, his mouth full of bread, a bullet hole in his forehead, the back of his skull dissolved into watery tendrils that floated away from him, and then hung suspended in the thick, oily space of the nothingness in which Roger found himself in.

And still he continued to fall.

A man with white hair, his body completely covered in blood, arcane symbols carved into his torso, screaming with pleasure as he was fucking a limp and unresponsive woman, until her head turned and the hellish grin of Roger's mother confronted him, drool dripping from her smile, her teeth broken and shattered, her grin turning into a picture of pure pleasure and terror as the man with the white hair turned into a shadow with burning red eyes and it fucked and fucked his mother until she started splitting in two, the skin pulling and ripping, the pain etched onto her face, her stomach opening up and then the Stag was screaming, for them both, begging for her guts:

letmeeatthemtheydisemboweledme

And still Roger fell.

CHAPTER 7
THE RED ROOM
(1949)

The echo of Peter Swan's final scream woke Roger up. He scrambled up and ran to the corner of the room, much like a dog will scuttle if it wakes up from a nightmare. His mother was half-lying under the bed, out for the count. His back burned and burned.

Roger rubbed his eyes. The room looked like it was pulsing under a translucent film.

The young boy got to his feet, shaking his head. The image of the man with the white hair, his eyeballs popping from his skull, his skin being ripped from him, revealing muscle...it was –

He stared dumbly at the book and the knife lying in the rather large pool of blood on the floor. It looked like the man really had vanished into thin air. Roger knew from blood-letting animals with his father that a ten stone deer had eight pints of blood in it.

He picked his clothes off the bed and put them on. He

touched his mother's face. No response.

There was only one person that Roger knew who would be able to help. The one person who had come to check up on him in the weeks and months when Roger had been told that he had been struck down by some virus and was very seriously ill.

Dr Hogarth.

* * *

Anne-Marie Casement had made it out of the room, past the pool of blood and halfway down the stairs, before she fell into unconsciousness again. Her head banged hard down the last few steps until she came to rest at the bottom.

When Roger returned with Hogarth, the doctor dragged her through to the living room and let her lie on the rug. He had brought his bag with him and in it was an opiate he'd use on her once she started to stir again. From Roger's frantic babbling about strange men being killed and lots of blood, when he reached his house, it sounded like there was a lot to do before explaining anything to her was to happen.

"Show me the room," he said, and Roger pointed up the stairs. His face was a mask of fear, he certainly didn't want to go back in there again.

Hogarth smiled gently and patted the boy on the shoulder.

"It's okay," the doctor said softly, his voice calm and reassuring, a soft wave against the sand bank.

Roger went up the stairs, slowly, his breathing fast, Hogarth could see his ribcage rising up and down against the thin fabric of his shirt. When he got to the top of the stairs he walked along the landing then turned to the second door on the right, turned to face the doctor who was right behind him.

"In there, it's all in there."

Even before Hogarth walked into the room he could feel that there was something *wrong*, something that was totally out of balance with the rest of the house.

The bed, a double, was at the far side of the room. A dresser, plain, and made, probably by Mr Casement, was underneath the window. There was no mirror attached like you would find on fancy or bought models. Anne-Marie Casement wasn't a woman who wore make-up. Not that it was an issue of cost, because she would have been able to afford it, before her husband had died, certainly, but because she had a natural beauty that make-up would never have been able to touch.

The puddle of blood spread over most of the floor and it was a wonder that neither the boy nor his mother had been covered in any of it. The rug would need to be thrown out.

“Do you have a bucket and a cloth?” Hogarth asked the boy, who was hanging by the entrance to the room, staring at the blood with dread fascination. He nodded and left, thundered down the stairs and in the next instant the pipes in the house started to creak and judder as he filled whatever he had found.

Dr Hogarth walked around the blood to the wall where there was a back scratcher; what looked like a jade hand attached to a length of bamboo resting on two hooks. He took it and knelt down by the edge of the blood pool and stretched until he caught a side of the knife and scraped both scratcher and blade until he had brought it to where he knelt.

It was a knife with a short, but very sharp blade. The handle looked as if it was made from black stone, and had into it, carved inscriptions that had been laid in with gold leaf:

Roger came up the stairs more slowly this time, the bucket of water weighing him down. He brought it into the room and put it down next to Hogarth, a slosh of water came up and over the rim, splashing into the blood.

Hogarth nodded silent thanks, picked up the knife and put it and his hand into the water, which immediately turned a pink colour. He sloshed his hands around the bucket, brought it out, and wiped it against his flannel trousers, it smeared dark.

He then used the back scratcher to hook the book and slide it across; it seemed to glide over the blood almost as if it were waterproof.

"Why haven't you asked where the body is?" Roger said quietly as Hogarth took the roughly bound book from the pool, laid it on the floor and then opened it up, bloody fingers smearing through the pages that were filled with carefully written passages and diagrams.

"There's no body, but there's an amazing amount of blood, and nobody could get up and walk after losing that amount. There's no trail leading anywhere, so, either someone's poured more than a couple of buckets of blood down on here..." Hogarth looked at the boy, who was nodding 'no' furiously, "So... the only other explanation is that he's vanished?" Hogarth said simply, his mind suddenly not able to cope with the question he had just asked.

Roger nodded and smiled, in complete agreement with the doctor's summarisation.

"His skin was being torn from him."

Hogarth felt like his heart had stopped. Years of training, dedicating his life to science meant that even thinking about the supernatural was an alien concept – the equivalent of eating slugs on toast. But ever since the boy had been found, the unknown had filled Hogarth's every waking moment, researching every possibility, responding to unusual correspondence...

Hogarth didn't think that Doctor Swan (if that was his real name) would be writing him any more letters in the future.

"I've never asked you anything about when you went missing, even though you said to the police that you couldn't remember anything; that you just 'woke up' by the side of the lake. Is that still the case? You weren't lying to them, were you?"

"I don't remember anything," Roger started slowly. "But I have dreams. I'm up in the mountains, but then I'm underground. It's dark and I have my torch...and there are these...things. I have a picture of them in my head, but they are not like anything...human." The boy looked utterly frightened again, but Hogarth thought that he had to push now, more than ever.

"Why didn't you say anything to anyone?"

"I didn't want to be taken away from Mother," the boy sobbed, and Hogarth chided himself angrily for making the boy cry.

"No, no...you're right. That's the last thing that anybody would have wanted to hear. But you could have told me, I would never have thought you mad or stupid."

Hogarth's statement was left in dead air as they both heard a moaning come from down stairs.

It was a risk to put the mother back under after what she had suffered was clearly a minor head injury, but Hogarth felt that he had no choice. It was his intention that after he left the house, that neither Roger nor his mother would remember anything that had happened.

He went to his brown leather doctor's bag and unscrewed a vial of weak barbiturates; injecting enough into her to make her unaware of what was happening for the next few hours.

The next plan of action was to stoke up the burner that worked the oven and the hob. In the meantime, Hogarth told the boy to stay by his mother while he drove back to his house to bring back towels, a mop that would soon need to be replaced, and a bottle of Clorox. It was going to utterly destroy the colour of the wood after the blood had been lifted.

He was sure that a repeat visit to the cottage was going to raise a few eyebrows if anyone happened to notice, but the good thing about the Casement's living so far off the beaten road, and that she had almost been abandoned by the community ever since the rumours had started after the young boy's re-appearance, that even if he had been noticed, if it was mentioned it would be a cursory thing.

There was talk of the boy being kidnapped by Black

Donald, taken to dance the dance of the cloven feet. Some thought the Shellycoat had come from the loch and dragged the boy under to live with him. The locals would all say that they were God fearing folk, but their belief in the stories, slights and wisps of the mountains were as strong as they had been a hundred years ago or more, no matter that the brutal realities of two wars should have taught them that fancy, made-up stories didn't exist.

Arriving back, forty minutes later, sweating, uncomfortable, his mind buzzing with questions, he tried as hard as he could not to let the persistent feeling of unease take and sweep him away. Time for reflection would come later.

The boy was sitting by his mother, and looked up at Hogarth expectantly when he entered the room. The doctor smiled, and Roger relaxed visibly. His hair was coming back slowly; there were only one or two small patches where his hair looked thinner.

"Is there a place we can burn these towels after they've been used?" Hogarth asked.

"We have a fire pit, and I'll get some sacks to put the towels in so they don't dribble down the stairs."

"Perish the thought of that happening, we'd have to drug your mother up for a month to clean the house!" It was a poor joke, but Roger smiled at it weakly, all the same. The boy had guts.

The towels soaked up the blood and were very heavy when Hogarth struggled with them into the thick hessian sacks. Blood was up his arms, splashed onto his neck, and covered his chest.

After the worst had been lifted, Roger bumped the sacks down the stairs, and apart from them starting to smear by the time they got to the back door, they held extremely well.

They then took the hot water off the hob and poured it onto the wooden floorboards; Hogarth actually went to the room underneath to make sure that no blood had seeped through and had attacked the ceiling, but the floorboards had been slotted together well.

Once the Clorox had been poured, the smell was unlike anything Roger had experienced before in his life, it made his vision blur, and he thought that he was going to pass out. Hogarth ordered him out of the room, to go and check on his mother. Roger left the room silently.

An hour or so later the job was done, and the rug from the guest room was dragged onto the bleach-stained wood, covering it. Hogarth made mention about him driving back to his house in bloody clothes and hoped that he didn't get arrested by the police. Roger went to the dark oak dresser and pulled out a clean shirt and flannel trousers. His father's. The shirt was slightly too big for Hogarth and he had to roll the waist of the trousers once so they would fit.

They threw the clothes onto the fire which was crackling away happily. Hogarth and Roger stared at the fire as it danced and ate into the air.

“What’s next?” Roger asked, turning to the doctor.

CHAPTER 8
TRAUMA
(1970)

Roger woke up screaming. He thrashed about the bed uncontrollably, the last vestiges of sleep not letting him go that easily.

He groaned as the muscles around his ribs pulled and his hamstring also popped, his body had been that tense. He rolled about the bed in agony, holding both legs. He felt a cool hand on his chest, there, vibrant, through the pain.

He opened his eyes. His wife was staring at him.

"I'm sorry," he whispered. Her eyes widened in horror.

"Oh, Roger..." she leant across and picked something from the mattress. It was his hair.

He sat bolt upright and grabbed his chest in agony. He looked around and all he saw was his hair.

"All gone?"

"All gone," she whispered at him.

"Mum, Dad?" Shaun opened up their bedroom door and walked in. It was too late for Roger to duck underneath the mattress, and couldn't have, even if he wanted to. He was stuck there in a stasis of pain.

"Dad, what happened to your *hair*?" Shaun asked, running across the room, jumping onto the bed and staring at the clumps. It looked like a mattress of dead rodents.

Roger sat there stunned, and could only cry, both in pain and despair as Amanda got the boy out of the room and went downstairs to phone the doctor.

* * *

"It's the stress of what you're going through," the family doctor, a notoriously grumpy man called Able Simmons said. "Your hair will grow back, given time. It's understandable, given the situation." He let the words hang on the air.

Everybody knew now that the family had been banned from shopping in the local shop, due to the connections with the deceased man. He was getting blanked by lots of people and someone had spat in Amanda's face when she was sitting in the hairdressers getting her hair re-permed. The fact that someone would actually do that. And it had been one of the staff, a second cousin.

But for all of the aggression they faced, there was a

lot of sympathy. People were rightly disgusted by the fact that Angus would have got into filming those kinds of films in the first place, and yes – while it might have been a pretend one – what was to say that he wouldn't have done, or indeed, might have done already. *Scum of the earth, the family should be ashamed* and on one occasion – *you've done the rat bastard a favour*.

It got too much for Amanda. Three days before Christmas she packed Shaun and the presents together and said that she was going to spend a little time with her mother and father in Tongue. Roger protested, begged, cried in front of her, but she shook her head, no. It was for their own good, she had said, touching his face gently. She wouldn't be gone long, just enough time for things to start healing.

But it's fucking Christmas! Roger had yelled, kicking the car twice as it drove off, denting the passenger side door in badly. He could hear Shaun's cries all the way down the drive.

A bottle of whisky was consumed on Christmas Eve. Christmas Day he got out of bed once, and that was to wish Shaun a happy day. The young boy was tearful. Roger hung up on him halfway through a sentence; he thought if he heard another word he was going to die of heartbreak right there on the spot.

Boxing Day came and went. Gavin Leader had decided not to invite him to the shoot. "Matter of taste and all that, you won't even be able to hold a gun, seem a bit off," was the excuse that was given to him. Days and bottles of whisky crawled forward. His beard grew but the hair on his head didn't. Hugh had come round a few times and had tried to rouse Roger to come to the door, which was locked.

The phone had rung constantly for days; Amanda, no doubt. But he had let it ring. If she was that concerned about him she would come back, wouldn't she?

In the first two days after New Year's, when nobody had come round to wish him a Happy Hogmanay, dreams that stayed with him for days on end started to haunt him,

But they weren't dreams, they were absolute nightmares – and in them, he was always a child, being chased by a tall man with white hair into a tunnel where he fell and fell into nothingness. Then the dream would switch to his mother, lying in her bed, her face covered in blood, screaming at him that it was all his fault that his father had died, that it was his fault that he had died up in the mountains.

His father. The only slight break in the nightmare that showed him any kindness, a smiling face. Calm, gentle.

Then the dream would turn ugly, horrific, more blackness than anyone deserved; flash to them walking up to an old shed, covered in moss, high up in the world, miles away from anyone and anywhere. Father would turn to him, his face would look puzzled and his heart would burst out from his chest, suspended in the air. Roger would scream and hold out his arms as a beast – half human, half stag; beautiful; its antlers covered in soft, delicate velvet, grabbed hold of his father and dragged him down off the hill, biting into his neck. Roger would be unable to move, only to look on in horror as the heart was left, still suspended and would pump out what blood it held until there was none left and fall to the ground and collapse into a bloody puddle.

The same dream, night after night after night.

* * *

Roger's solicitor, James Hibbert, phoned him on the sixth of January to say that there wouldn't be charges filed against him, that the police and the DPP wouldn't seek to take the case to court. Common sense, it seemed, had prevailed. Roger had never committed a crime that had come to the attention of the police before, was a good standing member of the community, was well liked, and even though there were a lot of people who would now think that he had got away with murder and the ramifications for the future were not to be sniffed at.

"Will I be allowed my guns back?" he asked, his mouth dry, his heart racing in his chest. He looked at the mess in the living room, the blankets on the sofa, empty bottles of whisky on the floor. It looked like a bomb site.

"That's where it gets tricky," Hibbert said softly. "The police don't want to give them back to you. You are, at the end of the day, responsible for the death of someone because you shot them. We can however, apply to the courts to get your guns back – you took the best course of action because you thought a life was at risk, and it is deemed that reasonable force was used. Remember that they've not revoked your firearms license, only confiscated it. I think you can get your guns back, and I'm willing to get them back for you.

"Thank you so much," Roger sighed, gripping the phone so tightly that his knuckles felt like they were going to pop. His neck didn't feel so tense, his shoulders started to relax for the first time in months.

* * *

He called Amanda and they talked long into the night. There were many tears on both ends. Roger apologising for everything that had happened since that fateful night. Amanda had asked him if he was going to be alright, and Roger lied, saying that he thought he really was, that he had turned a corner with the news. He just wanted his family back. He spoke to Shaun for half an hour, catching up, telling him the little white lie that he had been away helping a friend on a fishing boat for a couple of weeks while they waited for the police investigation to be over.

"Will you be allowed to go gamekeeping again, Dad? Are you allowed to use the guns again?"

"Only if your mum says that it's fine. I'm not going to bring guns into the house if it makes her uncomfortable." There was no reason to think that he wouldn't get his guns back. So why trouble the boy?

Of course there should be no reason for her to feel uncomfortable. He had never raised his voice in anger or even so much as thought about lifting his hand to his family. Deep down, he was angry at her for being so callous towards him, upping and taking the boy when he needed them the most. But he could get rid of those feelings; he would get rid of those feelings.

It looked like things were finally going to start looking up. Roger felt ashamed that he had let the booze dictate his stride. For a while if he had pushed it, he could really have been lost to the bottle.

There were happy tears when Amanda and Shaun came back. The nightmares however, continued.

* * *

Roger was too scared to go to the doctors. When the hallucinations started, during the middle of the day, when he was doing mundane things like washing the car or pottering about in his work shed, planing a piece of wood for the new bookcase that he was building, his special awareness would warp and distort, things would almost start to shimmer in front of him.

On one occasion when he was out in the garden – roughing up the ground for the parsnips, broad beans and early potatoes to go in – he looked up to the three hills far away, about twenty miles or so, and they seemed to compress before disappearing altogether. When he blinked, shook his head, they were back, as if nothing had happened.

He thought that he might have a tumour; something similar had happened to one of the old ducks in the village, Edith Sharples it had been, she had started to rave and hallucinate one day whilst in the middle of doing her weekly shopping in Fine Fayre – mainly that there were fire demons coming out of the ground and were 'fucking the meat counter, they're fucking the tills'. She was taken to the hospital, and was found to be suffering from one. She died only a month or so later.

Little by little, the mask that Roger needed to get through the day started to creep and slither and set over now haggard features. It helped him smile when he needed to smile, helped him laugh when he needed to laugh. It gave him the appearance of normalcy as the nightmares and daytime hallucinations ate into him. Amanda looked on at him with pride, knowing the burden he carried with his alopecia, but unknowing of the pieces of his mind that were breaking free and being cast off into utter darkness and despair.

She tried to protect them all from the worst of the gossip and the hatred that was felt towards them by a large section of the community; and that hatred would always be there, no matter the years that would pass, generation after the next would take up the mantle – it would be safe to say that two hundred years could pass and if both families were still living in the community together the Reivers would *always* hate the Casements.

Amanda had tried to broach the subject of moving, to start anew, putting the past behind them, but Roger pushed it away – he was still trying to get used to the fact that he might have to claim unemployment benefit if his guns were confiscated for good. He had talked to Gavin Leader about it, and his boss had agreed that he could come back and work for him, and to also store the guns on the Estate so that they weren't in the house. Gavin was immune to the gossiping and bickering of the community, his money saw to that and it silenced most people; he was the boss to many people in the area and would have no qualms in sacking the whole lot if word got back of their backstabbing and treachery.

In the end a middle ground was reached, and it was Shaun's idea. He and Roger left the house one morning, dressed for rough hiking – both wearing waterproof trousers and wax jackets, the boy wearing a deerstalker's cap that made him look like a miniature Sherlock Holmes – and both had good hiking sticks, whittled down by Roger from the thick branches of the Pussy willow. Lunch was cheese pieces wrapped tight and put in his pieces bag.

They sat by a tributary of the Sallow, shaded by trees, the sun had come out strong half-way through their hike, and even though they had to make their way through fierce bushes and brambles at times, off had come the wax jackets, to be slung over shoulders.

"I've been thinking, Dad," Shaun said thoughtfully as he bit into his piece, washed down with a small bottle of 'diluten' orange.

"Steady on, that's dangerous, isn't it? Thinking? You might get us all into a heap of trouble!" Roger grinned his false grin and forced himself to reach across and ruffle the boy's hair.

He was glad of the hike, it helped calm him down somewhat, getting into an automatic rhythm evened out his anxieties, made his heart slow from the one beat away from a heart attack that he lived with constantly.

"Don't be silly, dad. Is it okay if we go up to where you were a boy? Where you were born and brought up before you went to stay with Aunt Alice?

Something broke through. One sliver burst into

a tumescent shattering of something *pleasing* and it flooded his mind, soothed his synapses. He nearly laughed aloud when he realised what it was. It was *relief.* He had been resisting the call to go back, a deep unnerving that had become more persistent, especially after the shooting. To go 'home, or at least to go back to his roots –there was nothing there to tie him to the past. Aunt Alice had died years ago. They could go away, away from the scene of the crime, so to speak – take a few weeks out and reconnect, work on being a family. If he was away from the source, maybe the nightmares would *stop.* He could leave his number with Hibbert who could keep him notified on whether he was able to keep his guns or not.

"Oh, Shaun, it's an incredible idea!" Roger hugged his son, held him tight – the simplicity of the boy's suggestion carving the way forward, for the time being, at least.

"I love you, Dad," the boy said, his face full of love, big eyes filling with tears. "I'm sorry that you've had such a nasty time. But Mum and I are always here for you. We love you."

Roger started to cry and didn't stop for quite some time.

CHAPTER 9
MOTHER
(1949)

Anne-Marie came to. She thrashed this way and that, eyes wild, not seeing anything that was in front of her. Dr Hogarth approached her carefully, sat down with her, his touch cool on hot skin. He talked low. She stared at him as if he was a being from another world. Her face had puffed up and turned black, and she was having trouble looking out of her left eye.

Roger looked at his mother from the corner of the room, the events of the day catching up with him, and he began to cry. Hogarth left the mother who slumped back onto the sofa and came to the boy and led him out of the living room and into the kitchen where he ferreted about on one of the high shelves and brought down a dust-covered bottle of whisky – and through serendipity, chose the same glass Roger's father had drunk the 'water of life' from.

Hogarth poured a small helping and passed it onto the boy, who sniffed it, looked at Hogarth who nodded his approval, then in one, drunk the fiery liquid. Roger began to cough and splutter. His stomach burned, not unpleasantly.

Roger held out his glass for another, Hogarth guffawed and poured the boy another and poured himself a generous helping. Hogarth leant forward and clinked Roger's glass, to what, he didn't know, and took a sip.

"It was good that you came to get me, boy," Hogarth said quietly. "If the police had come...and they still might...we have to deal with your mother...but if they had come, things would have become impossible almost immediately. And the question...you'll have noticed that people react to change, however small, in very strange ways." Hogarth took a decent sip before continuing.

"You have a pool of blood, no body, a mother who is out for the count and you unable to say what happened–"

"But I told you when I came to your house." Roger looked puzzled. It seemed that a thought with a little more weight to it than normal was above the head of the drained looking child.

"No matter," Hogarth smiled, drained the rest of his drink, winced, ruffled the young boy's hair and walked through to the living room.

Once Anne-Marie was awake, he had to make some things very clear to her. And she would listen, and she would accept everything the doctor said and there would be nothing else mentioned about the day again.

* * *

Later, when Hogarth arrived home, he collapsed onto his bed, his back in agony. As he lay there, breathing in deeply, trying to make sense of the perfect storm he had walked into, he felt that he understood what Roger was. He represented danger; he didn't think to one or two people – but there would come a time where he would be responsible for something of such magnitude (*a holocaust? Is that what you're saying, you old fool? He's only a boy*) that there would be no coming back from it.

He took it upon himself to look after the boy and his mother if she didn't go back on her promise, but the more days that past, would anyone believe her? Hogarth made a mental note through all the jumble to keep his ear to the ground and listen out for anyone complaining that someone had left a hotel or bed and breakfast without paying or leaving behind their luggage. That would surely warrant some kind of police investigation, but Hogarth didn't think it would last long. Unless it was an outright case of murder, nobody really cared about outsiders coming into the area.

People drifted in, drifted out. It was the way it was.

* * *

(1951)

Anne-Marie followed Roger upstairs. Her eyes were blank, whisky heavy. She had a belt in her hand as she wobbled up after him. He ran, small, frantic steps, through to his room and closed the door, reaching for his chair that was left nearby for such an occasion. He hitched the door under the door handle, and no amount of trying on Anne-Marie's part could get the door open.

"Let me in you little bastard," she hissed, thumping on the door with frustration.

Roger sat on his bed and waited for her to go away, like she always did. She'd give up and get bored and go to sleep. He'd creep through, remove the bottle of whisky from her hand, pour it down the sink, and then play the charade they had played for over a year and a half. He'd be on the receiving end of a few thumps every now and again, but on the main he'd escape them. He was never drunk and a lot quicker than she.

* * *

An hour and a half passed. The boy was pretty sure that she'd fallen asleep. Maybe even slid down the wall and was fast asleep on the hallway carpet. Roger felt sad for her, but was unable to do anything for her. There was money coming in, from where the young boy didn't know – but that hardly meant that she was buying food for them. In all truth, Roger spent more and more time at Doctor Hogarth's, the only person who seemed willing to look out for him.

He unhooked the chair from under the door handle and as soon as he had done so, it flew open, smacking into his chest and throwing him onto his back, the chair falling over and clattering onto the wooden floorboards.

Anne-Marie Casement came in, her eyes now blazing with real anger, her hair mussed up and dirty, the belt in her hand. His father's belt. He had never used it on the boy, had never even raised a hand up to him in anger. She was swinging the belt back and forth. She meant to hit him with the heavy buckle. This was new. This was dangerous.

He scrambled to his feet as she roared into the room, swinging the belt up and over her head. He waited till the last moment and darted diagonally away from the heavy buckle, crashing into his mother's midriff and using his impetus to swing her around and make her fall onto the floor. It had the desired effect; she went down hard, the air escaping her in one big *woompf*, the belt leaving her hand.

Roger leapt over her, missing her flailing arms, and

half-rolled and grabbed the belt. He was crying now, this mother's punch bag, small and weak, standing in front of a hissing mad woman who would one day kill him. And Roger knew this. That one day she would go too far, maybe drink a little too much and that would be the end of little Roger Casement.

The boy screamed and smacked his mother across the head with the belt, catching her temple. She was out cold instantly, a trickle of blood running down her face. She started to convulse, angry, urgent movements, one leg caught a splinter from the flooring.

Roger knelt next to her, tears streaming down his face. His eyes closed and he too started to convulse, very gently. The air about him clung to the boy as if it was tar. His mind drunkenly lurched as he placed his small hand over his mother's mouth and with his other, pinched her nose.

After a while, the convulsions stopped.

CHAPTER 10
THE DEVIL'S FOOTSTEPS
(1970)

It was a happy family that packed the car that would take them out of the Scottish Borders, through Edinburgh, Perth, and then into the Highlands, and to Roger, his first home.

His body was buzzing with anticipation, hoping that he would remember some parts, hoping that not too much had changed.

The Triumph coped admirably with some of the hills as they drove through Aviemore and afterwards, the car nearly stalled trying to negotiate the often treacherous terrain as they drove through the Black Isle at Inverness. The further North, then North West they went, the bleaker it became, juts of bone white stone marked the way. *Blonde on Blonde* played and Roger even sung to some of Dylan's songs, much to Shaun's faux disgust.

The arrived at the small hamlet of Curtise Glen, only ten miles away from his home village, but Roger didn't want to have it as his base. They checked in, just before dusk; their host, an elderly lady who had a room with a double and a single, did they mind sharing? No, they did not and they were taken upstairs, the wind had picked up outside and started to whip against the house, shriek as the wind came in through a tiny sliver in the bedroom window.

The first thing Amanda did, after they were left be by the landlady was to stuff toilet tissue in the gap. The shrill was reduced to a muffled buffeting.

They sat in the room, the fire on and stoked up, Shaun always wondered at how the fire would take hold when the crackling kindling was buried with so much coal, and it would take time, wisps of slate grey smoke rising up from the centre of the pile. The volume of smoke would suddenly billow, coal dust and grit would suddenly ignite and send off tiny trails; spits of heat that would ruin carpets if there was no fireguard to hand.

Amanda had prepared a mountain of food, most of which had been consumed on the lengthy drive up, but there was still cold chicken to be had, and home-made coleslaw that looked a little ropey, but after a sniff from Amanda was deemed to still be okay. Shaun was permitted to have a bag of Smiths 'Fangs'. With heavy bellies, they unpacked, Shaun was tucked into the sturdy green canvas camp bed in the corner of the room, and the adults went to bed, Roger taking off the beanie he preferred to wear everywhere to hide his bald head; however there *were* peach fuzz hairs coming back in small patches, hair so fine that it could only been seen in a certain light.

In the pitch black of early morning, Roger the big spoon, snored lightly. Shaun sat upright in bed, hearing his father. He got up and climbed into bed with them, waking up father and mother and they all jostled for a comfortable sleeping position in the small double bed.

* * *

Amanda nudged Shaun gently. "Did you hear your father get up and go out?"

"No?" Shaun sat up, touched the empty space his father had left in the bed. It was cold. "Where do you think he's gone? To get a newspaper?"

"I don't know. We'll ask the landlady to see if she heard anything. He might have taken a wee jaunt up to the old house before he takes us up. Maybe just to see if he can remember the way!"

* * *

Roger felt pressure pushing on his face. His back was burning, in the place where his scar was situated. He opened his eyes and lifted his head. He was lying on dirt.

He moaned and pushed himself up and looked at

his surroundings. It was both completely alien and completely familiar at the same time. He looked out at the lake before him. His senses came to with a crashing start, had he really walked this far?

He got up to his feet instantly, wobbled a bit, his vision drunkenly see-sawing, and then his hand went to his back, tried to reach that impossible spot where his scar was, to rub it, try to sooth it. It was throbbing in powerful ebbs.

The lake was mirrored glass.

Roger winced as he began to walk. He lifted his foot, caught it with his hand and looked with dull shock at the many lacerations he had received. One of them looked quite deep and would need medical attention. He hobbled away from the lake, in no way remembering the area where he had once woken up, exactly thirty-three years to the day.

He looked up at the ragged peaks high above him, the tops hidden by mist. He felt overcome by the sudden urge go climb up, to explore – he must have come here when he was a child, surely?

Jagged and blistered memories evaded him. He could remember as far back as his mother's drinking. She was always drinking and always screaming at him.

Roger had brought a curse to the Casement home. He had cried and asked why. There were questions about the scar on his back, which he knew hadn't been there as a *young* child, from the very brief snatches of his past that he *could* remember. But before he knew it, he was carted off to his Aunt, and then the news came through that his mother had died.

The day after his Aunt had told him (and she had said it with such relish, there had been a glint in her eyes that proclaimed that the boy was all hers and she could do with him what she pleased) Roger packed up a change of clothes and stole money from the hiding place his Aunt didn't think he knew about, around thirty pounds, and snuck out and took a train to Edinburgh, never to return.

The adult Roger started walking to where he thought the bed and breakfast was, hoping that Amanda had the good sense to come looking for him. It wouldn't do any good if he was spotted in his current dishevelled state.

He got about ten minutes down the road when a police car pulled up next to him. Roger sighed, considered for the briefest of moments about making a run for it, going to the tree line on the furthest side of the lake. He could hide out there and come out when it was dark. But that would mean a search party for him if he didn't get back to Amanda. More hassle than was needed on a holiday.

What made Roger want to run was the stigma that would come once the policeman phoned through with his name and the humiliation that this pyjama clad sleepwalker was a cold blooded killer.

The policeman got out of the car, eyeing Roger warily, his brow furrowed with concentration. He looked Roger up and down, taking in the dirty feet, the splashed of mud that had coated the legs of the light blue linen pyjamas.

"Drunk are you?" the policeman asked.

"No, officer, it appears that I've been sleepwalking."

The sound of Roger's voice had the effect of a slap on the immaculately dressed officer of the law. He took off his hat, tucked it under his arm, and took a step towards Roger, trying to see past the bald head with tufts of hair growing here and there.

"Roger Casement? Is that really you?"

Roger tightened up, trying to think that his wife had put the call out that he had disappeared and wasn't dressed in daytime attire, that it -

"It's me, Neil Howie. Do you remember me? We used to play together when we were wee." Roger stood stock still. An instant migraine jumped into the front of his skull.

"Yes -" was all Roger could get out before he collapsed to the ground.

"Jesus Christ, man," Sergeant Neil Howie swore, then chastised himself for taking the Lord's name in vain. He picked the heavier-built man up under the oxters and dragged him to the muddy-white SETAC Land Rover, laying him on the ground whilst he opened up the front door, then pulled Roger up and managed to bundle him onto the leather seat with some difficulty.

As soon as Neil closed the door it started to rain, a persistent, but soft wave of water that came across the lake and hit the roof with a tiny pattering. Once he had started the engine up, put the machine into gear and released the handbrake, foot going down on the accelerator as he eased up the clutch, the pattering became a drumming, big fat droplets hammering down, making it impossible to see out of the windscreen. Neil sighed and turned on the windscreen wiper and crawled away from the spot – if he went any faster the danger would that he'd churn up the soft earth and have a bit of a problem getting out, Land Rover or no.

Once on the road he sped towards town, and three quarters of a mile away, a car approached him, its headlamps flashing away. He flashed back, then dropped the gears down, and came to a halt at the side of the road.

The woman pulled up alongside and rolled down her window. She was distressed and she had a young boy in the passenger seat next to her. His face was puffy with tears.

"Officer, have you seen a man - ?"

"Are you Roger's wife?" he asked. She nodded her head rapidly.

"I have him, he's no' well, follow me and we'll get him back to a place of warmth."

* * *

The rain was thundering it down by the time Neil beeped the horn of his Land Rover when he arrived at the police station.

A few moments later the desk Sergeant, Seamus Ward, over from Moville, County Donegal came out, with a newspaper over his head, looked at the prone figure of Roger in the front seat, shook his head and helped Neil carry Roger in. Amanda and Shaun followed, the young boy protecting his latest holiday book, a Hardy Boys adventure. Wife and son followed the head of the Casement family in.

The interior of the police station was duck egg blue, but looked colder in the harsh morning light. The two men moved Roger into its only cell and onto the thin mattress. Ward went to get some blankets whilst Amanda knelt by him, stroking his smooth head.

"When did he lose the hair?" Neil asked from the doorway. His foot tapped the heavy metal kick plate at the base of the steel door.

"A few months ago."

"He lost it when he was a child, did you know that?"

"Really?" Amanda's head snapped round until she met Neil's. The sergeant stripes on each of his arms seemed to glow.

"Yes, when he was found."

"Found?" Amanda stood up and drew herself to her full five foot six. "You mean he was missing?"

"Ye...s." Neil didn't know if he should go on or not. "Didn't you know? He went missing for eight months, vanished off the face of the earth. Was found at the lake, the very spot I found him today. In fact..." Neil tried to think of different times and dates in a different age, but it had suddenly become just that little bit too weird for his straight laced Christian way of thinking.

"Sergeant, I think you better tell me everything you know."

Neil shook his head. "No, ma'am, with all due respect, I can't. If Roger doesn't know anything about this, like you claim, it's only fair that he know when he comes to. And even then, I'm not the right person to tell him about this. Will you excuse me whilst I place a phone call?" Before Amanda could object, Neil left the cell and walked through to the small office at the back of the police cottage.

Ward returned with a blanket for Roger and towels for Amanda and Shaun to dry their heads; even leaving the car to do the short dash to the building had soaked them.

Outside, the weather got worse.

* * *

"I've had to phone for back-up," Neil explained as he drove Roger, who was awake, talkative and responsive, and just a little bit embarrassed. His migraine had gone, which was a blessing, and apart from Amanda saying that he wasn't to do anything like that ever again, and Shaun asking him how he didn't wake up when the stones were digging in at his feet, he felt good.

Roger still didn't know how to deal with Neil Howie. He tried to place the policeman as a young boy and couldn't. Neil didn't seem too fazed by Roger's apparent memory loss, though he did wonder at the way that Roger kept looking out of the Land Rover as if it was his first time in the area.

"I'm going to drop you off at the Doctor's, he'll see to your feet. I'll swing by to pick you up later and take you back to the bed and breakfast. I don't know when it'll be mind, what with this weather," Neil looked at the sky which was a dirty black, and looked to be the portent of one of the worst storms that would hit the area for a long time.

They drove deeper into the valley, at slow pace, the surface water on the road rising. Roger told Shaun that the small streams and brooks high up the in mountains would soon be building, and that the main river, given time, would burst its bank by morning, a statement that didn't fill Sergeant Neil Howie with any joy.

They drove past small waterfalls that poured from the high outcroppings of rock above them. Neil did most of the talking, to Shaun, who was asking questions about how long he had been a policeman and if he had had to arrest any baddies in his time.

The dirty white Land Rover pulled up to a lovely looking cottage with a carefully tended to garden. Neil got out, went to the gate, opened it and knocked on the door, and after twenty seconds or so, opened it and walked in, beckoning the Casement family to follow him.

Roger led the way, still draped in the police blanket, feeling very self-aware and slightly humiliated that he was walking into a stranger's home, even if it *was* a doctor, still dressed in his pyjamas.

The doctor on the chair took everyone bar Neil by surprise. He smiled when they piled into his lounge, and asked them to sit down. He looked at Roger and his eyes clouded with emotion.

"When Neil phoned to tell me you had come back...I couldn't believe it. So long...so long..."

Doctor Hogarth, ninety-three years old, held his hands up to his face and moaned.

CHAPTER 11
A CLEAN SLATE
(1951)

The young boy stood by the front gate.

Doctor Hogarth was in the front parlour, dusting. He caught a reflection in the glass fronted cabinet and turned around. It was Roger, his hands gripping onto the arrow shaped slats of the gate.

Hogarth smiled, it was always a pleasure to see the boy, but why wasn't he coming in? He went out to see the boy, who didn't say anything to him, no smiling, no salutations. It was as if he wasn't really there.

"What's wrong, Roger?" Hogarth asked.

The doctor then noticed a smear of blood on the boy's cuffs to his pressed linen shirt.

"My mother is dead."

* * *

Roger took Hogarth into the room where his mother

lay. He pointed to the belt in her hand, which he had wiped clean of blood before he left to fetch the Doctor. Roger then pointed at the bedpost that had a blob of blood on it.

"She came at me and tripped. She was drunk, I tried to..."

"Why didn't you phone?" Hogarth looked at the boy and instantly knew that he was lying. It was as plain as the moon in the night sky.

"We don't have the phone installed any more. She didn't pay the bills." Another lie. Anne-Marie had phoned the day before, begging for money.

Hogarth was destroyed by sadness. The boy had chosen a different path to the one Hogarth had hoped that he would take. He couldn't take the boy in, not with the knowledge he now had. He didn't want to believe that the boy had resorted to murder, but it looked staged, Roger wasn't even upset.

He didn't think that the boy was past saving, but he needed him to know that.

"Roger, I *know* that you killed your mother. That dent in the side of her head is long and thin – in no way did she clatter it off that round, soft wood bedpost. I don't believe it, you don't believe it, and the police certainly are not going to believe it when they come and see for themselves the mess that you've got yourself into."

There was fear in the boy's eyes. Real fear. He hadn't

seen that since the day of the clean-up. Good, it was great. It meant that Hogarth was getting through to him and if he could just get his crowbar in a little more he could break the boy wide open and save him from spending the next six or seven years in a home for boys before spending some time in an adult jail.

"What will I do?"

Hogarth's mind was racing. He knew what he was going to do, but by tomorrow, the boy would be out of his life and he wouldn't be there to look after him anymore.

"Have you heard of a person called Confucius? He lived a long time ago, he was a teacher."

Roger shook his head, *no*.

"There is a saying that's attributed to him, I read it once, when I was in my late teens and about to start on my chosen career path, that of a doctor. The saying is 'Life is very simple, but we insist on making it complicated.' Ordinarily, that's true, the human animal has a fundamentally easy life, it is born into a world where it is cared for, it grows up, it breeds, it provides food and shelter, it grows old, and it dies. Confucius knew that unless you were a priest living a solitary life, life will never be simple, no matter how many things you put in place to make it so. There's always someone there to poke a stick in the spokes, to mess things up.

"You're a child, Roger, and you should be leading that simple life. Something happened when you went up into the mountains that day with your father, and what, we'll never know. You can't remember. When you were brought to me when you were found, you scared me, your situation scared me, but most of all, I was scared for *you*. Someone had poked a stick in your spokes, but wasn't content in you falling off your bike the once. Once you jumped back on, the stick was thrust back in and you came off again.

"This time Roger, you got back on the bike and put the stick in the wheel yourself. You insisted on making your life complicated. Look at your mother, *look at her*." Hogarth grabbed the boy forcibly by the neck and pushed him down to her. Roger didn't struggle.

"You're *insisting* on making it complicated. No, you're *insisting* on making it near damn *impossible*! You've had an incredibly bad hand dealt to you, son, and I will help you this one last time. But you do realise after this you can't be in my life. Do you *understand*?"

His hand squeezed Roger's neck, making him cry out in pain. Hogarth let go as if he had been burned. He *had* been burned. A bolt of bad electricity had run up his arm and into his head. It was like someone had removed the top of his skull and punched his brain with all their might. He staggered back and steadied himself on the bloodied bed knob.

"What I'm going to do now, son, is what you should have done." Hogarth breathed in deeply, closed his eyes to compose himself, then went to the corpse and lifted her up by the shoulders.

"Pull that chair across here," he ordered.

Roger did as he was told and scraped the chair across the room. Hogarth rolled the body on to it, its head lolled onto its chest, hands dangling limply by its sides.

"Now son, this bit isn't nice, but you're going to have to do it. I need you to put your arms around your mother, under her armpits, and take the weight of her. It's only going to be for a few seconds, but this needs to be done."

Roger didn't understand what Hogarth was going to do, but did as he was told. He got in under the armpits and held the corpse of his mother tightly. He could smell her last drink mingled with a sweet, almost sickly smell. Maybe her perfume. He winced as the weight of the corpse bore down on him, heavy breasts pressing into his face, making it hard to breath.

Hogarth grabbed Anne-Marie's head by the hair and lined up the injury to the bed knob. He let the head fall back a bit, then with all of his might slammed it into the polished metal.

The crunch the impact made was truly sickening. Roger leapt back and the body slid off the chair and onto the ground.

"Now –" Hogarth said, breathing heavily, "now she's fallen and smashed her head on your bed frame."

CHAPTER 12
I'LL BE WITH YOU WHEN THE DEAL GOES DOWN (1970)

Neil made his excuses and left.

Roger and Shaun were sitting on the sofa. Roger was now wearing a pair of trousers and a checked shirt that Amanda had brought with her just in case she had found Roger first.

Amanda was through in the kitchen, making a cup of tea for them all. Shaun sat in the corner of the room, looking with some wonder at the stuffed hyena with long hair on its ears. It was attacking a cobra.

"So you were my doctor when I was a child. And you still practice?" Roger asked, his voice questioning, probing.

"Yes, I was your doctor, and yes, you'll need work on those feet, but as you can probably tell, I'm no longer practicing. I'll place a call with Jacob, the locum, who will come and see to your feet in a while.

"How are you still alive?" Shaun asked, looking up from the glass taxidermy box. "You're ancient, aren't you?"

"Shaun!" Roger retorted, but Hogarth held up a pale, liver spotted hand that was resolutely shake free and smiled.

"Let the boy be, it's a valid question. And son," he said, looking at Shaun, "Sometimes I ask myself that very same question. I think that sometimes I held on because...that one day I might have met your father again. I'm not going to deny it, there were times when I could have easily given up, when my son died, not so many years ago, of the cancer. That was a big blow. Me being a doctor and not able to save my first born. I could have given up the ghost then, yes."

Roger looked at the old man with wonder. Frail he was, yes, of that there was no doubt. But Doctor Hogarth's mind was pitch sharp, nothing could get past him.

"I'm sorry, but I really can't remember you. And did you know my mother, Anne-Marie? She died when I was staying with my aunt..."

"Yes, I knew your mother. She was a good woman." Doctor Hogarth was about to say something else, but Amanda came in with the tea, putting the doctors cup on a red leather placemat. Roger started to feel better and better with each swig he took, but the deep burning in his back and the pain in his feet were jockeying for position.

Hogarth phoned Jacob, who came round and tended to Roger's feet, which were better than were expected: lots and lots of superficial cuts and one deep laceration on the heel which was causing the most problems when he walked.

Doctor Hogarth was nice and funny but Amanda knew that he wanted to get Roger on his own. She looked at her husband, and felt, for the first time in a long time, that she didn't know who her husband really was, and she didn't think that he knew the answer either. He was a man made up of fragments of time that had been forged with him but without his knowledge, and maybe even without his permission.

She wanted to stay, wanted to find out what had happened, what *was* happening; she didn't trust Roger to tell her the truth. But, as ever, playing the dutiful wife, she smiled and asked Hogarth if there was a nice walk that she and Shaun could go on.

"Preferably under the cover of some good trees."

* * *

Once they were alone and the last of the tea had been

drunk, Doctor Hogarth got up from his chair, the first time since his guests arrived, and walked, quite ably, though slowly and with careful footing out of the room. "Follow me," he said to Roger, and Roger did as he was told.

They came to a wooden door at the dark end of the house, unpainted and locked. Doctor Hogarth undid the top button of his shirt with slow and rheumy fingers. He took a silver chain from his neck and on it, a black door key. It seemed to Roger to be slightly too large to wear around the neck, Hogarth said softly, as if reading his mind, "You'll see why in a second."

The lock clicked and Hogarth pushed the door open, swinging easily on its hinges. Hogarth reached in and fumbled for the light switch, the harshness of the bulb revealing a room of the likes Roger didn't even think could exist.

Hundreds, no, *thousands* of newspaper cuttings were tacked onto the walls, brittle and brown with age. Hundreds of books were piled up in every conceivable corner, folders full of notes and magazine cuttings were piled high on top of the bookcases, nine in all. The room was a cavern of dust and mania.

"This has been my life's work. You have been my life's work."

Roger looked at him, clearly thinking that the old man had gone insane.

"I'm your life's work? I don't understand."

"That scar on your back. Is it still troubling you much?"

The statement made Roger's blood run cold. Hogarth pushed past the younger man and went to a tall filing cabinet. He opened the bottom draw and started rummaging through decades worth of large envelopes that were the neatest things in the room.

"Ah, here." He pulled out a folder and showed it to Roger. He took it across to the table, pushed a stack of books to one side, some of them falling onto the ground. "Leave them, I'll get them later," and opened up the folder and took out a set of photographs. They were of a young boy, on his front, on what appeared to be a table. He was naked and there was an ugly scar on his -

"That's you, Roger. I took these photos when you were brought off the mountains in 1947. When you were found you had been missing for eight months, all hope was lost. Everyone, myself included, thought you were dead."

The words were like hammer blows to Roger.

"I don't believe you. It can't be true. What are you, a dirty old man with pictures of a boy like that? I should report you to the police."

Hogarth's hand snatched out and grabbed Roger's shoulder with considerable strength for a 93 year old man. His eyes blazed with fury.

"Don't be a fool, man. Top drawer of the cabinet. The first envelope. It says 'Roger Casement Clippings.'

* * *

FATHER DEAD, BOY, 8, MISSING IN MOUNTAINS

FUNERAL HELD OF CASEMENT. BOY STILL MISSING

SEARCH CALLED OFF

BOY FOUND!

VILLAGERS JOY AS MISSING BOY FOUND AFTER EIGHT MONTHS

POLICE HAVE 'NO CLUES' TO DISAPPEARANCE

"It was after that last headline there was what you would call a blanket ban on reporting your case. After you were found, there were many people in the community that wanted you out, the churchy ones, those that fear the de'il."

"Missing? What happened to me?"

Hogarth went to one of the shelves groaning with books and pulled down a white box, grey with dust. He walked out of the room. Roger followed him.

Once they were both sitting down, Hogarth told him everything he knew about his disappearance and stopped at the moment he was brought into his house, all those many years ago.

* * *

Roger was drained. It had been one of the weirdest days on record. That he had no memory of those days left him distraught and angry.

"Pour us both a whisky, and I'll bring you up to speed."

The two men sipped in silence for a while, letting the sensation of the whisky warm them up, revive the flagging senses, injecting a little bit of life back into tired bones.

"Can you remember anything about the months and years after you were found?" Hogarth asked softly.

"No. I remember my mother, I remember her sending me away. She was drinking heavily and it was a relief, to be honest. She sent me to stay with an aunt until I heard that she was dead. I ran away after that."

"And do you remember this?"

Hogarth passed the white box across. Roger opened

it and a knife with a black handle and strangle symbols carved into it lay in a bed of tissue paper.

"No. I've never seen this before in my life."

Hogarth smiled wryly.

"Can you help me up, please?" the doctor asked. Roger got up and reached across for him. Hogarth placed his hand on Roger's shoulder, squeezed and said, "Sleep".

Roger did as he was told.

* * *

Hogarth was a man with unfamiliar motives. He didn't even know why he should have got involved with Roger. He should have patched him up and sent him on his way. It was the wound on his back, fresh and angry and alien, that set Doctor Hogarth on the path of research and unfamiliarity that would stay with him for the rest of his life.

When the death of the boy's mother was reported, Hogarth said that he would take Roger into his home until his aunt, the only living relative, returned from a cruise to India. A telegram had been sent out and had been answered – she would come back in her own time, thank you very much.

Anne-Marie Casement's funeral was held a few days afterwards, buried next to her husband. Neither the boy nor the doctor were present. Sgt Amos Howie agreed to go and took his son Neil along. The Reverend Probert said a few words, and afterwards said, to his wife Kate, that the 'poor laddie was in for a life of woe and misery.'

Roger acted as if nothing had happened, read old books that had once belonged to the doctor's son, went fishing and helped around the house. Every evening, after supper, the doctor and young boy would sit in the parlour and the doctor would hypnotise the boy. He used the sessions to try and find out what had happened to Roger when he was missing, but there was only an unintelligible mumble and a strange, almost alien noise; something that came from the back of the boy's throat and almost sounded as if his windpipe was being pressed in.

Doctor Hogarth had first practised hypnotherapy when he was a teenager. His father had been a stage magician who had toured America before returning home and settling with Hogarth's mother. It was easy to hypnotise the boy, sometimes only took the word 'sleep' to put him under instantly.

He had thought long and hard on what he was going to do, and had 'programmed' him on his eighteenth birthday so that he would gradually forget about everything that had happened to him from the moment he was found up until the moment he finally left the doctors. Then his memories would begin when he was living with his aunt.

As the elderly doctor studied Roger Casement, his head slumped against his chest, breathing in and out regularly, he marvelled at the fact that his brain had tricked itself into thinking that his mother had died when he was staying with his aunt.

Little by little the old man unlocked everything that needed to be unlocked, memories tumbling back into the once-barren memory, what Roger used to call, a long time ago, his 'blank box'.

"Wake," Hogarth said.

Roger screamed.

CHAPTER 13
A PLAGUE OF STONES
(1970)

Amanda came in through the back door of Hogarth's cottage. She took her boots off and undid her jacket, sock clad feet padding through to the living room.

Shaun was in the garden staring at a toad on a rock. It regarded him with wet eyes.

Hogarth was lying on the floor, alert, but in pain. There was swelling to the right hand side of his face.

"It was too much, I gave him too much." The doctor tried to get up and cried out at the effort.

Amanda picked him up, he was lighter than she expected and dumped him into his chair.

"What did you tell him?"

"Mum?" Shaun came into the room.

* * *

Roger drove the doctor's car at breakneck speed. The

car was a Morris, kept in impeccable condition, and Hogarth managed a trip out at least once a week in it if the weather was calm.

Roger was screaming as he drove. His voice was starting to break with effort. He didn't think he would ever stop.

As soon as Hogarth awoke him the onslaught was like nothing he had ever experienced; even the hallucinations in the weeks and months after the killing was seemed weak in comparison. He slammed his hand on the top of the bald pate as hard as he could as if that would get rid of them.

fathermistbloodmothersnowsnowsnowwoodnaked coldsnowgungunholemoutainsalonealonesnowalone

"Oh Christ! Oh Jesus Christ, no!" Roger screamed as the car tore through the valley towards the lake.

"Who introduced the pheasant into Britain, son?"

"The Romans did, Father."

"Very good. And where do pheasants originate?"

"Russia, Father."

"Very good."

* * *

"I've called the police station, but there's nobody around," Amanda said, putting on her jacket, doing it up as tight as it would go.

Outside the rain was torrential, the front garden, once tended carefully, was water-logged. She nodded her thanks as Hogarth hobbled through from some part of the cottage with cellotape. She used it to tape the top of the wellington boots Hogarth had supplied for her, once his sons. She had to pack the fronts out with newspaper so she would fit inside them.

Once she was done she turned to Shaun.

"Your dad's not been very well lately, you know that." The boy nodded.

"He's not well again and needs our help. He's gone off in the doctor's car, but he didn't take a jacket or anything and I don't want him to catch a cold."

"Or drown," Shaun said solemnly.

"Or drown. The doctor will look after you until I get back. Be good for him." She kissed his forehead.

It was the last time she ever saw her son.

Amanda rushed out of the cottage and was nearly knocked over by the wall of rain. Head down she made her way to the forest that she and Shaun had walked through before to stay away from the worst of the rain. Hogarth had told her that if she followed it to its natural end, and crossed the two grass fields, each with standing stones in the centre and took herself into the thin strip of woods and walked that down the hill, it would bring her almost to the front door of the police station where she could pick up her car and go and look for Roger.

* * *

The mountains trembled at his arrival. He walked up the steep inclines, again the small child following his father, following the shadow of time past. His feet stung with every step he took, making him hobble over the sheer granite slabs that he had to cross over diagonally upwards otherwise he would slide down them and probably break his legs.

"Father?" Roger called out into the noise of the driving rain. He felt something, a presence up there on the mountains with him. Something was watching him.

He climbed faster, finger pads catching sharp ends of stones and tearing. His knee smacked against a rock sending a shear of pain up his leg. He crashed onto his side and rolled onto his back.

He looked up at the sky, breathing heavily, wondering idly if he just left his mouth open he would soon drown to death with the amount of rain that was falling. Then the earth gave way as the slab of granite cracked in two, the earth rendered with a noise that, as Roger fell, he remembered. It was a noise from the deepest darkest corner of his dreams, a noise that sounded like the blasting of a million foghorns.

He lay there dazed, looking up at the two slabs of rock above him, they were on a downwards angle, liable to go at any second. Small stones were falling free from the earth and...

?

...bouncing to a stop five metres above his head. They hung, suspended. Rain stopped there also, small puddles forming around the rocks.

He got up, crouched on his haunches, the palms of his hands completely flat on the smooth surface. In the distance were speleothems, some proud and standing, many crumbled, disintegrated into broken lumps of discarded mineral. Jets of yellow cloud shot up from the ground.

The foghorn noise didn't trouble him as he walked deeper into the cavern. The light that was coming in from above seemed to bounce of the walls, rays of light coming from such oblique angles that it was an impossibility. The whole place seemed to bend the laws of physics. He tried to breathe, but felt as if he was on the moon, and every breath he took threatened to suck the life right out of him, leave him a dry husk.

He collapsed onto the floor when the first wave of creatures came out from the rock. They came towards him hesitantly, staring at this gasping, retching thing that was thrashing about on the ground. They watched as he crawled across the piles of rubble.

Roger saw the rifle and had total recall. He grabbed it and was instantly taken back to the time he last used it.

He rolled onto his bum and sat up, hands fitting into the right places of the rifle. The corpse of the thing he had killed lay there, as if he had shot it only an hour before.

He pulled back the bolt of the rifle and ejected the spent rifle case. The creatures were now disregarding him, crawling up the walls and through the membrane that Roger had fallen through. More and more of them spilled forth, paying him no heed, and in the furthest end of the cavern came another massive tearing of the earth, and through it, he could see a mountain collapse in on itself.

"It's okay," he mumbled, his mind now gone. "It's just another hallucination."

He got up to his knees and walked away from the body and looked down with curiosity at his sandwich bag. He pushed it with his foot as he walked past. He stumbled into the very heart of the cavern, snow covering the tops of the rubble mounds, and snow hung in the air, but didn't fall.

* * *

Amanda arrived at the police station as Sergeant Neil Howie drove up by the front door. The sky had turned a pitch black, the rain was unforgiving and slashes of lightning ripped the sky open, revealing strange red wounds that glowed.

The wind picked up instantly, pushing Amanda to the ground. The noise of the wind screamed hellishly as the woman got to her knees, a look of panic on her face. Neil held his hand out to her, telling her to stay in the position she was in. Amanda didn't understand what he was meaning and managed to get to her feet again. Then a gust of wind, the likes before which had never been seen in this part of the country, no matter the ferocious gales which had gone before picked up and carried Amanda, smashing her into the cottage, killing her, crushing her skull. Neil had looked on in horror, seeing her look of surprise turn into horror before she was smashed in. Then another gust toppled the Land Rover, crushing the roof. Neil was thrown across both seats and waited till the Land Rover settled.

He lay there, his legs broken, wondering where Ward was. Then a strange blasting noise, louder than anything he had ever heard in his life began. It turned his bones to jelly, he tried to scream but no noise came out.

A hole, the size of three football fields appeared and the vehicle and the cottage were both swallowed up. The Land Rover was crushed flat, liquefying Sergeant Neil Howie.

* * *

The valley was slowly being destroyed. Roofs were

being blown off houses, livestock being carried into the air, before being carried away to another part of the valley. Rivers and streams started to bubble; massive cracks appeared in the landscape. People hid under their beds; many tried and failed to make it to the 'wee free' church, which had already been skewered by the oldest tree in the valley – one of the branches had taken the Reverend Smart's head clean off his shoulders.

The electricity went off. Houses that were lucky enough to have gas central heating started to explode, creating small, intense flashes across the landscape.

And finally, after one last slice of red burst across the sky, it went utterly, utterly dark.

* * *

Shaun looked out of the window.

"What's that noise?" he screamed, turning to look at Hogarth who sat there in his chair, his face slack with disbelief.

He had never found the meaning of what Roger's scar had meant, and had come up with many different theories. He had once thought that Roger might have been the son of God. But he knew what he was now, knew why he had come back. It was to bear witness to what had passed in less than a blink of an eye, ever since he was a small young boy, lost in the mountains.

It was End of Days.

"Ah, come here boy. I have a story to tell you about your father. It's a good one, you'll like it. He was a very brave soul."

Shaun started to cry. Doctor Hogarth stood up and went to comfort the boy. Then a tearing, renting awful noise, like that of a nuclear bomb going off. And a few seconds later, a one hundred foot slab of rock crushed through the cottage.

* * *

The earth shifted, Roger spilled forward losing the gun. He screamed when he landed, bone in his arm tearing through his skin.

A boulder fell from the ceiling, dislodged from the rift, indeed everything around Roger was starting to crumble and implode. It landed on the slab of rock he was lying on, propelling him into the air. He somersaulted, passed through the rock, his old childhood trick, and once more entered into dead space.

* * *

He was fully conscious, and the terrible, ancient creature was waking. And *beginning*.

Roger drifted towards it, carried up by the ascension of the being. A being that had breathed within the Earth far longer than any living thing above it.

Roger rose ever closer, now free of his cocoon, but in the moments before his body softened to a million silken threads, he told his son and his father that he loved them both.

Alison Littlewood is the author of *A Cold Season*, described by the Richard and Judy Book Club as "perfect reading for a dark winter's night." Her second novel, *Path of Needles*, is a dark blend of fairy tales and crime fiction, while *The Unquiet House* is a ghost story set in the Yorkshire countryside. Alison's short stories have been picked for *The Best Horror of the Year* and *The Mammoth Book of Best New Horror* anthologies, as well as *The Best British Fantasy 2013* and *The Mammoth Book of Best British Crime 10*. Visit her at www.alisonlittlewood.co.uk.

ONE NAMELESS THING

ALISON LITTLEWOOD

Part One: The Blue Perfection of the Sky

My mother used to tell me that the sky did not exist. I can still remember the first time she told me this. I was in the back garden, by turns kicking a ball around and being a smart alec, asking her questions I thought she couldn't answer. She explained, slowly and in words I could understand, that all I was looking at was white light striking gas molecules in the Earth's atmosphere, scattering the higher frequency blue light; that really, there was nothing there. I remember staring at her. Then I turned around and stared once more at the sky.

'But I can see it,' I said, and I pointed. It was summer and the sun was high, and there it was; a deep, perfect blue.

My mother didn't answer. She wasn't looking at the

sky at all. She was focused only on me, and in a way that made me think, for a moment, that she could never look away; then she did, and she laughed, and everything moved on.

Now the sky was deeply, almost painfully blue, so much so that it almost made me want to cry. I turned and looked at Kath, to see if she was moved by it. She only grinned back, like a kid, a kid going on holiday. Of course, we were no longer kids – Kath had a daughter who wasn't even a kid any more, who was studying literature at university – but we were going on holiday. The sky sat above a perfect sea and that, too, made me smile. The speedboat was coming to bring us to our island, home for the next two weeks. I had arrived in the Maldives, and I already thought it was the most beautiful place on earth.

So I knew why the sky was blue – but why was the sea? I'd never thought to ask and my mother hadn't told me.

I forgot such questions as we gave our names, got into the boat and set out, bouncing and scudding over the waves. It was rougher than I'd expected; from the shore, it had looked dead flat. The sun sparked and dazzled across it and after a time I started squinting into that light, not blinking, until tears ran down my face.

Kath dug me in the ribs. 'What are you looking at?'

'There are birds,' I said, 'flying just over the water. Look! But I can't seem to see them flying away.'

She followed my gaze and let out a loud, delighted laugh. 'They're not birds, idiot,' she said, 'they're fish. Flying fish.'

I saw that she was right. The fish were pale blue, almost aquamarine, and quick: it was hard to keep track of them. After a while I realised they were fleeing the boat: fleeing us. They were fish that flew – impossible things – and I felt myself filling up with joy. This wasn't just a holiday, I realised. It wasn't just a place. And I didn't quite know why I thought that as I leaned back on the hard seat and put my arm around Kath. Everything was perfect, impossible and perfect, and I let my eyes drift upward into that deepest of blues; gazing up at the thing which did not exist.

Part Two: The Fragility of Received Behaviour

We stood on the island's dock, waiting for the boat that would take us on the snorkelling trip. We could snorkel around the island itself of course, and had several times, but the trip was supposed to be better. It would take us out to another island, one that was more closely surrounded by a steep coral shelf, and apparently all kinds of things could be seen there: turtles, rays, even the occasional whitetip reef shark. Kath had read out a list of them from the sign-up sheet by reception, her voice becoming more and more excited.

Rays, I had thought. Sharks. O-kay.

But they weren't a danger to man. If they were, the staff wouldn't be readying the dhoni, a big old wooden boat built in the traditional fashion. The waters here were rich, too full of easy prey for the likes of us to tempt a shark. They'd swim around us or away from us. They certainly wouldn't bite.

I'd frowned when Kath had told me that, and I'd only been half in jest. 'How do they know?' I'd asked. She had murmured a reply, something about all the natural food that was in the water, there for the taking, but I hadn't really been listening. *Just one*, I'd been thinking.

It would only take one shark to act differently, to have different brain chemistry or different thoughts, a mad shark, or maybe a rebel shark, one that didn't accept all the regular patterns of shark behaviour, and everything would change. Limbs could be lost. Everything would stop.

But the men didn't stop. They were loading our flippers, tossing them down into the boat one by one so that we'd have to pair them all up again. They hadn't stopped, so it must be all right. Of course, it was all right. I turned to grin at Kath, and that was when I found she was watching the Frenchman.

I knew he was French because he had been talking with a group of others, all younger than him, and shorter, so that they looked up to him. His face was lean and his hair rough and long and grey; he reminded me at once of a wolf. He stood right on the edge of the dock, a little way from where the dhoni was moored, staring down into the water. He pointed and said something, a string of words we couldn't understand. Then he took off his t-shirt, stripping it in one single motion, and he dived clean and fast into the sea.

His friends didn't react, though my stomach clenched; it felt as if I'd just gulped down cold water. Kath exclaimed and we moved closer to the edge of the dock. The water was eight, maybe ten feet below. It was clear and I could see stringy weeds wrapped around the wooden struts and clinging shells and the flash of blue and yellow fish. Then there was the Frenchman, far below us, his white limbs passing clean and quick beneath. I knew at once I could never dive so deep. It was something else that was at once impossible and real, and as he surfaced, shaking water from his hair, holding up a black clicking tangle of legs and pincers and claws, I found I recoiled from it. I didn't like his neatness, his lean, muscular capability. I felt heavy, pressed down by the hot sun on the top of my head. I felt ungainly.

I watched as he held up the crab, then dropped it and arrowed towards the ladder. The boat was ready and I knew at once that he would be back on the dock and on board before any of us. He pulled himself over the edge, shaking his hair, the droplets showering everyone, and his friends laughed. He laughed too, relishing the attention; then he glanced at us and his smile faded. It was obvious that he knew, just from that single glance, that we could never swim like that; we could never *fly*.

We shrugged and picked up our bags. We seemed to have brought everything: towels, sun lotion, hats, a change of clothes. We joined the queue for boarding. The Frenchman, somehow, was indeed ahead of us. He said something loud to the staff and they gave him high fives as he headed for the sundeck on the roof of the boat.

The dhoni was ponderous and noisy, cutting into the day with its gruff diesel engine. The island's speedboat was for serious transport; this more decorative boat was for trips. It edged out into the water and headed north, rocking alarmingly as the current hit it side on. It took maybe half an hour before the next island came into view. The dhoni grew closer and closer, slowing and cutting the engines a short distance from the shore.

The waves here were lively, high. It wasn't like our own island, where they lapped the white beaches in soft caresses. There must be a strong tide. The island had no dock that I could see, no structures of any kind; its beach was white, its thick green crown a mystery. They had told us it was a nature reserve. We weren't allowed to set foot on it. If we were in trouble, they said, we just had to float and put a hand in the air and the boat would pick us up.

Kath shrugged. She was a better swimmer than I was. I knew she hadn't even thought to imagine a situation where she'd be in trouble. The French were already moving towards the prow and loud splashes announced their entry into the water. I looked over the side and saw the luminous flashes of their snorkels, then their faces appeared as they rolled, pulling on their flippers.

I glanced around at our abandoned things. *Just one*, I thought, and then we followed everybody else, heading for the sea. I jumped in, still wondering over the way we trusted ourselves to the received behaviour of creatures we didn't know and could never really understand.

The French were already about twenty feet away, moving further off, the tips of their snorkels forming a ragged line. Kath was bobbing nearby, waiting for me, hardly covering her impatience. I put my face under the water and just for a moment, wonderful things appeared; I caught sight of a shoal of silver-blue fish, then they were gone. The water was a cloudy blue-grey, not as clear as I'd expected, and there were particles floating in it. I briefly wondered if there'd been a storm, then water closed over the back of my head, shocking against the heat of my scalp, and I sputtered upwards.

'Over there.' Kath shouted. 'Further in. Come on, it's easy.'

I cleared my mask, clenching my jaw and gripping the mouthpiece. I let my face fall beneath the water again and there was a mass of blue-grey nothing and then I saw what she meant. I could make out the edge of the shelf, falling steeply into the deep. It was covered with fans of coral and being picked over by fish – butterflies, surgeonfish, damsels, other things I couldn't identify, and water splashed over my head again as a wave hit.

This time I ignored it. I didn't look up; there was too much to see. There were wonders down there. I let myself drift with the current, following a teardrop butterflyfish as it wove along an outcrop of coral before sinking out of sight. Then I saw the mouth of an eel, tucked beneath a crevice. I watched it from a distance, just floating, my ears full of my own bubbling breath, and it didn't approach and it didn't strike. It didn't do anything crazy at all. I couldn't smile but I felt it, amazement and yes, joy, and then I spun around in a lazy circle and looked into the deep at my back.

There were shadows down there. That was what I thought at first, just shadows, and I struck out and drifted over them.

There were dark shapes beneath. They were huge. They curled and spread black wings, gaining speed with a lazy flick of their muscles. I couldn't move. My eyes were wide open and I couldn't blink. *Huge*, I thought again, and I felt the cold in my belly, and the next thing I thought of was bats; giant, dark bats casting giant dark shadows, something that shouldn't be beneath the water but was, and I couldn't help it, I came up flailing. Above, there was the sea and the sky and flashes of the boat between the waves. Only that. But I knew those things were down there and I couldn't even see them, and that made everything worse. I tried to keep my face from going under as the waves kept coming, so rough up here, so still beneath, and I raised my hand. I couldn't see Kath. The others seemed a long way away.

Those things. I held my mask against my face and tilted my head downward, trying to see. I couldn't; my mask was clouded. And then I heard the dull deep throb of the diesel engine. It was too late to get myself together. The boat was already coming to pick me up.

* * *

The others started to get back on the boat, their voices suddenly too loud, the space too crowded. I hadn't been worried about Kath; I'd known she would be all right. She came up to me with a broad grin on her face. 'What happened to you?'

I shrugged. 'Came back a bit early.'

She didn't seem to notice anything odd about it. 'Did you see the turtle? And those fish!' Her eyes sparkled.

It's easy, she'd said.

I grinned back and nodded and agreed. She was right, it was easy, and I had been stupid, but it was only a thing of the moment; now I turned and looked out over the sea and saw how amazing it was. I had seen manta rays. Manta. And there was no need for Kath to know I had panicked, no need to tell her how pathetic I'd been. And yet that shadow was there, in the back of my mind; not just the panic but the reason I'd panicked, the overwhelming feeling that those creatures were something alien and strange, that I'd glimpsed into some unfathomable world I should never have seen. It wasn't something I could tell her, not something I could explain. When I thought of it, I shivered.

She grinned at me, pulling my arm around her, and I held her close, smelling the mixture of salt and conditioner in her hair. I could feel the Frenchman looking at me. I turned my head so that I could just see his gaze from the corner of my eye, the curl of contempt at his lip. I didn't look at him directly. I didn't look up again until we were drawing close to our dock, our island, our home.

* * *

That evening, we watched some TV before dinner. The evening was drawing in, the light turning blue. The news was on. There had been seismic activity off the coast of India, farther east near Jakarta, and in the Laccadive Sea. I frowned. So did Kath. 'That's near here, isn't it?' she asked.

But it was nothing to worry about, the reporter said. The effects would be slight, no tidal waves or other problems. And then it switched to an image of the Maldives, the green and white islands floating improbably in their sea of turquoise.

'A new trench has been discovered in the deeper

ocean beyond the Maldivian atolls, possibly the result of movements caused by a minor earthquake. Scientists are on the spot, exploring with the use of a deep sea submersible. One of the resulting images has been the cause of great excitement, hasn't it, Simon?'

The camera pulled back to reveal a man, presumably Simon. He was laughing. "It certainly has, Marie." The screen switched to a hazy shot, a spotlight shining in the dark, finding nothing but particles floating past; I thought at once of a night sky full of stars. Then there was the edge of something, a rock perhaps, or scales, and then it seemed to move, revealing something even darker behind it. I blinked. For a moment it had looked like something sentient; it had looked like an eye.

"Of course, it's nothing but an optical illusion," said Marie, "though it does look a little like an eye, doesn't it, Simon?"

"It certainly does," he agreed. "But they've calculated that, for it to appear that size . . . the eye would have to be a little over four metres across – that's about the size of a VW Beetle. In short, it simply isn't possible."

I glanced at Kath. She was staring at the set, a smile playing about her lips. 'How funny,' she said.

And then they showed other sea creatures that had been found in trenches, so deep that bones wouldn't be any use, would simply be crushed by the pressure.

Things that looked misshapen, that moved in odd ways; that were tentacular or gelatinous and transparent, or globular, or glutinous. Some of them carried lights within their bodies, and they glowed. They were things we couldn't conceive of; things we couldn't understand, or fathom how they could move, or eat, or live, or think.

'Amazing,' said Kath.

"It's a trick of the light, though it is rather fun," said Marie. "A little like when people thought they were seeing a sculpture of a human face on the surface of Mars, when really it was nothing but shadows."

Shadows. That made me swallow, hard.

'It's like those stories,' said Kath. 'The thought of something down there . . . it's like those old Cthulhu stories. Jess goes on about them sometimes. Old gods, alien beings, sleeping beneath the earth. Just waiting to be awoken and destroy everything. Dreaming bad dreams and infecting all our thoughts.'

I stared at her until she threw a cushion at me and burst out laughing. 'Come on, idiot. It's time to eat.'

I shook myself and smiled. It was time to eat. Suddenly, I was starving.

* * *

That night, I woke. It was dark and I was sweating. It was running down my face. The sheets stuck to me, suffocating, and I batted them away.

I turned and Kath was there, her eyes closed, her hair spread on the pillow. Behind her, the faint trace of insect repellent rose from a burner. I could smell it, a tang that rooted me, reminded me that I was here, really here. And then I remembered the thing she'd said yesterday, after we saw the news report.

I closed my eyes. It was all right: the dream had been dark and impenetrable and strange, but there was a reason for it. I couldn't remember it all, though snatches remained. There had been things rising from the deep, coming up through the layers of black and grey and blue and turquoise, like the sky in reverse; something malignant and infinitely strange. I shook away the shreds of memory. It had been bad, but after our trip, and her words, I could at least explain it. It was rational.

I shuffled across the bed to where Kath was sleeping. It was hot, but I didn't care. I wrapped myself around her. The weight, the heat of her was reassuring. I could feel her breathing, close and comforting and there, in her fragile shell. She did not wake, and I clung to her as if she was a rock in the middle of an agitated sea.

As I lay there, I could just see the glass of water she had placed on her bedside table. I stared at it for a while, searching for any ripples that might spread unbidden across its surface. It would be a sign, wouldn't it? I thought of that scene in *Jurassic Park* where the water betrayed the dinosaur's footsteps. *There's nothing,* I thought. *No earthquakes. No monsters.* But it was that eye I was thinking of, as tiredness crept over me. It was still in my thoughts, dark and unblinking, as I slept again.

Part Three: Dead Fish

There were ladies sweeping the paths outside the villa. We'd got used to this now; each morning they'd begin at our part of the island, getting rid of fallen leaves and anything unsightly. They used besom brooms, and their *fssssk-fssssk-fssssk* had become familiar. I lay awake, listening to the sound, letting it chase away the dreams of the night before.

The women didn't live on the island. I'd seen them come in by boat early one morning, along with a whole group of support workers. It had struck me how their manner was different from the tourists'. Every time we saw the sea, we stared in wonder. We stared at everything, the trees, the beach, the hermit crabs leaving trails across the sand like bicycle tracks, the dart-flash of lizards. These women stepped from the boat and barely looked up, as if they were already bending to their task. Sweep, sweep. *Fssssk-fssssk*.

Sometimes they brought gifts, yellow-green fruit a little smaller and smoother than a lime. They pressed them upon us and in return we gave them tips. Kath didn't want to eat the strange fruit, but I cut into them with a sharp stubby knife I took from the restaurant and tried the pale flesh. They tasted a bit like apples. I was discovering all kinds of fruit here; on the first day, I'd tried a curry made with jackfruit, and had been amused to find the texture a little like chicken.

The sweeping, as it always did, moved down the side of the villa and towards the beach. I waited for it to move across the deck and back up the other side, but it did not.

After a while I got up and went to peek out of the window. I couldn't see anyone on the deck. I looked at the narrow path that led through a narrow band of trees onto the sand and saw a figure standing there, just beyond our loungers. As I watched she bent and straightened again, lifting something that shone silver-grey for a moment before she dropped it into a large bag. It looked like a dead fish.

I frowned. The path sweepers didn't usually have bags; they didn't usually go onto the beach. But there weren't usually any dead fish, either. I watched as she turned and started walking back towards the villa, dragging the bag behind her as if it was heavy, and I let the blind fall across the window. For some reason I didn't want her to see me, to know that I'd seen her. It seemed it would be in some way rude, but I didn't know why.

Then Kath woke and summoned me with her sleepy

eyes and warm arms, and I forgot all about it, and went to see in the new day.

* * *

Our life on the island was falling into a pattern, but if it was a routine, it was a good one. Each morning we walked to the restaurant in the centre of the island and ate breakfast. Then we called by at the reception building to see if any new trips were on the notice-board. Then we headed further out, to the shore on the opposite side of the island, before walking back along the beach. The only variation lay in our decision to either turn right and walk clockwise past the island's dock or left and head anticlockwise past the water villas. It was a small choice to make, but for us, on holiday and free of responsibility, that was part of its charm.

Today we turned left and walked past the water villas. They were built on stilts over a shallow rocky shelf, so that the waves rushed in beneath them. Wooden walkways linked them with the sandy shoreline further in.

I paused when we drew level and saw what lay beneath.

There were more dead fish scattered beneath the villas. They were rolled and stirred by the incoming waves.

Kath exclaimed. 'What a shame.'

I still hadn't told her about the lady I'd seen that morning. There hadn't seemed to be any point. Now I stared. There weren't many fish; they were just dotted around, and apart from the fact that they all had washed up on the same morning, they appeared to have nothing in common. There were delicate yellows, the glow of amber, iridescent blues. They were beautiful and they were dead.

'What on earth is it?' asked Kath. 'Pollution?'

I shrugged. I couldn't see what might have been wrong with the fish. And then an image came into my mind, the plates of the earth shifting, sending shockwaves up and into the water, washing all before it. 'The earthquake, maybe,' I said. 'I certainly don't think it's normal.'

We stared a little longer, and then we continued our walk. There didn't seem to be anything else that we could do.

* * *

Back at the villa, I poured myself a glass of water. I stared at it for a moment without drinking, then set it down on top of the dresser. Kath had left some of her things there: a hairbrush, a bottle of sun lotion, a half-empty bag of Starbursts. She had bought the sweets at the airport, looking more than ever like an excited kid off on her travels. I tipped them out of the bag, orange, purple, green, and I stacked them, making a little square tower.

'What are you doing?'

Kath had been in the bathroom. It was reached via a quite ordinary-looking internal door, but on the other side, the room was open to the elements. It had walls but a thatched roof was suspended above them on wooden struts, leaving a wide gap between. The grandly named 'rain shower' was set into a curve at the far end, along with a couple of basins. The floor was tiled around the edges, with a stretch of fine sand in its centre. When Kath first saw it she had squealed with delight; I had immediately thought of how quiet we would have to be when using the toilet. Now, on waking, we would try to guess how many tiny white geckoes would be hiding in the shower; whether ants would be marching across the sandy floor.

What are you doing?

I shook my head and stared down at the tower of sweets, the glass of water; its surface was quite still. 'Nothing,' I said. 'Let's go and sunbathe.'

* * *

I laid next to Kath on the sun-beds. We spread lotion that smelled of coconut on our skin and let ourselves bake, letting the heat steam everything out of us: cares, worry, thought. I drifted as the sun rose higher in the sky. The sea kept up its constant lapping. Every so often I found myself pushing myself up and checking the shallows for dead fish. I didn't see any. I'd set a bottle of water into the sand at my side and occasionally I looked into that too, watching for ripples. There was nothing to see, and that was good. Occasionally a lizard appeared at the edge of the trees; occasionally a bird sang.

If I sat up fully, I could just see the couple from the next villa to our own. They were sunbathing too. She was young, in her twenties maybe, much younger than the man she was with. Kath and I had laughed about it. Their sun-beds weren't too close to ours and a fallen palm partially masked the sight. I could just see the bright red swimsuit she wore, like something out of a Special K advert.

Apart from that, there were only the crabs. The beach was littered with them, and at first Kath hadn't liked them; then she decided she did. They were hermit crabs, and what I saw when I half closed my eyes was small curled white shells, but all moving, heading on unknowable missions up or down the sand. On some nights, the staff gathered a few and wrote numbers on their backs and placed them in the middle of a chalked circle in the bar. Crab racing was a slow sport, but we'd laughed over it, picking number 66 or 72, cheering them on. Afterwards they'd released them again.

Kath had told me that the crabs didn't make their own shells. They lived in any they could find, claiming one until they grew too large and it closed in around them, upon which they'd abandon it and find something bigger.

When I looked at them closely I could see a couple of big claws and some smaller ones, salmon-pink and hinged, and feelers; lots of feelers, probing the sand before they walked on it. Behind those were two little protuberances, upon which were set their bright black eyes. Something about them made me uncomfortable and I rolled onto my back, throwing my arm across my face. It was too hot. I pushed myself up. 'I'm going inside for a bit,' I said, and Kath grunted in response.

Inside, I flicked on the television. It was still on the news channel; there was an image of people running in the street. Some of them had their mouths open, as if they were screaming. It looked a little like India. Behind them was a heap of what looked like bodies, or pieces of bodies.

'No one is sure why the incident broke out,' the reporter said. It wasn't Marie or Simon but an older man with white hair. "There were no demonstrations scheduled in the area. Eye witness reports state that it seemed to begin with just one man, who was wielding what some called a machete, others a sword. However it began, the violence rapidly spread, others laying hands on makeshift weapons and attacking people in the street. Many were killed and more were trampled to death in the panic. Officials say . . ."

I zoned out for a while. When I focused again they had moved on to something else, this time about America. The screen was empty but for an image of the stars and stripes above a ticker tape report. NO ONE CLAIMING RESPONSIBILITY IN WHAT SEEMS SPONTANEOUS OUTBREAK . . . SEVENTY DEAD . . . TERMS SUCH AS 'THE RAGE' OR 'INFECTIOUS MADNESS' UNHELPFUL, SAYS LAPD . . .

I blinked. It switched to a man on a street. He had a long beard; he looked unkempt. "It's the end," he said. "Been tellin' em for years. It's only the start. I told 'em, they're under the ground. They're under the ground!"

The report moved on to something about the economy and I switched it off. I looked around the empty room. Infectious madness? I shook my head. It didn't seem possible, as if I'd just watched a report from outer space. And then I thought of Kath, the thing she'd said:

Dreaming bad dreams . . . infecting all our thoughts.

I turned from the TV, half expecting the room to no longer be empty. I looked at the dresser. The glass of water was still there but the stack of sweets lay scattered, its colours spilt across the wood.

I heard footsteps and Kath walked in. She looked half asleep, almost dazed. 'Crap,' she said, 'it's hot out there.'

'I think you should call Jessica,' I said.

'What? Why, what's up?'

'There's been some . . . troubles. Riots. It seems to be international.' I knew it sounded stupid, even while I said the words. I pointed at the sweets and found my hand was shaking. 'I think there may have been another earthquake. It might even be connected.'

She let out a spurt of air, but she came to my side and put a hand on my shoulder. Then she pointed up towards the ceiling. There was a metal grille set into the plaster. 'Air conditioning,' she said. 'It blew them over, that's all. You should build your tower on solid ground next time.' She spurted that almost-laughter again.

Of course, she was right. And if she did call her daughter, what on earth would she say? Tell her to watch out for nutters wielding machetes? Such things didn't happen, not really. And if she told Jessica that it was me who'd said she should call, she'd think I was nuts too. I wasn't sure the girl liked me as it was. She wasn't out of her teens quite yet, and she had a teenager's air of practised disapproval.

'You're right,' I said. 'I'm sure it's fine.'

'Come on. Let's have lunch. I'm starving again.'

* * *

We decided to take another walk around the beach to clear our heads, rather than head directly inland to the restaurant. This time we headed in the opposite direction, past the dock; we saw the gathering as soon as we drew near. There were maybe ten or twelve of them standing around a barbecue that had been set up on the beach. There was music too, some fast-paced tune drifting towards us: a party.

Most of them were looking out across the water, and I turned and watched as the Frenchman appeared. He straightened from out of the waves, emerging like some smooth-backed sea creature. He was carrying something in his hands. I couldn't see what it was.

No one looked at us as we approached. They were all fixed on the Frenchman with the gray hair as he waded in to the shore. What he carried was some kind of spear, its wooden length hacked and sharpened into a series of barbs and then a point. Five or six multi-coloured fish flapped from it, stuck through their middles. He saw me watching and gave that wolfish grin.

'They're probably protected,' I said.

He answered in English. 'Not by me.'

He kept on walking until he was absorbed by the group. They cheered and clapped him on the back. Then they started pulling the fish from the spike, while one of them took out a knife. I focused on the fish. Their colours were already fading, their scales no longer catching the light. Their eyes were turning dull.

Part Four: At the Trenches of Madness

In my dream I was thrashing in the sea, but I couldn't move and I couldn't escape. I couldn't breathe. The water caught at my hands, clinging so that I couldn't get away. I was surrounded by fish. They were each pointing towards something deeper in, staring with unblinking black eyes. I knew all of their names, but I also knew there was something else down here; some dark, nameless thing. That didn't move, yet. It wasn't ready. It didn't open its eye.

I was on the edge of the world, on the edge of sleep; no, beyond the edge of the world and cast into the water, out of place in some alien environment. There were cries in my dreams, distant shouts cut through by screaming. I closed my eyes tighter, slipped under. Surrendered. I didn't know if I was a waking man slipping into sleep or a sleeping man awaking. Or was I a drowning man calling for help?

Kath pulled on my shoulder. 'Honey, wake up. Wake up.'

I did. Her hands were on me, on my skin.

'You're having some kind of nightmare.'

I pushed the sheets away, then pushed her. I was soaked. My body was covered in sweat and it was oily and cold. I muttered something, didn't know what; I wasn't even sure it made sense. It didn't seem like any language I was aware of.

'Honey? Wake up.'

I sat and turned and saw her face. 'Sorry,' I said. 'I was just dreaming.'

'What about?'

I frowned. I couldn't really remember. I only knew that there was water, lots of water, and I realised I could hear it now; the quiet room wasn't quiet any longer. I could hear, quite distinctly, the buzz of the mini-bar fridge; the slight gasping from the air con; my own blood in my ears. And beneath that, always present so that it so often faded from notice, was the constant sound of the sea.

Did you hear something?' Kath said. 'I thought I heard something.' She nodded towards the door; not the glass doors that led to the beach but the ones at the front of the villa.

I shook my head. I didn't say anything else. I somehow didn't want her touching me. I stared over her shoulder at the glass of water on her nightstand, but it didn't ripple. I told myself it was only water. After a while she shrugged and turned her back, and sometime after that, I slept again. There were no dreams this time, only the welcome dark.

* * *

I woke earlier than Kath and I stared at the ceiling, trying to work out what was different about the day. Then I had it; the sweepers hadn't come. It was better without the endless *fssssk-fssssk* of their brooms. I could hear the sea. Its constancy was reassuring. After a while I got up and went down to the glass doors that led onto the deck. I slid them open as quietly as I could, shoved my feet into sandals and went towards the beach. The air was pleasantly cool at this time; the sun was still low, though the sky was already a deep clear blue. The sound of the sea was soothing as I went down the little path. I thought I would sit on the sun-beds, while it was still cool enough to look out to sea. Sometimes little wooden fishing boats passed by; sometimes they were followed by dolphins.

I reached the end of the path just as the smell hit me. I emerged from the greenery and saw that there were dead fish everywhere. So many, silver against the white sand, and everywhere were crabs, not heading up the beach or down but creating a tangled web of trails as they feasted.

I glanced to the left and right. Through the fronds of the fallen palm tree, I could just see the woman next door; she was already sitting outside. I didn't know how she could bear it. I couldn't see her face but I could see the red flash of her swimsuit. I felt like I was spying. I turned to go back inside.

Kath woke as I was pulling glasses from the shelf above the mini-bar, pouring each one exactly half full of water. I was setting them around the room, on the coffee table, the cupboards, the dresser, the shelves. She sat up, rubbing sleep from her eyes. 'What are you doing?'

'It's them,' I said. 'They're coming. They're waking up.'

She stared at me. I put my hand to my mouth and tried to tell myself I couldn't remember what I'd just said, but I could. That was the problem.

She got out of bed. 'What the fuck?'

'Sorry. I'm tired. I didn't sleep well.'

She looked pointedly at the glass in my hand.

'It's just in case of any – movements,' I said.

I expected her to say something else, but she merely rolled her eyes and went into the bathroom. I closed my eyes. *Three*, I thought. *Three geckoes. And ants. Lots of ants.* Then I shook my head and started to pull on my clothes.

* * *

The path that led towards the restaurant was usually a place where we'd pass other couples and exchange a brief hello or a nod, but today it was empty. It usually bore some traces of the brooms which had swept it, but not today. At both sides of the path were gardens where tall palms sprung from the earth, which was carpeted with something that looked a little like grass. Sometimes bats swooped through the trees – big ones with fox faces and thin-stretched leathery wings. Usually there was the occasional gardener in blue uniform cutting stray palm fronds or moving irrigation pipes around. Not today.

Kath slipped her hand into mine and took a long, deep, audible breath. 'It's so nice,' she said. 'So warm.' I looked at her. She hadn't seemed to notice how quiet it was.

We reached the edge of the restaurant. The seating area was covered by a wide thatched roof that was suspended on wooden struts above the decking; there was no need for walls. Sometimes lizards came in and watched us eat, curries and rice or noodles or breads, taken from the buffet amid a clatter of knives and forks and plates and loaded serving dishes brought from the kitchens. But not today.

Kath exclaimed when we saw inside the restaurant. It looked as if a trail had been blazed through its centre; several chairs and even a couple of the big heavy wooden tables had been overturned. There was no one in sight – no guests, no staff, no chefs. There was an adjoining kitchen which was fully enclosed, a low white building, its doors shut. It had an air of stillness about it.

Kath walked slowly across the decking, looking vainly at the empty buffet, and I went to peer in at the kitchen. The doors each had a round glass porthole so that waiters could see the way was clear before they pushed through. We had the same waiter at each meal, and we liked him. His name was Dinesh and he hailed from Sri Lanka. He'd been here almost six months and would soon be going home for a visit. He was excited about it. Kath had laughed at his barely-hidden eagerness: I closed my eyes, now, and heard her words. *How could you ever leave?* She'd said. *This place is so beautiful.*

He'd smiled back. 'I have three children. I'm looking forward to seeing how they've grown.' And he'd looked happy, but there had been a little sadness there too, and I couldn't help but think of the words he hadn't said: that he wasn't looking forward to seeing how much he'd missed as they did that growing, the steps he hadn't seen them take, the words he hadn't heard them utter.

Kath was behind me. 'What on earth is going on?' she said. 'What are we supposed to eat? I'm going to ask about it. Are you coming?'

We trailed down another path, not speaking, until we reached the reception building. Usually at this time the windows would be thrown open, and often someone would be sitting at a desk outside. There was no one there; the desk was empty. I tried the door and found it was locked. Kath put her head against the wood. 'I think I can hear someone,' she said. 'I can hear someone inside. I heard them talking.' She listened again, shook her head.

I went to the nearest window. There were blinds but they weren't quite closed and I tried to peek between the slats. I saw a desk, discarded pens, papers, an empty chair. Then something else, something that looked like a man's foot, but that was wrong because it would mean he was lying on the floor. And I heard whispers, or thought I heard them, long and low and constant.

Kath grasped at my back. 'What does it mean? What is it?'

I shook my head. How would I know? There was no one there. We couldn't have heard a voice, not really, not through a closed door. I reached out and stroked her arm. I could recognise my irritation for what it was; hunger, clawing my belly with thin fingers. 'I really don't know,' I said, 'but we could maybe try the staff buildings.'

We had seen the staff lodgings in the distance on our walks around the island. Between the water villas and the beach villas, there was a wide path leading inland. It usually had service buggies parked along it, and beyond them was a large blocky building with narrow windows. There was a sign at the end of the track, a terse 'Staff

Only', and that was all except the gardens at the end of the path: a vivid lush green, planted in rows with different types of fruit and vegetables.

I felt another pang of hunger and thought suddenly of the Frenchman, striding out of the sea with his spear laden with fish. He'd done it so easily, just reached out and taken what he wanted. I glanced at Kath. Maybe we could have a barbecue together. We could borrow the equipment, cook on the beach, out of sight of other people. Then I thought of the glinting things I'd seen on the sand that morning, the little white hermit shells trailing and looping around them, and my stomach clenched. No, not fish: meat. I would have meat.

It was a short time after we set out that we saw the body. I glanced into the greenery at the side of yet another path and saw what I thought was a person lying on the ground. I thought at first of picnics or break-times, and then Kath gasped and grabbed my arm and froze. I looked harder. The person wasn't a gardener; their staff shirt was pale grey.

'Kath, wait here.' I pushed my way towards him. He was lying face down, one arm by his side, the fingers curled like an upturned sea creature. When I got close I saw the other was splayed outwards at an awkward angle and the stuff that was a little like grass was darkened with his blood. More blood had soaked into his shirt. I didn't pause to think, but knelt next to him, slipping a hand beneath his shoulder and prising him up. I whispered something in his ear; I don't know what, but I knew it seemed somehow important.

I could see his face. His eyes were only half closed, the white crescents shining, and I didn't want to look into them. I glanced down. His chest had been pulped. I heard the sweet-sticky sound of flesh sliding with the movement as I jerked away, and then the smell hit me, and there were flies, large and black, and red; everywhere, red. Things spilled from him and I thought of snakes but it was *him*, a part of him sagging and slopping from his belly, twining onto the green, and an image sprung into my mind of those trails the crabs had made, writhing twisting things I could not read. I let go and jumped away.

I felt Kath's hands on my arm. This time it felt good, and I turned and held her. She was crying. 'Shit,' I whispered. 'Shit.'

'We have to call someone. We have to do something,' she said. And my sight went out and up, floating to the tips of the palm trees, above the swooping bats and into the sky; and out, over the sea, the endless, foaming sea that divided us from anything at all.

'We will,' I said. 'We'll call someone.'

After that we forgot about the staff buildings. We

turned and headed for our villa, the place we felt safe, that was like home. There was a phone in there. I felt shaky and the sun was too hot. It bathed the top of my skull; it felt like some kind of baptism.

Inside, everything was as we had left it: the bed in disarray, the glasses of water still placed around the room. Had I really done that? I shook my head and went to the phone, hitting the buttons hard, trying reception and maintenance and then the kitchens and the dive centre for good measure, and each time the phones rang, or seemed to ring, but there was no answer.

'Here.' Kath threw a small card across the bed. It was a 24 hour emergency number from the travel agent. I rang the number and then she grabbed the phone from me. I went to the doors that let onto the beach. I'd left them open that morning, just slightly, and the smell of death had drifted inside. I pulled it closed, making sure the lock snicked into place. I remembered the girl I'd seen, the one next door, what seemed like hours ago, lying out on her lounger as if nothing had happened, that flash of red through the trees. Red. I felt sick.

'Yes – straight away,' Kath was saying. 'Yes. Yes.' I turned as she hung up. 'They're going to call the police,' she said. 'I asked them to send help. I asked them to get us home as soon as they can.' She put a hand to her stomach. 'God, I'm starving. How can I be starving?

After—' She clapped her hand to her mouth and ran for the bathroom. I heard her choking in there: *Quiet*, I thought, remembering those gaps between the walls and the roofing. It suddenly seemed a bad idea to let anyone know we were inside. At least we were on the beach, where the structures were further apart; if we were in a water villa anyone could have heard our steps on those wooden walkways. I wondered if their bathrooms, too, were open at the back. I had a sudden image of something dark rising from the water, reaching out with a muscular tentacle, probing through the gap to see what it could find. I put my hand to my mouth too. I suddenly felt dizzy, and I sat down on the bed.

Pork, I thought. That was what I wanted to eat: pork, stewed with those little yellow-green fruits a little like apples, or in gravy, or roasted in its own juices. I closed my eyes. I'd read something once about how pig meat was the closest thing to human flesh and that thought made my stomach roil. I closed my eyes. Anyway, this was a Muslim island; there would be no pork. There would be supplies, though, at the kitchen. We would just have to go and help ourselves. Then I remembered the mini-bar, went and grabbed a tub of peanuts and ripped them open, holding them out to Kath as she came in. 'This'll help.'

She shook them away. 'I'm calling Jess,' she said. 'I'll let her know we're coming home.'

It would be before dawn in England, but she called anyway. It took a while to get her daughter on the phone and then she spoke long and low and I tried not to listen. It didn't include me; I wasn't party to their family unit. It would have felt like an intrusion.

When she'd finished she sat there with the receiver on her lap, staring at nothing, and I went and put my arm around her shoulders. 'She says she can't wait for me to get back,' she murmured. 'Some kind of trouble there too. People fighting, in the streets. Not just fighting . . .' She leaned her head on my shoulder and she started to cry. I moved back onto the bed and held her. After a while she went quiet, and a while after that I think we must have slept, because I woke and the bed was shaking. There was a sound too, a constant low vibration. Everything was moving, as if the earth was nothing but some kind of skin and now whatever lay beneath was stirring. I pushed myself up and staggered to the dresser. The water was trembling in its glass, circles spinning across its surface. The glass too was moving, sliding across the table in little starts. I could hear something else, beyond the room, and I realised what it was and started to laugh. So careful I'd been, setting out those glasses, and there wasn't any point; I could hear the disturbance in the sea, the stutter and catch in its whisper, and I knew at once where the turmoil was coming from. Down there, in the depths, something was moving; turning in its sleep perhaps. Opening its eye. And the water had carried its dark message to my door.

Kath stirred, brushing her hair from her face. I grinned at her and she looked at me, her expression confused. I could feel the power in the ground beneath my feet, spreading upwards, gathering. Suddenly I wanted her. I wanted us to be close, as close as a man and a woman could be; closer. It was like something primal, undeniable, something I couldn't ignore. The power rushed through me and I went to her and pulled the sheets away and touched her body. She responded, reaching out for me, and her eyes were wide, her lips warm. It didn't take long. The heat inside her was burning. When I'd finished I lay on top of her, breathing; just breathing.

When I pushed myself away, I was hungrier than ever. I switched on the TV, though, before I went out. There was no fighting there, no sign of infection, no madness. No news at all. There was only a blank grey nothingness where it had all once been.

* * *

Nothing was moving through the trees or in the seating area of the restaurant. There was no sound coming from the kitchen block. Maybe no one else had tried it; maybe it had been cleared out already. The door looked intact though, and when I went around the back I saw the windows were too. I winced at the sound of glass shattering, waiting until silence returned before I moved again. I wondered how far the sound would have travelled.

Inside there were rows of burners, all cold, and racks of cooking implements and polished metal work surfaces. Furthest from the window – and my escape route – was an open doorway leading into the food store. It smelled of dryness and spices, turmeric and pepper. There were stacks of boxes covered in writing that I couldn't read. I pulled a few of them open and found flour, dried pulses, rice. Further in there were vegetables stacked in crates and further still there were large trays of fish, these plainly coloured with dead black eyes. They didn't look as fresh as the ones on the beach and their scent was sharp; it didn't seem so bad. If we could eat these, perhaps we could eat the washed-up ones too. That meant there would be plenty of food, as long as I brought it in out of the sun. I found myself calculating how long it might last before it turned rancid and pushed the thought away.

I realised I had picked up one of the fish without thinking about it. I could feel its scales, smooth if I ran my finger in one direction, coarse in the other. My fingers were darkened with a thin watery substance: blood. I threw it aside before grabbing a box and tipping out the contents. I began to pile stuff inside, fish, vegetables, whatever came under my hand. I wasn't even sure how I'd cook anything. If I had to, I could make a fire on the beach.

I brushed my hand against my shirt and looked down. It had left a smear, but below that was something worse; a thick red line, crusted and dark, at about the level of my waist. It hadn't been there before. I frowned. I must have cut myself when I climbed through the window, though I hadn't felt it; adrenaline perhaps, or fear. I turned back towards the window and found I couldn't see it from here. It was blocked by rows of shelving. I hefted the box of supplies under my arm and set out to go back.

* * *

The girl was standing just under the edge of the trees. She wore a light summer dress and was quite motionless, one hand outstretched, resting on the trunk of a palm. She looked as if she was posing for a holiday picture, until she pushed herself away from the tree and took a hesitant step. I shifted my grip on the box so that I could wave with one hand. She still didn't move. I glanced down, remembering the blood on my shirt, but the box was covering it; everything must look quite normal, except, of course, for the way I'd just climbed out of a window.

'I – I thought you were one of them,' she said as I drew closer. She wasn't as young as I'd thought. She was slender, blonde, with fine lines across her forehead and around her mouth. I shook my head. Did she think I was staff? I didn't know what she meant.

'I'm so glad to find someone normal,' she said.

I got the impression she didn't quite mean those words, that they were some kind of a test. I nodded down at the box I carried. 'I was after some breakfast,' I said. 'They didn't make any.'

'No. I suppose they didn't.' She looked away; her eyes filled with tears.

'It's okay. You can have some.'

She shook her head. 'I'm looking for our friends, Mark and Deanna. Do you know them?' I must have looked blank because she added, 'They're in the next villa to ours.' She pointed somewhere vaguely behind her.

'We're on the other side of the island.'

'We think they went on the sandbank trip yesterday. Then they didn't appear at dinner, and then–it all happened. You know.'

I didn't, but I thought I might have an idea. I remembered the member of staff I'd found; the cries I thought I'd heard in the night; the flash of red through the trees on the beach that morning.

'I haven't seen them since,' she said.

I had heard of the sandbank trip. We had been on it ourselves, in the first days; it was part of the regular schedule for the island's dhoni. In the mornings it went out to the snorkel reefs. In the afternoons it went to the sandbanks, a chain of white mounds that protruded from the sea like the humps on a monster's back. The water there was shallow, clear, beautiful. The sand was pure white. There were no crabs, no trees, no grasses, no life at all. The final mound was tiny, only a couple of metres across. It looked like something from a postcard, turquoise sea below, blue sky behind, only that thin white line in the middle. We'd taken it in turns to swim out to it and have our photographs taken.

I could still remember the way Kath had laughed when she'd seen her first glimpse of them, the way she'd turned to ask the crew: "What's the difference between an island and a sandbank?"

And the way he'd smiled back as he handled the great wooden tiller: "An island is there all the time. A sandbank . . . a sandbank is only there at low tide."

"I haven't seen them since," the woman had said.

A thought struck me, and I took another step towards her. She stumbled back, then looked awkward; I ignored it. 'There's a way we can check,' I said. 'I doubt if the dhoni's been taken snorkelling this morning. If it came back . . .'

She met my eye, her expression brightening. 'It'll still be there. At the dock.'

* * *

The dock was a dark line above the blue and sparkling water. We had chosen – I had chosen – not to approach it directly along the main path but to cut through the nearest patch of garden so that we could take a look through the trees first. The dhoni was there. I could see the edge of its prow jutting from behind the side of the dock, its blue paint a little lighter than the sea. It bobbed in the water. I could hear the tap of its sides against the wood and the slap of water against the struts. It looked peaceful. It looked like holidays. But there was something else in the picture; something that didn't belong.

A group of people were sitting on the dock, out there in the full sun. They had formed a rough circle and they weren't moving. They looked as if they were waiting for something. One sat a short distance from the others and I recognised him at once. The sun was behind him but I knew his lean form, his straight posture, the hair hanging loose to his shoulders. It was the Frenchman.

I felt the girl's touch on my back. She'd said her name

was Rachel. Her hand felt small and ineffectual. 'It's there,' she said. 'It's there!' And I sensed her working through the implications of that and her hand went still, a small warmth against my spine.

'Shit,' she said. 'It came back.' And I heard the unspoken words: *but my friends didn't*.

I didn't know what had happened to them – I don't suppose anyone ever would, now – but I could imagine. Infectious madness, they'd called it. The Rage. They might have been beaten or cut or thrown overboard. They might have been left behind. For a moment I could picture them, standing forlorn on the sandbanks while the boat receded. There was no shelter on the sandbanks. There was no food, no water. Just how long would they last? But then I remembered; they wouldn't have had long to wait after all. I could only imagine how they must have felt as the water began to rise, the islands on which they stood growing steadily smaller; swimming from one to the next, perhaps, as they were submerged one by one. And then what – drifting, trying to float? To swim? I closed my eyes. I could taste their fear. It would have gone to *it*, I thought, into the sea, their terror and their despair, spreading from them like a libation.

My head felt heavy. It was starting to ache. The sun spilled over everything, too hot, and I realised I was thirsty. I was still hungry too. I looked around for the box of supplies, but couldn't see it anywhere. I didn't remember deciding to leave it behind.

'They're gone,' Rachel whispered.

I didn't say anything. There was nothing to be said. There was only the truth, and she'd spoken it already.

I felt her shifting. 'I have to go,' she said. 'I have to get back to Ryan. That's my husband. I have to tell him about this. He'll know what to do.'

I turned and looked at her. What was she talking about? No one would know what to do. The Frenchman maybe, but they wouldn't be good things. They wouldn't be things she wanted to hear.

'I'm going,' she said again, but then just stood there, shading her eyes from the sun. Her face was red. 'I – I have to go back, don't I – to Ryan. I should see if he's okay.' She paused. 'He's been acting weird.'

I wet my lips. They felt rough, like cardboard, as if they didn't belong to me any longer. 'Weird how?'

'Just weird.' Then she turned and marched away, disappearing into the undergrowth, leaving only the faint trace of rustling behind.

I stared into the space where she had been. Then I turned and walked out onto the beach.

The sand was soft and I sank into it. It was silent under my feet. The sun pierced the shoulders of my shirt, feeling almost abrasive on my skin, as if it was intent on scouring me away. For a moment I thought of the sweepers: *fssssk-fssssk*. And for some reason I thought of what Kath had said: Old gods, alien beings, sleeping beneath the earth. Just waiting to be awoken and destroy everything. Dreaming bad dreams and infecting all our thoughts. It would be the quickest way, I thought. She had been right, all along. The quickest, cleanest way to get rid of man, to scour us all away . . . it would be to infect our dreams, to drive us mad, turn us on each other. To clear the way for – what? I thought of that eye beneath the water, slowly opening while it shifted. Waking.

I shook my head and focused on the dock. The Frenchman was standing now. He was staring directly at me. I was sure he could see me in every detail; I felt he knew me somehow, could see my thoughts. As I watched he nodded, just once.

I grimaced, remembering the blood on my shirt. Was that what he had seen – was he giving me his approval? I didn't know if I wanted it. I didn't know what it was he thought I'd done.

And then I remembered his spear and I took a step away.

It was as if the spell binding us had broken. The Frenchman turned towards the sea and flung his arms into the air, as if greeting the sun. It lit his hair, turning it golden, touching him; it was like a blessing. I looked up into the blue, into the thing which did not exist. Is that where they had come from? Aliens, Kath had called them. Old gods.

That was when I heard a cry, a long ululation, coming from the Frenchman's throat. I almost thought there were words in it, but I couldn't make them out. I probably couldn't understand them if I did. But I knew it was primal, and visceral, and malevolent. I knew it was an offering. He was worshipping something that lay beyond the waves.

I didn't think after that: I only turned and ran.

* * *

When I got back to our villa, I found everything quiet. I slipped inside, relishing the coolness. I'd left the air con cranked up high; within a couple of seconds my neck felt cold and it had chilled the sweat on my back. My head swam. I strode across the room to where I'd left the peanuts and crammed them into my mouth. They were too dry, but there seemed to be glasses of water everywhere. I grabbed one and gulped it down, spilling it onto my chest. More cold. I glanced down and stared at the front of my shirt.

My stomach roiled, queasy, and I realised I needed the bathroom. I rushed for the door and grabbed the handle, turned it; then stopped. A chill sweat was prickling along the length of my spine. There was something inside. I couldn't go in there. My guts were hot, furious. I rushed instead through the villa and out through the far doors, pounding across the deck and into the edge of the trees. I yanked down my trousers and let it go, then scoured the mess away with fallen leaves.

When I'd finished I edged around the trees and stepped out onto the sand. I couldn't smell the sea, only the sour stench of spoiling fish. They didn't smell like anything I'd want to eat, and I remembered the supplies; I hadn't gone back for them. And now there was the Frenchman, sitting at the edge of the island like some kind of king. I suddenly knew, if I went near him again, he'd know: he'd see.

I looked out at the water as a faint breeze brought with it briny air and the smell of the moving tide. Out there, everything was blue: clean.

Some of the fish had been washed away and some hollowed out by crabs, but some had flesh still clinging to them. I forced myself to pick up one or two, vaguely wondering if they would be all right if I cooked them. I could use fallen leaves as fuel, and things from the villa: wooden shelves and cupboards and pictures.

I threw the fish back down, noticing now that the crabs were almost absent from this stretch of beach. There were only one or two shells dotted around, their legs and feelers no doubt pulled tightly inside. Perhaps I'd disturbed them. I could still see their trails though, looping in whorls and straight lines and intersections that seemed almost like symbols written across the beach, everything in some language I couldn't read.

I glanced to the side. The flash of red I'd seen that morning had faded to something dull and darker. I pushed away the image that rose into my mind and told myself it was only the sun, momentarily disturbing my vision. I walked a short way down the beach so that I could see better and slowly, their sun-beds came into view.

The young woman was lying on her back, quite still, her eyes open and looking straight up into the sky. They had filmed over, fading as if bleached. She hadn't been wearing her red swimsuit after all. She was naked and her skin had been opened like a fruit. And like fruit left out in the sun, she had begun to stink.

There were white blotches too, everywhere, and I rubbed my eyes. I thought for a moment I was going to faint. Then everything slipped into focus and I saw it was the crabs, hundreds of them, crawling over her exposed flesh. Her belly had been ravaged and the contents were pale, white twisting intestines against something deeper and richer beneath. Her chest was open and a large crab was trying to crest a raised line of drying skin.

As I watched it lost its grip and fell, toppling inside her. Other crabs were already in there, their shells stained, gorging themselves. Another was flexing a claw against the burnt pink skin at her clavicle and it suddenly gave as if it were tissue paper. One of the crabs had a number written on its back. I remembered the races, cheering them on, and I bit my lip to keep from laughing. I buried my head in my hands. Everything was boiling, furious, the sun burning everything away.

Her limbs had been slashed. Her palms were turned upward like some deposed saint and they too had been cut; it looked as if she had been trying to defend herself, but I knew that couldn't be true, couldn't be real, because here is where she was supposed to be; opening herself, offering herself to the gods that waited in the world and beyond the world.

For a moment, there was something I needed to remember; then I saw only the dark shadow of a manta ray, its wings spreading wide in the viscous water. Something that looked a little like a bat, improbable and infinitely strange, infinitely unknowable, swimming far beneath me in the deep.

* * *

The air was blessedly cool and the sand was soft beneath me. I had lit a fire and it sent heat into my face and across my belly. I ran my hand across it. I had thought I must have cut myself, but my skin was whole, left intact for some purpose I couldn't fathom.

I jabbed a limp dead fish onto a sharpened stick and thrust the other end into the sand, watching the flesh curl away from the heat. The crabs had been eating it first, but what did that matter? They had merely led the way, following instinct as animals do. It was humans that had forgotten how.

I let my head fall back and listened to the crackling of the fire. The sky was purple at the bottom, deepening at its height to stygian black. Where it was darkest, the stars shone out most brightly: it made me think of the image that had been captured from a submersible, the dark water full of bright particles caught in the spotlights, drifting past like stars. And then that single dark eye beneath the water.

Aliens, they'd said. Was that really how they had come – falling from the stars, descending to a strange, unknowable world? Drifting down through the deep black to grey to cerulean, finding nothing solid there, no barrier to stop them, nothing but gas particles and light, nothing that could keep them out. And then finding the ocean, its layers of turquoise and blue darkening as the light was left behind, growing darker still as they descended into the midnight zone; finding peace, finding somewhere they could sleep, somewhere they could dream.

I put my hand to my head. My vision kept blurring. The fish wasn't cooked, but I grabbed the stick anyway, pulling at the rubbery skin, ignoring the pain in my fingers from the heat. Pain didn't matter; pain was what they wanted. Clearing the way. Scouring. I bent the skin back and forced the flesh between my teeth and felt the life rushing into me.

Afterwards, I think I danced. The light falling from the stars fizzed against my skin, each granule of sand simmering and turning, rejoicing as my feet stamped new symbols into the ground. And it sang to me, and I heard its song and I answered: that dark thing, unfathomable and strange, just beyond the surface of the black lapping water.

Part Five: One Nameless Thing

In the early morning I woke in bed in my own villa. I didn't remember going to sleep, and I didn't think there had been any dreams; my head felt clearer, lighter. I stretched and walked down to the beach-side doors, onto the deck, where I emptied my bladder into the trees. Then I frowned, not sure why I'd done that. I had a vague idea there was something wrong with the bathroom, though I wasn't sure what it was. I thought it might be something to do with the gap between the walls and the roof. I glanced back inside, into the cool dark room. No one had come in the night to drag me from my bed, to slash or kill. No one knew I was here. I shook my head: no, the Frenchman knew, or at least he knew I was alive. That was probably not a good thing for him to know. Perhaps I should reinforce the doors or push cupboards in front of them. But then how would I get out, if I had to? The rep had said that help was coming. I wasn't sure I wanted it any longer, but I went back inside and switched on the television to see if there was news. The screen filled with endless grey static. *Blue*, I thought. *It should be blue.* I wasn't sure why I'd thought that.

Next, I tried the phone. There was nothing at all, not

even a dial tone; only the dead sound of a dead line. A failed call from a place at the edge of the world. Had the rep actually sent help at all? They might have had enough problems of their own. I had no way of knowing. Maybe the rest of the world wasn't even there any longer. If it was, and I couldn't communicate with it, did it even matter?

But I was putting off the thing I needed to do.

I turned and looked at the door to the bathroom. There was definitely something wrong with it. I walked silently across the room, cringing when one of the tiles clicked under my feet. I reached for the door handle. I knew I didn't like it in there; I never had. There was something about that gap just over my head, the way that anything could get inside. Small things, slipping through the spaces we left for them; things that crept or clung or crawled. All the same, I had to know what it was. I couldn't have that room at my back, waiting, holding nothing but a question I couldn't answer. I turned the handle and opened the door a crack. A smell emerged at once, warm and foul: a miasma. It was rich and sweet and bitter, choking, and I staggered back, grasping to pull the door shut. It was no good, I could still smell it. I took deep breaths anyway, trying to expel it, telling myself that it was only the gap, that was all; it must have somehow trapped the scent of the fish rotting on the beach, concentrating it there.

I had a sudden memory of pushing one of those dead things onto a spike of wood, setting it by the fire, pulling cloying flesh from the fine bones, and I gagged. I doubled over then ran for the back doors, spattering the frame, spilling vomit onto the runners, forming new patterns on the glass. A different stink filled the air; it was bad, but not as bad as what I'd smelled in the bathroom.

I opened the beach doors and gulped in air. It was clean and I stayed there until I realised I could hear a faint noise, carried on the breeze. It sounded a little like pain. I shut this door too and sat on the floor, putting my head in my hands. What was happening? I shouldn't be here at all. I couldn't even remember why I'd come.

But somehow I was still hungry. I still craved meat, something to fill the emptiness in my belly. My mouth filled with saliva at the thought. So hungry. There must still be people on the island, people who knew what to do. Running this place took a lot of people; they didn't all ship in daily from the neighbouring islands. I never had investigated the staff building, the one where the live-in staff stayed, with its neatly tended garden outside. I never had found out where everybody was.

I glanced back into the villa. I didn't want to walk through it and catch a trace of that smell again, didn't even want to think about it. Instead I slipped outside, pulling the door to behind me. I couldn't lock these doors from the outside, but hopefully they would appear locked, if anyone should pass by. Anyway, what could it matter? The only people I'd seen around were dead, and although the Frenchman knew I was alive, he didn't know which villa was mine. If he did he could have come and attacked me last night, while I was in the open and vulnerable, standing on the beach and doing – what, exactly? I couldn't altogether remember.

I went down to the beach front. The breeze was stronger today. I breathed in deep and swung my arms about my torso. They felt stiff but began to loosen as I set off, heading anti-clockwise around the shoreline. There were fewer dead fish on the beach now. Some must have washed away, or perhaps the crabs had finished them off; they were dotted around, the sun shining on their little white shells as they tracked their way over the ripples in the sand. I spotted one that was bigger than the rest, almost as big as a fist. As I approached it withdrew its limbs, the shell clamping down, as if that's all it was; an empty shell. I picked it up and peered into the opening, seeing the odd shapes crammed inside. It was impossible to tell where each small leg or claw or feeler began. It struck me that if I got really hungry, perhaps I could eat them too. I set the crab back down. I kept looking back as I walked away, but it didn't emerge again.

The sea was peaceful, settled into its old rhythm once more. Perhaps the disturbance had been only another dream, an anxiety dream maybe; the sort of thing I might have had back at home when I was worrying about my job or paying the bills. Now those seemed like odd things to worry about, so impossibly distant they couldn't actually be real.

As I walked I went past other villas, each hiding behind its mask of greenery. The windows were strangely blank, reflecting back the sky but in some darker, shadowy way. I couldn't see inside them, couldn't tell if anyone was watching me. And then I reached a hammock, slung beneath a twisting, desiccated-looking tree. The white twine had weathered to grey where it wasn't stained red-brown. I think the thing that hung there had once been a girl. It made me think at once of pig carcasses hung to drain and I looked down to see that the sand too bore a stain. A lizard was sitting right in the middle of it, its black eyes fixed on me, bright and motionless.

There were pieces missing from the body. She looked as if she'd been hacked into with a machete. I stared at her until a noise drew my attention towards the villa. It had sounded like the gritting of soft footsteps on the path. Then came the more hollow sound of a footstep on wood. For a moment, there was something else: the dry scraping of a blade. I froze, twisting to see around the greenery. A young man was standing there. He looked like an all-American boy, blond and blue-eyed and tall, though his tan was marred by livid burns across his shoulders. He seemed to feel no discomfort, though, as he raised the thing he carried – it was a machete, like those the gardeners used to crack open coconuts for the tourists – and patted the flat of the blade into his palm.

He tilted back his head and sniffed the air.

I knew, somehow, that he was scenting for me. There was a part of him that knew I was there; he didn't have to catch sight of me to know that. I eased one foot back and retreated a step. I knew at once it was a mistake. My thoughts fuzzed for a moment – *fight him, kill him, sweep the way clear* – and then clarified. This boy had killed. He was sniffing, now, for blood. It would never be enough.

There was a quicksilver flash as the lizard ran, its splayed legs blazing a trail down the path, sending up little sprays of sand. This time it didn't stop when it saw me, it just kept on running. But the footsteps I'd heard were retreating. I heard the heavy slide of doors as the boy went inside. I hurried away, hoping he wouldn't see me as I passed by.

I didn't see anyone else as I headed around to the track

leading to the staff area; no one living, anyway. I heard sounds though, the rough growl of an engine starting up – I thought first of a boat, but it was coming from inland – and then hoarse, ragged screaming. I paused for a moment, waiting until the screams stopped, and then I faced forward and I carried on. That was what people did, isn't it? In the face of change, of disaster, they had a choice: to carry on, or stop and despair and die.

The sand here thinned to a narrow strip that was barely longer than a sun-bed. It was a reminder that, although this island seemed like a permanent thing, nothing was still; not even the beach. The tide swept it around the island, elongating the beach on one side while it narrowed on the other, again and again in a never-ending movement. I had a sudden sense that everything was connected, the movement of the sand and the tides and the currents and beyond that the moon and outward to the stars, everything linked, as if the lines and connections could draw some alien symbol that was almost complete.

I shook my head and squinted. There was something – no, two somethings – in the water, just past the island. They were being carried away from it, in the direction of the current. One of them rolled in the water, part of it lifting into the air before submerging again, light turning to dark turning to light once more. I thought it was a person, someone with dark hair, but if it was they were already dead. Saliva flooded my mouth and I swallowed hard, telling myself not to think of it, not to allow myself to be sick; my stomach must be empty enough. And yet I didn't feel sick.

I should eat soon. It might steady the continual hot pulse in the centre of my skull. It would be better then. If there were no dead fish, I could always catch fresh ones. There was a dive centre on the island, and they must have equipment there. Fishing rods maybe, or nets. And yet the thought of eating fish now, their slippery silver skins, their soft white formless flesh, their staring lidless eyes, did make me feel sick.

I had reached the track with the Staff Only sign at its foot. The sign looked as if it had been kicked in, the board splintered and broken: Staff O it said now, its shattered appearance belying the cheeriness of the letters. I sniffed. Somewhere, something was burning. I looked inland and saw smoke hanging low in the air, blurring everything, as if the island had been swathed in an unaccustomed fog. I walked towards it anyway, not troubling to try to stay hidden or stick to the edge of the path. The gardens around me were thickly planted, as if to screen off the area where the staff lived from tourist eyes. It was as if being on holiday meant that people shouldn't have to see that for some, this was work; real life, a means of survival. I remembered Dinesh's face when he'd spoken about his family, and words drifted through my mind:

How could you ever leave? This place is so beautiful.

I jerked my head, pushing the thought away.

The staff building was a square-edged block with no pretence at beauty. I could see it in glimpses through the trees, and it looked as if it had been painted white at some time in its past. The windows were narrow, some of them at the top of the building propped open with washing slung from loops of line. Lower down, all of them were firmly closed. Ahead of me, the gardens became a matter of business; there were lines of beanpoles up which creepers twined, the low spread of salad leaves. The smoke was thicker here and I slowed as I rounded the corner. Then I saw the fire, a pile of branches and smashed-up furniture and what looked like pieces of a boat; an oar jutted from the top like some kind of pennant. The earth around its base had been pressed flat, as if people had been sitting there, or walking around it perhaps. That made me think of my night on the beach and I remembered the way I'd stood under the starlight and danced, reaching over the ocean to whatever dwelt beneath its dark skin. No. Whatever madness had taken me had passed. And yet my head wasn't clear, wouldn't seem to settle on anything. I needed to eat. I needed to speak to someone, to find out what was happening, to have it explained to me in words I could understand.

The main door was away to my left. I glanced up at the windows; slices of sky looked back. The entrance, as I had expected, looked firmly closed. A glass panel was set into the top of the door but I couldn't see into it from where I stood; I wasn't sure if it would be low enough for me to see in even if I was closer. There was little choice, though, and anyway, the place appeared to be deserted. I couldn't hear any sounds – no one talking, no radio or television blaring into the day. It seemed stupid, something in equal parts insane and audacious, but in the end I walked straight up to the door, in full view of anyone looking out of the windows, and tried the handle. It turned a small way before it jammed and I pushed, hard, but the door didn't move. I had been right about the window; it was too high for me to look inside. I stood on tiptoe and tried to pull myself up, caught a glimpse of dark lines criss-crossing the space – some kind of wooden frame maybe, or something written on the wall, I wasn't sure.

I walked around the building until I reached a larger window. This time it was lower and I looked in on a small communal kitchen, pans left filthy next to the burners, what looked like sauce smeared across the walls. Then I drew myself taller and saw the body where it lay by the units, face and hands blistered. It looked a little like severe sunburn, but somehow I didn't think that was what had happened. The room was otherwise empty, unless someone was hiding behind the units. And a kitchen was good. I could perhaps arm myself, find a knife or something bigger, a cleaver or another machete for splitting coconuts. I'd seen the gardeners when they'd done that for the tourists, letting them drink the fresh clear liquid inside. They'd tapped all around it first, knowing just how to weaken the shell before one last hard strike opened the fruit. It would probably be easier still to crack open a man's skull.

I slipped my shirt over my head, finding it filthy, dampened with sweat and crusted with old blood. I couldn't believe I'd been wearing it. My stomach was still smeared too. I grimaced, wrapped the filthy cloth around my fist and struck the window, once tentatively, then harder when I felt it vibrate under my hand. It shattered into irregular sharp points and I knocked them from the framework, unable to lessen the noise. Then I placed my shirt across the ledge and boosted myself up.

I landed on the other side, on shards of glass that ground under my feet. More noise: I may as well have hammered on the door. I stepped over the body, trying not to see his face but unable to look away. It looked as if he'd been doused in boiling water, or, judging by the waxy look of his skin, hot oil. The room was full of the charred scent of roasted meat and my stomach made a pained sound.

There were no knives in the first drawer, nor the next. I had images of myself sneaking through the building bearing nothing but a rolling pin and my lip twitched; it was almost a smile. Then I found a heavy wooden meat tenderiser, and in the next drawer, four thin metal skewers. Another image: myself as vampire hunter, using the tenderiser to hammer the skewer-stakes into someone's chest. I let out a dry spurt of air that wasn't quite a laugh.

The only door let onto the hallway I'd glimpsed earlier. It was difficult to get through. The thing I'd seen was an old bed-frame leaning against the main entrance, heavy and wedged into place. I ducked under and around it and into the hall. There were stairs in front of me, concrete, uncarpeted. Before I reached the stairwell, though, I'd have to pass more doorways; there were three, all closed. More communal areas, maybe. I imagined most of the lodgings would be upstairs. But if I headed up there and those doors began to open, I'd be trapped. I had no idea how many people might be in the building, or how many of them might still be alive.

But the fire outside had still been smouldering, the body in the kitchen relatively fresh.

It was too late to exercise caution. I headed straight for the stairs, alert to any sounds. There were no concessions to aesthetics here; the walls and floor had no decoration other than old stains. I reached a small landing with a long clouded window, turned ninety degrees, took two steps forward and turned another ninety degrees to see another flight of stairs crowded with people and I saw their eyes, all fixed and staring straight at me.

They had been ready. Of course, they had been ready.

No one moved. There didn't seem to be any point in running. There was nowhere to hide, no way I'd make it even to the kitchen. They were clutching an assortment of weapons: knives, mallets, other things; gardening forks and a hoe, the flat of the blade still caked with earth, the tip shiny. I stared at it. It hadn't yet been used, I could see that. I knew that because the other weapons were coated with old blood and shreds of other matter, the nature of which I didn't want to think about.

I looked down at the meat tenderiser I held. My grip on it had involuntarily tightened or I think I would have dropped it. My bowels felt cold, watery. I knew I had no time left in which to contemplate how stupid I had been, entering a place where I clearly should not have trespassed, a place where inside, everything had already turned rotten. I had known, underneath, that whatever I found here could never have been anything good.

And then one of the people on the stairs – his chest was bare, no staff uniform now – stepped forward and spoke. It sounded like a question, but I could not understand the words. It didn't sound like any language I knew, nor like any of the languages I'd heard spoken here: Dhivehi, Sinhala, Tamil. But they didn't seem to be in any hurry. Perhaps I had a little more time yet. I looked from face to face and realised there were tourists here as well as staff, all of them together, standing shoulder to shoulder. Several had bared their torsos, their skin streaked with smears of filth and blood. I glanced down at my own skin, at the smears across my belly. Perhaps they'd read in the marks some kind of kinship, but there was no recognition in their eyes; all of them were blank.

Their leader opened his mouth and spoke those words again. It wasn't like anything I'd ever heard and yet he seemed to expect I would understand. I nodded, as if in answer, and opened my own mouth to speak. Although they hadn't attacked, there was still no use in running. As soon as I moved, whatever spell it was that held them here would break; I'd be cut down, that hoe first maybe, drawing its first blood. There was a thirst here that I could feel. It answered something in me. I gestured, as if to underline the words I was preparing to speak, and then I turned and hurled myself at the window.

It broke at once and I closed my eyes against it. The shards were bright and sharp and pierced my skin, and I flailed at nothing and caught the ledge, just for a second, before something bit into my hand and I fell. I did not fall far. There was a walkway outside the building, more flat concrete, and my legs jarred under me as I landed. I rolled at once, knowing the window was not far above and that some of those weapons were mounted on long handles, and I got up and ran. The walkway ended in a stair that headed down to the back of the building. I glanced around and saw the broken teeth of the window, the glimpse of faces, and beyond that, an open doorway.

I kept going, around the side of the building and cutting through a cluster of trees across to the track – Staff O, I thought – and then the ground started to move, and I swayed, and then I almost fell. I bent double, touching my fingertips to the earth, but I hadn't been mistaken: the earth was moving again, trembling, and I realised I could hear it, a low sound that vibrated through my ribcage. I took another step and staggered. For a moment I wasn't sure if it was really the ground that was shaking or if I was having some kind of fit.

I stumbled into a thick patch of shrubbery, ducking

beneath branches and wading in to the thickest part. Once I was hidden I fell back onto the ground. The leaves above were trembling, making a constant rushing sound a little like water. Then it slowed and started to quiet. The earth felt more solid, no longer a living, twisting thing. Then it was silent. I brushed the twigs aside, trying to see the building. There was a nasty cut across the palm of my hand, and as if angered by my gaze, it began to sting. My arms had escaped with a couple of light scratches but there was a nasty cut across my right thigh and another that deepened as it traced a line from my ankle to my calf. I could feel the blood dripping from it, as if sensation had only now begun to return. The heat of the sun matched the heat in my opened skin.

There was a small black spider in front of me, crawling across a leaf. I heard the sudden low buzz of a fly, but didn't see it. I leaned back against the branches and looked up. There was a bat hanging from the tree above me. It had found a large bundle of under-ripe bananas and was embracing them with its leathery wings. Its face was intelligent and furry, its eyes bright and sharp and looking at me. Each wing ended in a large unwieldy claw.

Then it gathered itself and it flew.

The thing rose through the leaves, rising higher, into the clear air. It spiralled upwards until it was way above the trees, above everything, spreading its wings wide as it formed a lazy circle. It made me think of the manta ray, distant and strange and beautiful, and suddenly, I wanted to cry.

It had looked at me as if it had known me; as if it understood what I was.

* * *

When I got back I let myself in at the villa and went straight to the cupboard with the mini-bar inside. I couldn't find the fruit knife, but I grabbed the corkscrew and pushed it into my pocket. There must be something here I could use as a weapon. I could always sneak around the gardens, see if I could find one of the gardener's machetes. Or I could stay here and barricade myself inside.

There was a bottle of water left in the mini-bar. I was thirsty and drank, then resisted the urge to tip the rest over my head or using it to scrub at my wounds. It might soon be too precious to waste. There was still the bathroom, provided the water supply hadn't been cut off or contaminated, but my mind pushed that thought aside as if it were closing a door. Still, I could dress myself in something better, cleaner. I went to the wardrobe and opened one of the doors. I didn't recognise any of the clothes inside; they didn't appear to be mine. I side-stepped to the next and pulled it open and saw my shirts. Someone else must have been here, everything mixed up in the confusion. I found a loose-fitting grey shirt and pulled it free of its hanger. Then I caught a glimpse of something wooden propped against the back of the wardrobe.

I pushed the clothes aside and stared down at what I'd found. I didn't blink; I didn't move. It was incomprehensible. I knew then that my mind had slipped somehow. Slowly, I put out a hand, one finger outstretched, and touched it, half expecting it to disappear. There was a narrow wooden rod with short protrusions, blunt at one side, sharpened at the other. It ended in a sharp point. I opened my mouth as if to speak, but there were no words; I had none.

I had seen this thing before, but not in my hands. I closed my eyes and pictured the grey-haired man wading out of the sea. *Four*, I thought, *or three*. Some of the fish had still been alive. I had seen them flapping against the wooden shaft, and I didn't think it had been from the movement or the wind, but their eyes had already been turning dull. The thing hidden here was a spear.

I had no recollection of how I'd come by it. The last time I'd seen the Frenchman he'd been standing on the dock, stretching out his hands over the sea in some kind of benediction. Had he had it with him then? I had no way of knowing. I reached out and took hold of it, feeling its weight. It was exactly as solid and heavy as I had expected, as if I was used to carrying it, and my hands wrapped tight around the smooth wood. I held it at my shoulder, ready. I already knew how straight it would fly, how satisfying it would feel as it entered its target. The almost comically surprised expression that would pass across their face before their eyes, too, dulled in death.

No, I thought.

Four, was it? Or three? Or five?

And I knew there was something else I had to see, something that had been hidden in a distant corner of my mind, something upon which I'd closed the door. Now that door was opening, and a light was shining through. No, not a light. A smell. A smell at once sweet and bitter and rich.

I turned and stared at the bathroom door. I didn't want to move but somehow my legs were taking me there, to the place I didn't want to go. I reached it and this time I didn't hesitate; I put out a hand and turned the handle and the door opened, so easily, and the smell was there, overblown and heated, but it didn't seem so bad any more. It wasn't nearly as bad as the thought of the smell, of where it might be coming from. I remembered how I'd rationalised it earlier, telling myself the scent had come from the beach, the rotting fish. Then the way

I'd gone to the beach doors, breathing in deeply of the clean air. I think a part of me had known, even then, that it hadn't made sense.

How many geckoes, honey? Will there be ants?

I shook my head. I couldn't think to whom the voice belonged, and I pushed the door wider and I saw her, lying in the shower, her legs buckled under her, cold and blue, and her body spattered red – I thought of a swimsuit, a bright swimsuit, but knew that was wrong, that wasn't her – and then I saw the places it had darkened to a deeper colour as it dried, and I saw other things: hanging from her body, everything the wrong shape or the wrong angle, and I looked at her face and was glad her hair was hanging over it, covering her eyes, though it was darkened on top; there was a great clotted mass on top of her head. I started, but something wouldn't allow me to look away, to run. And I saw that she had been right, there were ants, but not on the sand. The ants had found her, the woman I had once loved; they had formed new lines across her skin.

I made an odd sound in the back of my throat. My eyes were dry. When I blinked, they felt like sand.

Two, I thought. Two geckoes clinging to the wall, small and white, in the shower. *Two, honey! You were right!*

I went to her side and knelt. I put out a hand and

smoothed the hair from her face. I put my fingertips to her cheek. It looked bruised. I looked at the back of my knuckles; the skin there was rough, reddened. Then I looked down and I saw the knife, the knife I'd used to open the yellow-green fruit and slice into my lover's body, paring and dividing until it had nothing left to give. I closed my eyes. I could see it now, could remember the way I'd thrust against her, the madness upon me, wanting only to be close: *close. Closer*.

And I had been. I had.

I touched her face, just once more, and then I turned and left. I went back to the wardrobe and forced myself to look at her clothes hanging next to mine. I felt empty. Numb. I turned and looked around the villa, everything roughly in order, everything in place, the cupboards and the television and the phone. There was a small card next to the handset, Call in case of emergencies. It had been so like Kath to hold onto that, to make sure she had it safe. And then she'd called her daughter, talking low and long in that steady murmur, and I found myself wishing that I'd listened in after all. I wished I knew what it was like, inside that circle they'd formed together.

I went to the dresser and saw a half glass of water and I drank it. My gaze moved slowly across the things that had been left there: a bottle of sun lotion, the lid still sitting damply on the wood. A hairbrush, clogged with her hair. And a little scattering of brightly coloured sweets, yellow, green, purple; no orange ones left. *She had liked those best*, I thought, and then I knelt in front of the dresser and I began to cry.

I don't know how long I stayed there. When I stirred, I shifted and sat with my back to the dresser and I ate the sweets, one by one, my eyes still leaking tears.

Like a kid, I thought. *An excited kid, going on holiday*.

The sweets were too sugary, cloying. I forced myself to swallow anyway, but the memory was of something else; sitting by a fire, tossing a half-eaten fish into the sea. Cramming instead something darker into my mouth, something with more substance, rich and stringy and good.

I frowned. I remembered the body in the hammock, the way it had looked as if pieces had been cut from it, *missing*, and I turned my head and looked at the bathroom door. Had she—

But no. I couldn't think about that.

I was done with this place. Whatever happened now, I wouldn't need it any longer. I didn't bother to wash my skin or to dress my cuts, but I did pick up the spear on my way out. When I left, I didn't bother to close the door.

* * *

I found the first of them by the path that led into the

heart of the island. He was just standing there, his chest bared, under the trees. If I hadn't been alert I wouldn't have seen him. I wasn't even sure it mattered. His eyes moved as I drew near, but he was otherwise motionless. He held a knife loosely in his hand; its blade was dark.

I could remember when I'd first met him, the way he'd smiled at us. He was maybe in his late twenties, but that smile had struck me as innocent, almost too open. We had liked him at once. Now he didn't smile. His hand twitched, once, on the weapon, and his head swivelled slowly and he looked in the direction of the sea.

'They're coming,' he said. His voice had always been soft; now it was almost without expression.

He smiled. It was no longer his old smile, no longer guileless. It was no longer something I wanted to see. I raised the spear and he looked at it as if in approval. The ground seemed alive again; there was a constant low tremor, as if electricity were running through it. I closed my eyes. I no longer needed to sleep in order to dream. The haze had passed. I could see everything clearly now, the eye, the thick smooth skin turning in the deep. I could sense the thrill of life returning to its limbs, the way they were writhing, preparing to unfurl. And I knew its eyes were turned upon the world, fixed on me. For some reason, something I'd heard as a child floated through my mind: Through a glass darkly.

Old gods, she'd said. Alien beings. She had almost been right, but it was more than that; it was the sum of all the black dreams that reside inside us, the faces we turned towards the dark. And it was coming.

Dinesh drew back his lips over his teeth. Now his expression looked more like a snarl and I felt the strength coming over me, the veil dropping across my vision. They had known, all of them; they were my brothers, the ones who had felt its call and answered, shared in its dark baptism. And yet they didn't know; they didn't even suspect. This thing would have blood. The thirst was growing stronger, in the earth, in the air, rising through my body. It was sending out its glory, into the ground and through my feet and into my limbs. My hands raised the spear, tightening around it. I think I smiled.

Dinesh looked dazed when it went into him. He jerked away, took a step back to save himself from falling, and he blinked; he seemed almost to wake. He opened his mouth as if to speak, but only the shadow of a word came out. *You*, I think he said, or it may have been something else, something a little like a name. But the thing in the deep had no name, not really; we could give it nothing but approximations. There was no word that could hold it. It was boundless.

I stood over his body for a moment, paying him

tribute. He was an acolyte and he had served his purpose. In the end his god had not saved him, but I felt no pity; it wasn't that kind of god. He must have known that. His had not been to receive but to clear the way, to scour the earth for its coming: and ultimately, to surrender.

How could you ever leave? She'd said. *This place is so beautiful.*

I shook my head. There was nothing left; only one thing that remained to do.

* * *

Evening had started to fall as I made my way to the dock, and everything was silent, as if the world was holding its breath. It did not take long before I reached the edge of the trees that fringed the shore, and when I did, I saw that not everything was still: the bats were flying. They had taken to the skies, not whirling and circling above the trees, but heading straight out, over the water and away, leaving the island behind them.

The sky was still blue, but it was deepening, growing shadowed. It looked like the beautiful sky at the end of a holiday. It even seemed for a moment as if it held promise in it, as if there was some escape to be found there; and happy times, a mother who couldn't take her eyes from her son, a lover who couldn't wait to reach a beautiful island. I had to remind myself now that it was all gone. Even the sky, that beautiful pure blue, was nothing but a lie.

They had lit a fire on the dock. I didn't know what they were burning, but it was heaped in a great brass bowl that shone with the glow of the flames. Behind the figures I could just see the dhoni, still bobbing in the water. The sea itself was agitated; the surface in the distance appeared calm but the waves clawed at the edge of the sand like a drowning man.

For a while I only watched. The sky darkened and began to turn a lurid purple that was streaked with spilled blood. The fire, by contrast, seemed brighter still. That was when I started to walk towards them, in full view, heading across the beach and up onto the main track that led to the dock. I could see their faces, bronzed by fire and sun and blood.

Some of them turned to look at me as I approached. They remained seated, as if they didn't see me as any kind of threat, and somehow, their silence spoke of acceptance. It was like the men barricaded into the staff quarters; they knew that I was one of them, a follower, a brother. Only one of them was different. The grey-haired man pushed himself to his feet. His eyes were shining. The sky was bright behind him, but I knew who it was. The wolf had seen me, and he had understood at once. He knew me for what I was.

The others began to stir, taking their lead from him. He gestured towards one of them, a man with close-cropped hair and a broad face and shoulders. He stood. He wore only beach shorts, a brightly coloured design of pineapples just visible under the dirt and the blood. His arms were sweat-slicked. At his waist he wore a length of twine, and from it dangled a scalp; long hair clung to it, crusted and matted with dried blood. I recognised it. It belonged to the woman who had stood not far from this place, watching with me as people gathered on this very dock. Back then, her husband had not been among them. What was it she had said? 'I should see if he's okay. He's been acting weird.'

Now he drew a knife from his waistband.

'No,' I said. 'He's not enough.' I pointed straight at the wolf. 'You.'

The Frenchman's lip twisted. At first he didn't move; then he pulled a knife from his own belt. He turned to the woman's husband – Ryan – and gestured towards the other man's knife. Ryan held it out and he took it from him. Now he had two. He held the second one out to me, and I understood. It was the right thing. I threw the spear, hurling it towards the water, and it disappeared beneath the waves. I looked back at the wolf. I remembered his slick limbs slipping through the water, clean and fast, and I saw his leanness, his muscularity.

He didn't speak. He simply stepped towards me and closed in, the knife flashing as he passed it from hand to hand.

I knew I couldn't match his speed or his agility. If I let him lead me in some dance I would become exhausted, easy to finish. I didn't plan to be easy to finish.

His expression was sly, full of the contempt with which he'd first looked at me, so long ago, back on the boat. But there was something new in his eyes; he knew that I wasn't the thing he'd first taken me for. *Just one*, I had thought, back then. It would only take a single shark to behave in a new way, an unexpected way, and everything would change. But it hadn't been just one, after all: we had been given a choice, adapt or die, and both of us had chosen to adapt.

He swiped with the knife and I leapt back. He darted in again, quick as a lizard, and carved a new line into my skin. I didn't look at it, didn't need to, it couldn't matter now. Blood spilled onto my belly, warm and painless, and for a moment it seemed almost comforting.

The time was nearly upon us. The sky was livid, the sun just touching the horizon, hanging there as if everything had been suspended. Someone once told me that when the sun appeared in just that position, it was nothing but a mirage caused by the bending of light in the atmosphere; that the sun had already gone, sinking below the horizon. It was nothing but an illusion, something else that did not exist.

Directly above it, a bright star had appeared in the sky. *The alignment*, I thought, without knowing why, but the wolf seemed to feel it too. He stood back, half turning towards the light. I had an opportunity to strike, but no, he should see it coming. He deserved that, at least.

Then he looked at me. 'He's ready,' he said.

The boards beneath us began to shake, wood rattling against wood, and there was a higher, vibrating sound, as if the bolts that held it together were trembling, shaking themselves loose.

I merely nodded. We knew that; we could all feel it. The others were getting to their feet, moving away from the fire, which had started to hiss and spit. Around us and beneath us, nothing was solid. I glanced down and saw dark water below the slats, seething and angry. The sound of the waves had changed, becoming inconsistent, irregular.

The Frenchman smiled. He stepped towards me, stumbled, and I struck. I almost caught his face, but he jerked back and I took only some loose strands of his hair and a slice of his shoulder. He didn't cry out or catch his breath, but whirled and came in hard, using his knife like a sword, aiming for my neck. It was my turn to duck and I missed my footing, almost fell, but I used the movement and struck from beneath, rising fast and relentless through the air, the blade becoming my teeth, my claws, the focus of my intention. I knew I had him before I felt the resistance of his skin and flesh. The blade scraped on bone then found a new course, plunging deep between his ribs and into his chest. I could feel his heart beating. I could hear it. In that moment, as he met my eyes and almost smiled, we were connected; we were one. And I withdrew the knife and bathed the boards with his blood.

I could smell it, sharp and clean, and I knew that for now, this moment, it was enough. The thing would have blood, and here was the blood it craved; loyal, pure. After that . . . blood would have blood, and its thirst was endless. It would never die, never end, not until all of us were gone and only this earth remained, a burnt dead shell. That was the sacrifice it craved.

The others were jumping into the boat, as if to escape the uncertain earth, to flee their god, but there was nowhere they could go that would be far enough. One of them fell from the edge of the platform, landing half across the prow, screaming his pain into the wind that was gathering, cold and sharp. Someone else cut the rope that bound the dhoni and there were shouts of protest, others jumping into the sea. Someone screamed as miscreant waves smashed them against the dock. Blood spread from him, blooming into the water. I smiled. Perhaps the dead men would be able to see clearly at last, eye to dark and lidless eye, and they would know, they would understand, see the mysteries that until now I had only sensed. For a moment I envied them.

The sun – the deceiving sun – had now sunk far beneath the darkened seas. I could see the curvature of the earth, and yet something out there moved, breaking the smooth line. I grinned. I couldn't help it. It was time for everything to change, for all that we held dear to pass away. The cities, the world, the island, the circling of the bats and the migration of the sand around its shore; everything would come to an end. It was the end of pain, the end of the knowledge of everything I had done and what I had become. It was the answer, perhaps not one we had craved or imagined or wanted, but now the time for wondering had passed. It was here: the truth had come to find us out.

The sky wasn't blue any longer. Perhaps it never would be again. I stared at the new bright star that lit the sky, shining down on the water. Out there, miles from the shore, the sea was boiling. And the forgotten god began to rise, its hideous visage breaking the surface, its leathery wings spreading wide, darkening the world with their shadow. Its face, for a moment, was lost, shrouded in the foam and the water, but I could see its eyes; I could see their endless depravity, their ancient hunger.

I knelt. I couldn't help it; the dock was vibrating now as if it would shatter into nothingness, as if everything would. And I could hear its call, though not in my ears; this thing had no need of words, though somehow, deep inside my being, I could sense it, reaching for me and all that remained, compelling me to join with it, in the endless worship of death.

It was calling my name. Calling me home.

About the Editor

Scott Harrison is an award-winning scriptwriter and novelist whose books include *Remember Me: The Pandora Archive*, the official computer game tie-in for Capcom, *Star Trek: Shadow of the Machine* for Simon & Schuster and *Blake's 7: Archangel for Big Finish.* He has written audio plays for a number of different genres and ranges including *Sometime Never* (starring Simon Jones and Rosalyn Landor), *The Confessions of Dorian Gray* and *Blake's 7: The Liberator Chronicles*, as well as stage plays that have been produced in both the U.K and America. His comic book scripts and short stories have appeared in a variety of anthologies, such as *Into The Woods: A Fairytale Anthology, Faction Paradox: A Romance in Twelve Parts, Resurrection Engines, Twisted Histories* and *Beside The Seaside*. He lives by the sea with his wife and a stack of books he will never get around to reading.

Visit him at scottvharrison.blogspot.com